Praise for *The Su*

'A deeply satisfying, deftly woven n
and resistance, and of feminisms both implicit and explicit.
Early and late 20*th* century Iceland are both beautifully
evoked in Kat Gordon's rich, captivating prose'
Anna Hope, author of *Expectation*

'Thoroughly bewitching. Kat Gordon's spare prose is
as beautiful as it is haunting'
Freya Berry, author of *The Birdcage Library*

'In beautiful, crisp prose, *The Swell* examines the saga of
one family and the often complicated role of the women
within it. An addictive and twisty read'
Liza Klaussman, author of *Tigers in Red Weather*

'Gripping, bewitching, and laced with atmosphere,
reading *The Swell* was a wonderfully sensory experience'
Harriet Constable, author of *The Instrumentalist*

'A skilful, measured, atmospheric mystery set in Iceland
and weaving across two timelines. Kat Gordon is a
master storyteller'
Cathryn Kemp, author of *A Poisoner's Tale*

'Beautiful and powerful, a story of courage and survival
that echoes across generations'
Emily Critchley, author of *The Undoing of
Violet Claybourne*

'Set against a dramatic and treacherous Icelandic
landscape, *The Swell* is a cinematic and compelling story
of hope, autonomy and transformation'
Elle Machray, author of *Remember, Remember*

Kat Gordon was born in London in 1984. She has published two books, *The Artificial Anatomy of Parks*, which was shortlisted for the Guardian Not the Booker, and *An Unsuitable Woman*, which was a Richard and Judy Book Club pick and translated into multiple languages. Her writing has been anthologised in *Underground: Tales for London*.

She has lived in Reykjavik, and is currently settled in London with her partner and young son. She loves Iceland, but is not a fan of fermented shark.

THE
SWELL

KAT GORDON

MANILLA
PRESS

First published in the UK in 2024 by
MANILLA PRESS
An imprint of Zaffre Publishing Group
A Bonnier Books UK company
4th Floor, Victoria House, Bloomsbury Square, London, WC1B 4DA
Owned by Bonnier Books
Sveavägen 56, Stockholm, Sweden

This is a work of fiction based loosely on historical events. It is not
intended to be a true and accurate version of the events depicted,
and characters are either entirely fictional or used fictitiously.

A CIP catalogue record for this book is
available from the British Library.

Hardback ISBN: 978-1-78658-352-9

Export ISBN: 978-1-78658-436-6

Also available as an ebook and an audiobook

1 3 5 7 9 10 8 6 4 2

Typeset by IDSUK (Data Connection) Ltd
Printed and bound in Great Britain by Clays Ltd, Elcograf S.p.A.

Manilla Press is an imprint of Zaffre Publishing Group
A Bonnier Books UK company
www.bonnierbooks.co.uk

To an extraordinary mother, and the first feminist I knew, Janet Gordon, 1947–2021. To the Camden girls, for carrying on the legacy. And to my son, Noah, always.

Thorkell's sons and Bárdur's daughters played together in the winter on the ice on nearby streams called Bjarnaár. They played hard and with great zest. Thorkell's sons sought to dominate, for they were stronger; but Bárdur's daughters would not be subdued any more than they could avoid. One day they were playing and as usual there was competition between Raudfeldr and Helga. There was an ice field off the shore that day. There was a thick fog. They were playing close down by the sea. Raudfeldr then pushed Helga onto an ice floe. A great wind was blowing from the shore, so that the floe drifted out to the ice field. Helga then went out onto the ice field. That same night the ice drifted away from the shore and out to sea.

from the Bárđar Saga
edited by Jón Skaptason and Philip Pulsiano,
Garland Publishing, 1984

PART ONE
Shipwrecked

1910

THE NIGHT BEFORE, GUDRÚN had seen Hidden People fighting in the cove. Two men grappled with each other in the water, but their skin and hair stayed dry and no ripples went out from where they were. Over and over they went down and came up, first one in a headlock, then the other. Eventually, they went down and stayed down.

'It's a bad omen,' their father said, when she told him before supper.

'Of what?' Gudrún asked. 'It's not fishing season yet.'

He shrugged.

Freyja helped him off with his overalls and boots and inspected them for holes. Gudrún knew she'd found some by the way her shoulders hunched.

'Let's eat,' she said. 'You can mend them later.'

She watched Freyja set their father's things out before the fire to dry and sit silently at the table. She was often silent since she'd returned from the Big Farm a few weeks ago, especially when asked why they'd let her go.

Papi sat opposite her and inspected the salt cellar, the same one they'd had for twenty years. He wasn't much of a talker either. Gudrún left them to it and went into the kitchen.

It was more than two months since midsummer, but the evenings were still warm, and through the open kitchen window she could see sunlight streaking the grass.

Flies buzzed around the bowl of skyr she'd left out. A ptarmigan cackled nearby. Gudrún stood in the doorway soaking up the peace. She could smell the angelica that they'd planted last spring, earthy and a little spicy, mixing with the sourness of the skyr and the smoke from the fire in the next room.

Her father saw bad omens everywhere; they didn't always come to pass.

She gathered the dinner things together: smoked mutton, ewe's-milk cheese, blood pudding, anchovies. She carried them through to the badstofa and they tucked in.

'What do you think, Papi?' she asked. 'Will we get as much hay as last year?'

It was their mother who had first called him Papi, Gudrún remembered. When Mamma was younger, her own mother had had a dream that her daughter would marry a mute, Spanish prince, and Gudrún's mother had said Papi, with his dark eyes and his few words, must have been the one she'd seen. And now it would seem strange to call him anything else, even though Mamma was gone.

'Maybe,' Papi said.

'What about the fishing? Do you need me this time?'

'You'll need to look after this place.'

She didn't volunteer Freyja to look after the farm; it wouldn't change his mind. Papi would never let her join him on the boat. Their mother had fished with him every winter until her death, but she'd been different, *fiskin*, their father called it.

'They swarmed to her,' he always said. 'One time she brought so many of them it was more fish than water.'

Her mother. Freyja looked just like her, everyone said. Tall and blonde and delicately boned, with big blue eyes.

Gudrún was taller, and looked like their father. Broad-shouldered. Brown-haired. Her eyes were the same as Freyja's though.

Gudrún stole a glance at her sister; she was pushing her cheese around her plate with a fork.

'Not hungry?' she asked.

Freyja looked up. 'Not really.'

'Don't give it to Jules Verne again. He stank the whole house out farting last time.'

Freyja didn't return her smile.

'Don't give him anything,' Papi said. 'He should be catching mice. Why else do we have a cat?'

The wind started up after dinner. They heard it creaking through the beams, then it got louder until it was throwing itself against the house, and Gudrún smelled earth and knew rain was soaking into the turf walls. She went to the window, even though the fields were out of sight, and pressed her forehead against the glass. Four more weeks of haymaking, unless this bad weather held. She tapped her forefinger against her heart twice for good luck. They couldn't afford for it to hold.

Behind her, Freyja muttered something under her breath. Gudrún turned to look at her. 'What was that?' she asked.

'I've dropped the needle again.'

Freyja got down on her hands and knees and scoured the floor. Papi, who was sitting in his armchair in front of the fire, spoke without opening his eyes. 'Gudrún will find it.'

Ever since she was little Gudrún had been able to find lost or hidden things. Freyja had asked her about it once, and she hadn't known how to explain it. She just saw things, she'd said, and shrugged. But only things that were really there. Freyja could put down a cup and lose it straight away, but she could see things that weren't there. Or had done once. When Gudrún was four and Freyja was one, the two of them had been playing in the garden while their mother hung up the washing. Freyja had pointed at her. 'Mamma go to sleep,' she'd said. A week later their mother had died suddenly of a heart attack.

Gudrún joined her sister.

'Your finger,' she said. 'You've pricked it.'

Freyja lifted her hand to inspect it, then wiped the blood on her skirt. 'Sometimes I dream of a fabric that doesn't need mending.'

'Don't hold your breath. The people who invent things aren't the people who stay up darning clothes. Besides, would anyone trust it?' Gudrún nodded at Papi, then at his rubber boots lined up inside the door. Rósa Gudmundsdóttir had bought them for all the tenant farmers a few years ago, but Papi didn't believe in keeping his feet dry and filled them up with water before he put them on.

'It's just newfangled nonsense,' he said, every time he did it. 'You'll see.'

Freyja shook her head at the boots. 'I suppose not.'

Gudrún turned and saw a flash of silver. 'Found it,' she said.

At eleven o'clock Freyja was still bent over Papi's overalls. The light from her lantern reached their bed and stained the inside of Gudrún's eyelids red until she rolled over and buried her face in the pillow. She could still hear

Freyja's soft breaths. Lately, Freyja hadn't been coming to bed until the early hours of the morning, and Gudrún knew it meant something. *Stay awake*, she told herself. *Find out what's bothering her.*

She fingered the ring she wore on a chain around her neck – their mother's wedding ring – and for a moment she let herself think of her. Their mother. Just a long, golden plait, and fingernails crusted with dirt from the garden. Maybe a snatch of her voice – low? Calling them indoors. And the two of them throwing themselves into her arms. She couldn't remember much about her mother, but she remembered how easy she'd made everything, how warm—

She must have fallen asleep after all. Her shoulder was being shaken and Freyja was looming over her, her face pale and hair dripping icy water onto the sheets. She was talking so quickly Gudrún couldn't understand at first.

'Why are you so cold?' Gudrún asked. 'What time is it?'

'It's sinking.'

'What's sinking?'

'The ship. The one I've been talking about.'

'What ship?'

Freyja tugged at her and she let herself be hauled out of bed.

'Where's Papi?'

'Down on the beach. Come *on*. And bring a lantern.'

Gudrún snatched up a lantern and put on her coat and boots while Freyja paused in the open doorway. Her fingers were clumsy with sleep, fumbling with the buttons, and the next time she looked up Freyja was running ahead, her coat flapping out behind in the wind. Gudrún called after her to wrap up properly, but Freyja was already too far away to hear.

Gudrún struggled after her. The rain had stopped, but the wind kept up a shrill whistle, and whipped her hair across her face. It was early morning, she judged. Maybe four o'clock. Everything was colourless in the grey, pre-dawn light, but she could easily pick out the path ahead and more: the boulder to the right that marked the way down to the beach, the fields beyond where their sheep and cow would be huddled together, and farther away still, Snæfellsjökull – or Freyja's mountain, as they called it in the family – the volcano that dominated the landscape, rising up as if straight out of the sea, dark and jagged, with the glacier at its peak hidden behind swirling cloud. Then round past the boulder, the beach, black sands smooth and glistening, and the water, blacker still, and boiling away.

And the ship. A Pacific steam whaleship, beautiful, almost two hundred feet in length, bark rigged, with a strongly raked bow. She was three-masted, and Gudrún guessed they'd been using sails when the storm blew up; the cotton was torn to pieces. She was taking on water, too; they'd obviously handled her badly.

Gudrún turned away, feeling sick. She'd seen enough wrecks to know what would happen next.

Farther down the beach, Papi and Freyja were holding up their swaying lanterns, as if to search for swimmers. *There won't be any*, Gudrún thought suddenly, surprising herself. But why should she be surprised? For four months of the year she was a fisherman's daughter; she knew about the killing force of the sea.

There was a loud groan as the waves lifted the vessel up, then a splitting sound as she hit the rocks. Gudrún looked again. The ship's back was broken properly now and she started to sink faster.

Over the noise of the wind, she heard Freyja shouting something and saw her point at the water. Gudrún started to run to them as fast as she could. The sand sucked at her boots and spray smacked her in the face, but the tone of Freyja's voice – half excited, half terrified – spurred her on.

'We've got to do something, Papi,' Freyja was shouting when Gudrún came within earshot. She was almost at the water's edge, and Papi had her by the elbow, his fingertips white as if he were holding on for dear life.

'Too dangerous.'

'Look – they're still there.' Freyja pointed again.

Gudrún looked. She saw two heads, briefly, before they disappeared behind a wave.

'Freyja,' she called. 'Come away from the water.' They were both strong swimmers, Gudrún maybe stronger than Freyja, but she knew, just looking at it, that the sea would overpower them tonight.

'Gunna, you can see them, can't you?'

'Yes.'

'We need to get the rowing boat.'

Gudrún took her other elbow. 'It's too rough. We'd all drown.'

'*Look*,' Freyja said.

The two heads were in view again. Gudrún could just make out arms and shoulders above the water too. One of them was thrashing around more than the other, and as she watched he grabbed his companion and they both went under. Freyja let out a cry and started forwards, dragging Gudrún and Papi with her until they were up to their ankles in cold sea.

'He'll kill them both.'

'Wait,' Gudrún said.

The two heads were above water again. The head belonging to the man being held onto was jerking away, as if trying to shake the other off, then suddenly they were apart, and one of them was swimming. Gudrún felt her heart hammering in her chest. The one left behind thrashed around for another few seconds, then went under.

'Oh God,' she said.

'Had to do it,' Papi said.

The waves were sucking at Gudrún's feet and she shifted to steady herself, feeling the sand underneath shift with her.

'Papi, he's getting tired,' Freyja said. She was staring at the swimming man. His strokes were sure and steady, but he was close enough now for the three on the beach to see his face, which was scrunched up as if in pain, and the heaving of his chest.

Papi set down his lantern and waded farther into the water. Gudrún held Freyja tighter as they watched him strike out towards the man, reach him, and grab him underneath his armpits. Then Papi was swimming back to shore, hauling the sailor behind him. They collapsed in the shallows and Gudrún and Freyja ran towards them, helping them both up and away from the water. The ship was completely gone now.

They staggered up the beach, the sailor mumbling something as they walked. Gudrún stole a look at him out of the corner of her eye. He had dark, curly hair, and a dimple in the middle of his chin. His eyelashes were absurdly thick and long. He must have shed his coat in the water, and his arms, which dangled across her and Papi's shoulders, were lean and tanned. He smelled of tobacco and salt. It felt odd to be so close to him, a stranger.

'We can stop here,' Papi said when they came to the bottom of the cliff.

Gudrún unwound the sailor from her neck. He took a step away from them. For a moment it looked like he was about to start running, and Gudrún had a sudden, alarming notion that he was in trouble, or he was the trouble, and they'd made a mistake helping him. Then he was just a man again. A boy, really, very pale, and trembling. He opened his mouth.

'Thank you,' he said, and fainted.

*

They put him in Papi's bed. Doctor Jóhann from Hellnar village came to see him and said he would live. After a week he was walking around and opening drawers and looking in pots, laughing at the contents.

'What in the name of God is that?' he said when he came across the dried fish. 'It looks like feet shavings.'

Papi ground his teeth.

His name was Tomas. He was Danish, and young, only nineteen – one year older than Freyja and two years younger than Gudrún. He was strong, and he didn't take life too seriously. When he wasn't laughing he was always singing, in a clear, tuneful voice. Not for the first time, Gudrún marvelled at how easy it was to understand the language, especially in song. 'The language of our oppressors,' Papi called it and muttered

11

that Tomas was probably a spy sent to undermine the fight for independence.

'Danish men or Icelandic men,' Gudrún said. 'You all sound the same to me.'

Nine days after the wreck they were all in the badstofa after supper, Papi in his usual chair, Tomas poking at the fire, Freyja holding the wool while Gudrún wound it.

'What tune is that?' Gudrún asked, and Tomas put down the poker and turned to face them.

'Was I singing?' he asked.

Freyja smiled at the wool in her hands.

'Something about whales,' Gudrún said.

He stretched and grinned. 'Could be any of them.'

'If I had the wings of a gull, my boys, I would spread 'em and fly home,' Freyja said. 'That's how it starts.'

'Oh, that one,' Tomas said. 'The first mate used to sing it. I must have picked it up from him.'

'It doesn't sound like he liked being on the ship much,' Gudrún said.

'The first mate? He was born to it,' Tomas said. He put his hands in his pockets. 'He was the first one to know something was up with the whales.'

'What was up with them?' Gudrún asked.

'The Atlantic's almost empty. That's why we were going to Canada; our captain was getting desperate.'

Gudrún caught Freyja's eye. He hadn't spoken about his time on the ship before.

'What happened?' Freyja asked.

'The storm happened. We were caught by surprise. Most of the men were below. I was port-watch, so I was on deck.' He frowned. 'We loosed the main sheet, but it was too late by then. The lower deck ports had been opened and the water went into those and washed everyone before it. The captain was still trying to get the boats launched when we broke in two.'

'Were you scared?' Freyja asked quietly.

'I was angry.' He didn't look at them. 'It shouldn't have happened. One hundred lives.'

'She was a good boat, too,' Gudrún said.

There was silence for a moment, then a sudden, explosive creaking as Papi stood up. Gudrún jumped; she'd almost forgotten he was there.

'No use dwelling, it's done,' Papi said. 'What are your plans now?'

'Do you need an extra hand here?' Tomas asked. He seemed the closest Gudrún had seen him to being embarrassed. 'I can do anything.'

'We need help with the haymaking. You can work for your lodging.'

Tomas bowed his head as if in agreement; Papi grunted, and it was done. Papi left the room and Gudrún followed him to the cowshed.

'We've always managed with the haymaking before,' she said, watching as he collected sacking from the shelf.

'He can't stay here with nothing to do – it ruins a man not to be useful.'

'But why allow him to stay at all?'

Papi stopped and turned to her. 'I don't know what happened to Freyja, or why she's been like the living dead these last weeks, but since we rescued that boy out the sea she's been smiling again. Haven't you seen it?'

'I suppose so.'

Papi turned back again and spoke to the sackcloths in front of him. 'Your sister's got a soft heart. Like her mother. If it pleases her to help out a stranger, then that's what we'll do.'

'If you think it's best,' Gudrún said, but his words left a sharp pain, like a needle had been stuck into her. Freyja had barely known their mother, she told herself. If anyone should be like Mamma, it was her.

Papi gave him their old farmhand's clothing; he also moved him to the cowshed.

'Papi, you can't,' Freyja said.

Tomas shrugged. 'I can sleep anywhere. As long as there's a floor, what's the difference?'

Papi knocked the old tobacco out of his pipe bowl. 'I'm sorry if our house seems like a barn to you.'

Tomas laughed. 'I didn't mean it like that.'

Gudrún tried not to smile, out of loyalty to Papi. She wondered what the house did look like to Tomas. It was much like every other farmhouse in Snæfellsnes, a series of small chambers connected by a narrow corridor: badstofa – with Papi's and their separate sleeping areas partitioned off by curtains – kitchen, pantry and a small hut for keeping manure. All the doors were low, the floor was stone, the walls and roof were turf and there were timber gables facing south. It wasn't a palace, but Freyja kept it clean, especially now.

'Just show me where to go,' Tomas said.

'The cowshed is behind the kitchen,' Gudrún said.

'And it has its own entrance?'

'No.'

He laughed again, louder this time. 'So your cow has to go through the kitchen to get outside?'

'In the winter,' Gudrún said. 'The rest of the year she stays out in the field.'

Papi got up. 'Better than sleeping on the lava fields,' he said, stiffly. 'It would be a shame indeed if Axlar-Bjorn were to get you.'

'*Papi*,' Freyja said.

Papi left the room.

Tomas looked after him. 'Is Axlar-Bjorn a particularly unpleasant character?'

Freyja dipped her head and Gudrún thought she saw her cheeks flush.

'He's no character at all,' Gudrún said. 'He murdered almost twenty people who travelled past his farm and threw their bodies in Íglutjörn pond. But this was in 1596.'

Tomas raised an eyebrow.

'He had a special axe that he found on Mount Axlarhyrna – apparently a stranger appeared to him in a dream and told him where to find it. And when he did, it possessed him and drove him to kill.'

'But he was caught?'

'They broke all his limbs with a sledgehammer and beheaded him. And just to be safe they cut his body into three pieces and buried them in different locations under cairns.'

'I feel a little sorry for Axlar-Bjorn,' Tomas said.

'Don't,' Freyja said.

'But if he was tricked into killing those people—'

'If you believe the story of the dream,' Gudrún said. 'Which no one does.'

'Some people do,' Freyja said.

Tomas grinned. 'You know, I've never been anywhere quite like this country.'

That evening Freyja was restless in bed. After thirty minutes of struggling to keep hold of the blankets, Gudrún kicked her in the shin.

'Ow.'

'Go to sleep.'

'I can't.'

'Then stay awake, but keep still.'

Freyja propped herself up on one elbow. Grey light seeped in past the drawn curtains, but she had her back to the window so when Gudrún looked at her, half her face was in shadow.

'Do you think Papi offended Tomas?' Freyja asked.

'I think it's the other way around.'

'Papi's so stern with him.'

'Hh-mm.'

'What do you think would have happened to him if we hadn't been there that night?'

'I think he would have survived anyway. Tomases always survive.'

'Still, I'm glad we were there.'

'Freyja—'

'Yes?'

'How did you know about the ship?'

'I saw it.'

'But why were you outside?'

'I don't know.' Freyja wouldn't meet her eye. 'I felt like I should go out for some reason, and then I saw it.'

'Out in the rain?'

'Yes. Are you angry with me?'

'No. Why should I be?'

'I know I've been different. Since I came back, I mean.'

'You have.' Gudrún sat up. 'What happened at the farm? Was Rósa unkind to you?'

Freyja was quiet.

'Was she?'

'Why do you dislike Rósa so much?'

Because she's Rósa, Gudrún thought. The sheriff's daughter; the Snæfellsnes beauty. 'What's to like?'

'It wasn't that.' Freyja closed her eyes. 'I wasn't a good worker, I suppose.'

'So they let you go?'

'Yes.'

'Is that what's wrong?'

Silence again.

'Freyja?'

'I felt ashamed.'

'Don't.' She stroked Freyja's forehead. 'You *are* a good worker, whatever they thought. And we need you here too.'

'I know.'

'And they haven't said anything to Papi about it, so they can't be angry. Rósa is too busy being the most important person in the peninsula anyway.'

Freyja turned away. 'Goodnight, Gunna.'

'Goodnight, darling.'

*

Tomas was still with them in October, when the light started to change. In the summer it was brilliant, without being fierce. Every year Gudrún wondered at how clear

17

the air was, how far she could see into the distance. Sometimes she thought she could see the coast of Greenland, a clear, dark line, or, more than a hundred miles in the other direction, the distinct shape of the volcano, Hekla, where Saint Brendan once conversed with the prisoner, Judas Iscariot.

In October the light was hazy, creeping towards darkness. The colour on the lava fields changed too, to red and gold, as the moss put on its winter coat. Freyja had spent late August gathering bilberries and crowberries from the shrubs and heather around the farm, and what fruit she hadn't picked was now rotting sweetly on the ground.

With the hay safely stowed away they spent more time walking along the coast with Tomas. They showed him where the eider ducks nested, and the cold-water spring dedicated to the Holy Virgin Mary, who had appeared there to Gudmundur the Good in 1230, accompanied by three angels, and bade him consecrate the water. They showed him Arnarstapi, the trading post surrounded by ravines and grottos, and the cove at Dritvik, with its black lava sea stacks. They taught him to gather colourful kelp from the rock pools, and crab and rock eels.

'Are those seals?' he asked when they were making their way back from Dritvik, pointing at the slick, grey heads far out in the water.

'Yes,' Gudrún said. 'There's a bigger colony farther along the coast.'

'Don't you eat them? It would make a change from lamb.'

'Some people do. We don't.'

'Why not?'

'In Iceland we say that seals are the Pharaoh's soldiers who drowned in the Red Sea,' Freyja said. 'It'd be like eating ghosts.'

Tomas grinned. 'I could really eat a ghost.'

'Don't,' Freyja said, hitting his arm. He caught her around the waist and spun her around, laughing. Freyja laughed too.

Gudrún looked away.

'What about whales?' Tomas asked.

'What about them?' Gudrún said.

'I haven't seen any here.'

'There used to be lots. Killer whales, Minke whales. Porpoises.'

'Gone?'

She nodded.

Without talking about it, the three of them had lined themselves along the cliff edge. Gudrún looked down at the sea below. It was calm now, and a deep turquoise. Small bursts of white showed where the waves were breaking, but the sound of it barely reached them. Above them, gannets wheeled past. Papi had told them the birds could fly up to a hundred miles out to sea each day. If you saw them with fish in their beaks you could follow them back to shore because they were returning to their nestlings.

They'd lived by the sea for her whole life, Gudrún thought. It was so familiar to her, she felt safe near it. She knew it could change completely with the weather, but the tide came in and out even so.

'There are monsters out there,' Papi always said. 'They hide themselves in the depths so you don't know until it's too late.' But that was Papi.

'Ah well,' Tomas said. 'You never know with the sea. She's just like a woman.'

'What do you mean?' Freyja asked.

Something in her voice made Gudrún look over at her. She was closer to the edge than the other two, still looking out.

'She makes life, doesn't she?' Tomas said. 'Seaweed, and the rest of it. But she's unpredictable, indestructible. She has a violent temper.' He grinned.

'That sounds more like men,' Gudrún said.

'No – we're more like the mountains. Solitary and dominant.'

'Not the mountain behind us.'

'That one too.'

Now Freyja looked at them. 'I've lived by Snæfellsjökull all my life and I know she's a woman.'

Tomas held up his hands. 'Maybe Icelandic mountains are different.'

'Or Icelandic women,' Gudrún said.

'That they are.'

'You should listen to Freyja when it comes to Snæfellsjökull. She knows it better than anyone in the region.'

'Not everyone,' Freyja said.

Gudrún smiled. 'We called her "Goat Girl" when she was younger, she was so good at climbing.'

He laughed. '"Goat girl" – I like it.' His expression changed, grew wistful. 'I had a sister like that. She was faster than I was – our mother used to say she was born during a storm and she never stopped blowing around.'

He leaned his head on Gudrún's shoulder and sighed deeply. His hair tickled her nose and some bony part of his face – cheekbone, or chin – was digging into the flesh around her collarbone, and yet nothing had ever been so delicious as the weight of him, the heat of his out-breath on her neck. She found herself holding her own breath so as not to disturb him.

'What was her name?' Freyja asked.

'Clara.' He lifted his head again. 'She died two years ago, giving birth to my nephew.'

Gudrún clucked her tongue. 'Such a waste.'

'Gunna doesn't believe in babies,' Freyja said.

Tomas grinned. 'She doesn't believe they're real?'

'I don't think women should spend all their time making them,' Gudrún said. She saw Tomas and Freyja exchange a look and felt her cheeks grow hot. 'How can that be it? Sex. Babies. How can that be all we get to do?'

'Well—'

'I know, I know. It's our fault for being born women, I suppose.'

'You sound like my sisters too,' Tomas said. 'All members of the Danish Women's Society.' He stooped and picked two small yellow flowers. 'What are these called?'

'Scots lovage,' Gudrún said.

He presented them with one each. Gudrún looked at Freyja, who smiled and tucked the flower behind her ear.

'Thank you,' she said.

*

The fruit Freyja had picked they made into jams – Gudrún, Freyja and Tomas all together in the kitchen, stirring and chopping and jarring.

The day after their walk to Dritvik, they were in the middle of a batch when the parish priest stopped by on his way to the Big Farm.

Gudrún answered the knock.

'Father,' she said, and took a step back. Maybe it was that his eyes were always rimmed with pink, and his breath stank through years of sinus trouble, but Father Fridrik always left her feeling slightly ill. He wasn't yet forty, but something about him seemed to be decaying already.

'My child.'

She looked past him to where his horse was grazing in their vegetable patch. 'If you're here for Papi, I'm afraid he's in Arnarstapi today.'

'No, no. I just needed a rest.'

She hesitated, then stepped back further. 'Come in, then.'

He entered the badstofa. 'I won't be long,' he said, and sat in Papi's armchair. 'I'll just have a coffee.'

'Make yourself at home,' Gudrún said, and smiled when he looked at her suspiciously.

In the kitchen she put the kettle on the range and tugged Freyja's sleeve.

'You have to come back out with me, both of you,' she whispered.

'Who is it?' Freyja asked, leaning in to hear her answer. 'Father Fridrik.'

Freyja straightened up with a snap. 'I'm not going out.'

Gudrún rolled her eyes. 'I know he's tedious, but you can't leave me alone with him.'

'What's he like?' Tomas asked.

'The worst gossip,' Gudrún said. She nodded at him. 'He'll want to know all about you.'

He raised an eyebrow. 'Shall we have some fun?'

'No,' Gudrún said. 'We want him to finish his coffee and go.'

The kettle started whistling and she gathered the roast coffee from its pot above the fire.

'Did you put the butter in here?' she asked Freyja.

Freyja didn't seem to hear and Gudrún took her shoulder in her hand and shook it gently to rouse her.

'Butter?'

Freyja clasped her hands together. 'I forgot.'

Gudrún sighed. 'Never mind. He can have dull beans. Everyone in the peninsula will just have to hear about our inferior coffee from now on.'

She tipped the beans into the grinder and went to fetch the cream and sugar. Freyja lined the brewing pot with its cloth filter, and laid out four cups and saucers. She moved so slowly Gudrún could have shaken her again, but harder.

'Come on,' she said. 'The sooner we give it to him, the sooner he leaves.'

Tomas grinned.

When the coffee was ready, Gudrún carried it through to the badstofa in the cups, while Tomas and Freyja brought the cream and sugar behind her. The priest stayed seated, but his eyes lit up when he saw Tomas.

'Thank you, my dears,' he said.

'Cream? Sugar?'

'Both, thank you.'

Tomas tipped cream into the cup Gudrún was holding out. The priest winced.

'What?' Tomas asked.

'You should put the sugar in first,' Gudrún said. 'Otherwise the drinker won't marry for seven years.'

'Doesn't matter to him, surely?'

The priest coughed delicately. 'Next time,' he said. 'You *are* in the presence of two maidens, remember.' He shot a look at Freyja, skulking by the doorway.

Gudrún bit her tongue.

'Sit, sit,' the priest said.

Gudrún and Freyja sat in their chairs and Tomas sat cross-legged in front of the fire. Fridrik simpered at them all.

'Freyja – I was sorry to hear you'd left your position. I hope Rósa wasn't displeased with your work?'

Freyja opened her eyes wide and looked at Gudrún.

'I would have thought you had enough on your plate without worrying about us all the way out here, Father,' Gudrún said.

Fridrik's smile grew. 'I spend a lot of time at the farm.'

'Oh?'

'Such a gracious young woman, Rósa Gudmundsdóttir.'

Gudrún smiled tightly.

'You're lucky to have her as a landlord,' Fridrik continued. 'The whole family is a credit to the region.'

'Well, it's been two months since Freyja came back,' Gudrún said. 'If there were any real concerns about her departure surely they could have been raised before now.'

The priest shook his head sadly. 'I've also been sorry not to see you at church, my dears.'

'Isn't the church fit to burst already without us?'

'Thank you, child. My sermons do seem to strike a chord with the congregation.' He wiggled in the chair as if settling in. 'In fact, I've been speaking with the sheriff about funds for a new church. The older members find

24

it hard to climb up to the clifftop. And Hellnar has seventy
inhabitants now – far too many for the building.'

'Well, we wouldn't want to take anyone's place,' Gudrún
said. 'And we've been so busy with the hay this year.'

'Not too busy for God, surely?'

'They pray all the time,' Tomas said, untruthfully, and
Gudrún saw Freyja nod, once, and had to hide her confusion. He blew on his coffee. 'It's a wonder that anything
gets done around here.'

'I'm glad to hear it.'

'They've been trying to get me into praying too.'

'Are you not religious?'

Tomas opened his mouth then closed it again.

'My boy?'

'You remind me of our priest back in Denmark,' Tomas
said. 'He was . . . conscientious too.' He fixed the priest
with a strange smile.

Freyja spoke up suddenly. 'What business takes you to
the Big Farm?'

'Bjartur of Dofri is missing, and I want to speak to the
sheriff about it.'

'We're sorry to hear it,' Gudrún said.

'Very worrying.' He took a sip of the coffee. 'You don't
use chicory root in your brewing?'

'Chicory root?'

'For flavour.'

'*My* priest also liked chicory root in his coffee,' Tomas
said, slapping his knee.

Freyja made a strangled sound that she turned into a
cough.

'Forgive me,' Father Fridrik said, turning to Gudrún. 'I
knew you had a visitor, but I don't know how he got here.'

'He was shipwrecked,' Gudrún said.

'Ah yes. The whaling ship?'

Tomas laughed hollowly. 'The doctor said I'd like whaling. He said it'd keep my mind off other things.'

The priest stirred uneasily.

'You believe in God's plan, don't you, Father?' Tomas said.

'Of course I do, my son.'

'I think it was his plan that I end up here. All last year I had the same dream – a stranger came to me and told me to look for a special tool on a mountain in Iceland.'

'A tool?' Father Fridrik asked weakly.

'Tomas, you mustn't talk about it anymore,' Freyja said gently. 'Don't let yourself get worked up again.'

'He said it would make me famous.' Tomas stretched out the arm holding his cup and slowly rotated it until the coffee poured onto the ground. 'Can't you see its shape in the grounds? The axe, I mean.'

The priest stood up quickly. 'I should be going,' he said.

'I'll see you out,' Gudrún said.

Outside, he climbed straight onto his pony. 'Are you quite safe with him?' he asked.

'He's harmless,' Gudrún said.

'But the dream about the tool—'

'Just a dream, Father.'

'Poor soul.'

A ripple of laughter stirred within her and she bowed her head. 'Thank you for thinking of us.'

'Bless you.' He turned the pony and trotted briskly out of sight.

Gudrún went back inside. Freyja and Tomas turned smiling faces to her.

'A bit much, don't you think?' she asked Tomas.

'It was funny though, Gunna,' Freyja said. 'Admit it.'

'Who's going to clean the coffee up?'

'I will,' Tomas said.

'Good.'

'Hopefully he won't bother you again for a while.'

He wasn't looking at Freyja, but Gudrún understood anyway that his words were for her and felt a softening towards him that he'd sensed Freyja's embarrassment. She looked at her sister, trying to catch her eye to show that she'd sensed it too, that she was on her side, but Freyja was inspecting the hearth.

'Poor Bjartur,' she said.

'He said Bjartur of Dofri,' Tomas said. 'I thought Hellnar was the nearest village.'

'It's one of the farms near Hellnar,' Gudrún said.

'How many farms are there out here?'

'There are seven of us, including the Big Farm belonging to the sheriff, all named for the Bárdur Saga. Dofri was Bárdur's foster father.'

'Why Bárdur?'

'He's our guardian spirit. He sailed here from Norway centuries ago with his wife and nine daughters and other people who didn't like the Norwegian king, and lived at a farm called Laugarbrekka.'

'What did he do?'

'The usual. Fighting. His nephews, Solvi and Raudfeldr, pushed Bárdur's daughter Helga out to sea on an iceberg, so Bárdur killed them.'

Tomas raised an eyebrow. 'How?'

'He threw one of them into a gorge, and another off a cliff.' Gudrún shrugged. 'His half-brother found out, and fought him, of course. Bárdur broke his brother's leg, then disappeared into the ice cap of Snæfellsjökull.'

'You don't approve of him?'

Gudrún gave him a look. 'I don't approve of killing young boys.'

'Even if they've killed your daughter?'

'She didn't die. She floated to Greenland, where Erik the Red lived. And she met Skeggi there and fell in love, apparently.'

'But Bárdur didn't know that,' Freyja said.

'No.' Gudrún stopped, suddenly uncertain. It was the same as when the three of them had stood on the clifftop; Tomas and Freyja were in alignment, almost as if they were speaking another language underneath the words that she understood.

'What makes him your guardian spirit?' Tomas asked.

'He tried to atone afterwards, I suppose,' Gudrún said. 'People called on him when they were in trouble.'

'He's been seen walking across the glacier,' Freyja said. 'He dresses in a grey cowl and carries a cleft staff.'

'I see.' Tomas looked around the badstofa. 'And who's this farm named after?'

'It was called Gestr, meaning "guest", after Bárdur's son, but Papi changed it to Sigrídur after Mamma.'

'Guest?'

'Yes.'

He smiled. 'So it was fate, after all, my ending up here.' He stood and ran his fingers through his hair. The bottom of his shirt rode up, revealing a flat, brown stomach, and Gudrún felt the same fear that had come over her after the wreck, when she'd looked at him properly for the first time.

'We should get back to the jam,' she said.

That night, Tomas helped Gudrún prepare the meat soup. Freyja mended Papi's fishing clothes by the fire while Papi read. There was an easy silence between them all, even throughout dinner. Afterwards, Jules Verne jumped up on Tomas's lap and went to sleep.

'He thinks you're one of the family,' Gudrún said, and was suddenly embarrassed.

Papi raised his eyebrows but went back to his book.

'It's a lot quieter than I remember my family being,' Tomas said, and laughed. 'There's thirteen of us in all.'

'Thirteen mouths,' Papi said, and swore under his breath.

'I should write to them,' Tomas said. It was his turn to look embarrassed. 'If someone will help me?'

'I will,' Freyja offered. 'We can do it tonight, if you like.'

They stood up, and bumped into each other, and smiled. Gudrún stood too.

'I'm going to read in bed,' she said.

'Goodnight, Gunna.'

'I'll turn in, too,' Papi said. 'I need to check on the boat early tomorrow.'

They left them by the fire with a sheet of paper, a pen and some ink. For thirty minutes or so Gudrún could hear whispers and stifled laughter, then she fell asleep.

Freyja woke her climbing into bed.

'What time is it?' Gudrún asked, half asleep.

'Did I wake you?'

'Yes.'

'Sorry.'

'What time is it?'

'It's late.' She felt hot to touch and Gudrún moved away. 'Go back to sleep, Gunna.'

'I'm trying, but you keep talking to me.'

In the moonlight she saw Freyja smile.

'I love you.'

'I love you too.'

1975

SIGGA WOKE SUDDENLY IN the October cold. She lay there for a moment, trying not to disturb Olafur, who was snoring gently next to her, or her cat Loki, curled up at their feet, then turned her head to look at the alarm clock, blinking 6 a.m. on the bedside table. Early.

She wriggled out of bed. Loki opened one eye.

'Coming?' she whispered.

He yawned, shook himself and jumped to the floor. He followed her down the steep staircase to the lobby, then veered towards the front door.

'You want to go out?'

He twitched his tail.

She opened the door for him, then shut it again and made her way into the kitchen at the back of the house, where the back door faced the Atlantic and the Esja mountain range. It was still dark enough outside that with the light on all she could see was her reflection in the glass, but she loved that the view was out there anyway. She loved the view from the front of the house too, onto Njálsgata, and, a few streets over, the bone-white tower of Hallgrímskirkja, the cathedral-in-progress.

She made herself a coffee and ate a slice of toast and butter, leaning against the kitchen counter, inspecting her reflection. She looked tired. She wondered what it was that had woken her, what had been ticking away in her brain. It could be the rally – the once-in-a-lifetime rally, nine days from now. Sigga was meant to be helping organise that, and they were saying now that at least fifteen thousand women would be there.

And then, in December, there would be the ceremony in London, the prize-giving for a story competition her teacher had entered her for. It was most likely that. She could still remember when she'd heard she'd won, how *sparkling* she'd felt. And now she could barely stand to think about it; every time the telephone rang she worried it would be them saying they'd made a mistake, saying there was nothing special about her after all.

She finished the toast.

'Sigga.' Her mother was in the doorway. 'I didn't hear you get up. Did Olafur stay over last night?'

'I was trying to be quiet, and yes, he's still in bed.' She brushed crumbs off herself. 'Why are you up?'

'I feel awful.'

Mamma sat at the table and Sigga put a palm across her forehead. 'You're burning up.'

'Do you have to go to this meeting with Amma?'

'Pétur will be around if you need anything.'

'Can you really see Pétur doing the cooking and cleaning?'

'Pabbi's going to work, you're ill and I'm out. Pétur's twenty-two, he can do it if he puts his mind to it.'

Her mother shook her head.

'*Mamma*. Promise me you won't cook for him.'

'I wouldn't have to if you stayed.'

Sigga rolled her eyes; Pétur had always been Mamma's favourite. Gabríel would have cooked and cleaned without being asked to, but he and Ragga lived in

Heimaey now they were married, and didn't often get the chance to visit.

Mamma held out her hand and Sigga took it.

'You're almost nineteen. When I was your age I was running the family home—'

'I'm not you, Mamma. I'm still at school. Like Pabbi was at my age.'

'You're hardly going to be a doctor like him though, are you?'

Sigga clenched her teeth and counted to ten. She never won arguments with Mamma if she seemed angry.

'Not that I want to be a doctor,' she said, 'but why not?'

Mamma shrugged. 'What are you supposed to do with all this education when you have children and you're at home all day long?'

'Who says I want children?'

Mamma gave her a look. 'You won't think like that when all your friends are having them, Sigrídur.'

Sigga shook her head. 'Do you want anything to eat or drink?' she asked.

'No, I'm not hungry.' Mamma had been on a diet for as long as Sigga could remember. Sometimes it meant bottles of small pills that the doctor prescribed, sometimes it meant eating nothing but toast and coffee. It didn't seem to matter to her that she was tiny already, birdlike almost, with big green eyes, and black hair that fell in ringlets to her shoulders. Completely different to Gabríel and Sigga, with their blonde hair and long legs. Pétur shared Mamma's colouring, if not her height. Maybe that was why Mamma took his side so often.

'Okay. Why don't you lie down in the living room – I can bring you a book and a blanket.'

'Good girl.' Mamma squeezed her hand.

'It's not a big deal.'

'See – you're already looking after me. Motherhood is just that. Unless your children are anything like you were. I've told you, haven't I, that you cried so much when you were a baby I thought you might actually have had a demon in you?'

Sigga looked away, counted to twenty for good measure. 'You've told me.'

'Well, I'm glad it went away.'

She got her mother settled, gulped down her coffee and went back upstairs. She could hear Olafur in the shower, so she undressed and waited in her room, running her hands over her body. It had been so long in developing, it was still an alien thing to her. The puppy fat that had clung for so many years had just melted away a year or so ago and now her waist was smaller than Mamma's, even. And these breasts – where had they been for so long? At least she'd look her age now when she went to university, that was important. Especially, for some reason, if she went abroad, as she'd just started to consider doing. But then how would it work with Olafur?

Olafur came into the room in a cloud of Brylcreem. A teacher had once told him he looked like a young Gary Cooper, and now he wore his hair in a side parting, like the American soldiers who'd been stationed in Iceland during the war. His favourite film was *High Noon*, with Cooper and Grace Kelly; the previous summer he'd started calling her 'Grace' and asked her to call him 'Coop'. She'd pretended to forget so often he gave up, which was a relief because 'Coop' was a dumb name, and because she didn't really look anything like Grace. She had the same wide, full mouth, the heavy brows, the strong jawline, but that was where it ended, and it burned to think people would assume she had such a high opinion of herself.

'If you're ready in five minutes I can give you a lift,' he said.

'I can walk.'

'I'm going that way anyway.' He banged his head on the sloping ceiling and swore. 'I don't know why your family loves these old houses so much,' he said.

She shrugged. It was true, she loved them. She loved the creaky wooden floors. She loved the paint on the corrugated-iron exterior. Even if it was peeling, it was part of their identity: she lived in the red and cream house, her amma lived in the blue and grey house.

'When we're married, we'll live in a modern apartment,' Olafur said.

'What a romantic proposal,' she said. 'Maybe I'll say no.'

'I thought men weren't supposed to be romantic anymore.' He tucked his shirt into his trousers. 'No more opening doors or pulling out chairs. Buying flowers.'

'Is *that* your idea of romance? You do that for your grandmother.'

'But I don't do this.' He crossed the room and took her in his arms, pressed her into his chest. She breathed in his smell – earthy, woody, a slight tang from the Brylcreem.

'Besides, she's a wonderful lady; she deserves a bit of romancing.'

'Gross.'

'It was a joke, Sigga.'

'I *know*.'

She pulled him even closer. There was a sudden, strange ferocity coursing through her and the only way she could think of getting rid of it was by touching him, kissing him, pressing her mouth against his so forcefully her lips hurt. His hands came up underneath her jumper and she pressed her breasts into them. He stroked her nipples, but she kept on pressing. She wanted him to tug them, squeeze them until her eyes watered, then suddenly the violence dissipated and she pushed him away, feeling cold all over.

'What was that?' he asked.

She knew what he was getting at. Over the last two months they'd only slept together three times. She barely even wanted him near her apart from moments like these. But she didn't know what that meant or what was happening to her, so she shrugged, looking away, and said, 'I needed air.'

She heard him fidget for a moment, then he went to the door. 'If you don't need a lift, I'd better go. I've got a lecture.'

'Okay.'

She showered then dressed: black shirt, orange sweater. Then her brown miniskirt. The zip jammed just below the waistband and she paused, sucked in her stomach, and forced it up the rest of the way.

She could hear Pabbi and Pétur stirring when she went back downstairs.

'I'm going to Amma's house now,' she called to her mother. 'Can I take her some kleinur?'

'There's some in the bread bin,' her mother called back.

She grabbed the bag of doughnuts and, as an afterthought, an orange from the fruit bowl, then pulled on her coat and left the house.

No one was out yet, and the only movement came from a paper wrapper from the Co-operative Bakery skimming the road in the breeze. Loki was sitting in the rowan tree in their small front garden, eyeing a raven that was pecking around near the white fence that separated garden from sidewalk.

'I wouldn't if I were you,' Sigga told him.

She was halfway to the garden gate when she heard a woman's voice shouting, just one word – *no* – then immediately afterwards the distinctive tinkle of broken glass. She looked up, instinctively, and saw the windows of the neighbouring house were open on the raised ground floor. Of course. They were always making some noise or other: breaking things, having loud sex. Once or twice she'd heard them argue, really screaming at each other; that was the only thing she wouldn't miss when she moved out.

The husband worked in a bank, or some other job where the employees wore expensive suits and left early in the morning. He always smiled when he saw her, said hello. The woman, on the other hand, was practically invisible; she'd worked in the national library when they'd first moved in, but she seemed to have left it since, and now she didn't go out much. They'd passed each other on the street a few times and Sigga had always pretended to be in a hurry. She didn't have anything against the woman personally, but she didn't want to be sucked into any part of their lives.

Sigga turned up the collar of her coat and headed left out of the gate.

Her grandmother's house was in the opposite direction to Lækjartorg, where the rally would take place, and closer to Sundhöllin swimming pool. Sigga crossed Frakkastigur and turned left towards the sea, then right again on

Grettisgata. On the left side of the road was a row of street lamps, bathing the sidewalk in a dim, orange glow. The right side of the road was crammed with parked cars, mostly Fords. Brown Ford Cortinas, cream Ford Escorts. One green Mini. Olafur wanted a Ford. Mostly because they were reliable, but also because he approved of President Ford. He thought he was exactly the person to get everyone past Watergate.

Sigga took the orange from her coat pocket and started peeling it. She dropped the empty peel back in her coat pocket and ate the segments quickly, one for each house that she passed. She didn't need to look around to tell exactly where she was on the street. She'd half lived at Amma's house, helping her bake skúffukaka and chop wood, listening to her stories. She'd loved staying the night, lying there in her bed as Amma told her all about Bárdur, the protector of Snæfellsnes, part giant, part troll, part man. She could still remember wondering what it would be like to be inside Amma's head, and if she shrank very, very small and climbed in through her ear whether she would find herself on a mountainside, following Bárdur through the snow. She'd liked the idea of the snow falling quickly as she looked back down at the whole world sunk and buried, all the houses, the sea, all flat and white, and in the middle of that idea she'd squeeze her eyes shut, because if she opened them she knew she'd see snow piled up against the window of *their* house, and then it would be pouring in and filling up all the air . . .

Then she'd open her eyes, and Amma would be sitting at the end of her bed, and Sigga would sigh happily, and burrow deeper inside her blankets, safe and warm.

38

Amma never raised her voice, or nagged her to keep up her ballet classes. She was funny, but firm. Kind, but blunt. It was Amma's voice in her head that had recently helped Sigga write the story.

Her knees were feeling the early-morning chill, so she hurried her pace and arrived at her grandmother's breathing slightly fast. The door was unlocked as usual, and her grandmother was in the kitchen. She was standing at the sink, her back to Sigga, so only her fluffy white hair was visible above a brown roll-neck jumper.

'Hi, Amma. I brought kleinur.'

Her grandmother didn't move. A half-drunk cup of coffee was at the table next to a half-eaten bowl of porridge. Sigga wondered if something was bothering her too, then dismissed the thought. Amma was fearless, it was legendary in the family, even at eighty-something years old. She'd come from the Snæfellsnes peninsula years ago, when Pabbi was a baby, and raised him by herself in the city. Both her parents and her only sister had died, and Sigga had never heard her speak about Pabbi's father.

'Amma?' she said again.

Her grandmother turned and fixed her eyes on Sigga. They were big and dark blue, bluer still against all that white hair.

'Sorry, darling,' she said. 'My mind was elsewhere.'

The radio on the kitchen counter was on, and a news-reader was interviewing somebody about the Government's decision to extend Iceland's fishery limits.

Amma motioned for Sigga to sit down and turned down the volume. 'Same old news,' she said. 'Either I'm going crazy or Elizabeth Taylor married Richard Burton again.'

'I heard that too,' Sigga said. 'In Botswana.'

'Good for them. Anything to drink with your kleinur?'

'No thanks.'

They sat opposite each other at the kitchen table.

'I feel weird,' Sigga said.

'How so?'

'On edge.'

Her grandmother ate a corner of the doughnut. 'Me too, actually.'

'Mamma's ill.'

'That's a shame. Another of her migraines?'

'Probably. I made her promise not to cook for Pétur.'

'You didn't trust her not to?'

'It's Pétur.'

Amma smiled. 'Women are taught that men are useless from such an early age that we find it hard to shake the idea.'

'She doesn't think he's useless; she thinks he's a genius.'

'She thinks both,' Amma said. 'But it does him a disservice to think he can't look after himself. It does her a disservice too.' She swept kleinur crumbs from the table top into her cupped hand, then tipped them into her coffee. 'Anyway, I'll wash up. The meeting's at Ava's house today, did I say?'

'No, you didn't.'

Ava was Amma's old landlady from when she and Pabbi lived in an attic on Frakkastigur. She was 'different', as Mamma would say. Her hair was short and stuck up in tufts and she carried liquorice in her pockets to give to children she met on the street. She was a composer and Sigga had always liked visiting her house, with its grand piano, and old furniture, and all the oil paintings on the wall.

Amma stood, then paused, resting one hand on the back of her chair. 'What about Karen? Is she coming?'

'She's away in Denmark. Her sister's just had a baby.'

'Okay. Hand me the cup and bowl?'

'I'll wash up,' Sigga said. 'You get ready.'

Amma clucked. 'What did I do to deserve you? I'll dig out an extra jumper, then.'

She left the room. Sigga went to the sink, started running the tap, then turned up the radio. The newsreader had obviously gone back to an earlier story. '*The headlines again,*' he was saying. '*A body has been found, perfectly preserved in the ice on Snæfellsjökull . . .*'

She turned off the tap and paused, hands submerged in warm water, to hear the rest.

'*According to the report, the deceased has lain there undiscovered for over fifty years. More details to follow.*'

1910

DECEMBER BROUGHT SNOW. LOOKING out of the kitchen window on Yule's Eve, Gudrún saw a white, cloudless sky and white ground. There was no more smell of angelica when she breathed in, only cold air that burned the back of her throat, and the birds were silent, although she saw tracks in the garden leading up to where she'd thrown down scraps for them to eat.

Tomas and Freyja had been decorating the tree in the badstofa with candles and oranges and garlands of popcorn, all from the sack dropped off by one of Rósa's farmhands early that morning. Gudrún went into the corridor, where she could hear Freyja explaining the Yule Lads to him, and laughter.

'Tell me their names again,' Tomas said.

'It's easy: Sheepfold Stick, Gilly Oaf, Stubby, Spoon-licker, Pot-licker, Bowl-licker, Door-slammer, Skyr-glutton, Sausage-pilfer, Peeper, Sniffer, Meat-hook and Candle-beggar.'

'That's a lot of licking of kitchen utensils.'

'Says the man who drinks soup straight from the bowl.'

'It's quicker.'

A laugh. 'Oh, and they live in the mountains with their parents, Grýla and Leppalúdi.'

'So they're trolls?'

'Yes.'

'Not elves.'

'No.'

'So they're bad?'

'They like to steal things.'

'And lick them.'

There was silence for a moment. Gudrún moved to the badstofa doorway and looked in. They were standing close together, on one side of the tree they'd placed in the centre of the room. Tomas was holding the end of a popcorn garland while Freyja untangled it in the middle. Freyja's skin was rosy in the firelight, almost luminescent. Her head was bent forwards in concentration, and Tomas was smiling down at the exposed nape of her neck, a softness in his eyes. For the first time, Gudrún felt a prickle of envy, and a small voice wondered why Freyja and not her.

She started to back out, until they both looked in her direction.

'Gunna,' Freyja said, smiling. 'Can you help me?'

She came into the room properly and took the garland from Freyja.

'Whatever's cooking in there smells good,' Tomas said.

'It's just ptarmigan.'

She didn't have to look up to know they'd exchanged glances, and realised her tone had been sharper than she'd intended.

'Can I do anything?' Freyja asked.

'You're busy with this.' Gudrún ran her finger lightly along the string until she felt an almost imperceptible knot, then started to pick at it with her fingernail. She looked at Freyja and saw the small crease around her sister's mouth that meant she was chewing the inside of her lip. 'It looks good – the tree, I mean.'

Freyja leaned forwards and rubbed her nose into Gudrún's neck, like she used to do when they were little. 'Thank you.'

Gudrún rested her chin on Freyja's head. 'Here – I've started it for you.'

Tomas took the garland. 'I'll take over. You ladies sit down and rest.'

Gudrún and Freyja broke apart and looked at each other.

'What a gentleman,' Gudrún said, and saw Freyja trying to stifle a smile.

'I need to repay your hospitality somehow.'

'Tell us about Christmas in Denmark,' Freyja said, settling herself into Papi's chair.

Tomas perched on its arm and lifted the garland up to his face. 'It's Christmassy.'

'Not one of your better stories,' Gudrún remarked.

He shrugged. 'Hymns, candles, families, rice pudding. We have nisse instead of your Yule Lads.'

'What's a nisser?' Freyja asked.

'A small man in a red cap. Every farm has one as a guardian. They're supposed to help with work and protecting livestock but they take offence easily.'

'What happens then?'

'They go on killing sprees. Some of them can shape-shift.'

'Much more believable than the Yule Lads,' Freyja said.

Tomas smiled at the popcorn. 'Much.'

Gudrún watched his fingers deftly unpick the rest of the knot then run up and down the string as hers had done. They were long and wiry, but she could imagine they would be gentle if he ever touched her. Ever stroked her arm, brushed hair out of her face—

He looked up and saw her watching him.

'That was quick,' she said.

'I'm a sailor, remember?'

'Yes.' She took up the poker and jabbed at the wood in the fireplace.

'When's Papi back?' Freyja asked.

'Soon, I'm sure.'

'I don't like him being outside in this weather.'

'What weather?' Gudrún smiled. 'It's not even snowing now.'

'It will.' Freyja looked at her. 'They found Bjartur, you know? Papi told me this morning.'

'The man who went missing in October?' Tomas asked. 'Where did they find him?'

'At the foot of Snæfellsjökull.'

'Did he fall?'

Gudrún shrugged. 'They think he meant to get lost.'

'Up the mountain?'

'He wouldn't be the first.' She looked back at Freyja. 'Papi's fine. Bjartur's wife died last Yule – his farmhands said he never got over it.'

'Last night, I dreamt we found Bjartur in a cave halfway up the mountain,' Freyja said. 'At least, I think it was him.' Her expression was strange, and Gudrún was suddenly reminded of how, as children, when they used to run up Snæfellsjökull every summer, Freyja was always barefoot. So she could be closer to it, she'd said. Was that when they'd started calling it Freyja's mountain?

It was almost two thirty, and the sun, which had barely risen above the volcano's peak, was beginning to set, flooding the snow-packed garden with a deep blood-red colour. Shadows stretched out from the corners of the

46

room and curled over the furniture, leaving everything grey and formless in their wake.

Freyja stood and plucked a candle from the tree. She brought it to the fire and lit it, then went back and lit all the other candles with it. The room flickered from gold to darkness and back again. In the grate, the fire crackled enthusiastically, and from time to time they heard the thump as melting snow slid off the roof and hit the ground, but otherwise all was quiet.

Gudrún joined Freyja at the tree. Close up, she could smell the freshness of pine, and the sweet zing of orange. Jules Verne appeared and curled himself around her ankles, and she picked him up. His fur was covered with a light layer of frost. She turned him to face her.

'I suppose you're hanging around for the food too,' she said.

He mewled pathetically.

'We'll see what there is in the kitchen then. Don't tell Papi.'

Freyja smiled. Tomas stepped aside for Gudrún to pass. For a moment she considered asking him to help peel the potatoes, but he wasn't looking at her.

She spent the next few hours hard at it, peeling potatoes, chopping fruit for the jam, stirring the peas and beans. She heard Papi come home and clomp around and the church bells pealing at six, signalling the start of Yule. At five past six she carried the food through to the badstofa, where the other three were sitting by the fire, and placed it on the table. They looked up when she came in, and as irritated as she was at having spent all day cooking alone, she savoured the roundness of their eyes as they looked at her work.

'Gunna, it's a feast,' Freyja said.

'Papi, can you carve?'

They sat. Papi at the head of the table, Tomas at the other end. Papi cut up the bird and dished out the portions; Gudrún ladled the accompaniments onto their plates, while Freyja poured them wine. They raised their glasses to each other.

'*Glædilig jul,*' Tomas said.

'*Gleðileg jól,*' Gudrún and Freyja said in unison.

Papi drank half his glass in one. 'Danish was always a ridiculous language,' he said.

Gudrún saw the frown ruffling Freyja's brow and felt her own answer. Papi wasn't usually so argumentative.

'Papi,' Freyja said. 'That's not exactly the Christmas spirit.'

Tomas grinned.

Papi speared a potato. 'I've earned my right to speak my mind, haven't I? I've worked hard enough all these years.'

'That's not how it works,' Gudrún said.

'Isn't it?' He pointed his fork at her. 'You'll see. You'll end up old and alone too and you won't be bothered with politeness.'

Gudrún sawed furiously at her meat, trying to cover up her red cheeks. 'God help me if I turn out like you.'

'You won't end up old and alone, Gunna,' Freyja said. She sounded like she was close to tears and Gudrún felt a momentary irritation; *she* was the one Papi had attacked.

'Having daughters is a curse,' Papi continued. 'Daughters leave you, and then their husbands take everything.'

'What?' Freyja said.

'Property,' Papi said. 'It's unnatural not to pass on your property to your children.' He fixed Tomas with a glare. 'Your *blood* children. Bárdur knew it – his dream about the tree was all about the end of his line.'

Gudrún realised he was slurring. 'Papi, where did you go earlier?'

'I went to Gudmundur – to pay my respects for the holiday.' Papi dropped his fork. 'He had some very good wine. Quite a bit of it, actually.'

'You're drunk, aren't you?'

'Maybe.'

'For God's sake.' Gudrún pressed a forefinger against her mouth to stop herself from laughing. Across the table she could see Freyja cover her face with her hands. 'We thought you'd lost your mind.'

'Have I? My head's killing me, you know?'

'Papi . . .' Gudrún started, then had to press harder. Papi had barely drunk since they were little, and she couldn't imagine how he'd seemed to Gudmundur. The sheriff probably had wine with every meal.

'Oh my girls.' A large tear suddenly appeared and rolled down Papi's left cheek. 'What did I do to deserve you?'

'You're an old fool, you know that?'

She got up and went to Papi, and Freyja did too, and they hugged him while he sobbed alternately into their shoulders. Tomas continued eating, a grin on his face.

'Let's open our presents,' Freyja said, after Papi had wiped his nose on his sleeve. 'Wait here.'

She went to their bed in the corner of the badstofa and slid something out from underneath her pillow. She came back holding it out; it was a parcel tied up with string. Gudrún took it from her and opened it. Inside were four woollen scarves – one deep blue, one red, one green and one grey.

'When did you get the chance to make these?' Gudrún asked, fingering the red scarf. It was bouncy and incredibly thick, and she thought for a moment of Kristin, her favourite sheep, who had wandered onto the beach last year and drowned.

'I've been working on them for a while.' Freyja handed the blue scarf to Tomas, the green one to Papi and wrapped the grey scarf around herself.

'Now you won't be eaten by the Christmas Cat,' Gudrún said to Tomas.

'I beg your pardon?'

'The Christmas Cat.' Gudrún draped the red scarf over her neck. 'He belongs to Grýla, and he eats anyone who doesn't receive new clothing at Christmas.'

'You haven't got a Christmas Cat?' Freyja asked.

He shook his head.

'Do they have *no* traditions in Denmark?' Papi exploded, and had to be calmed down with another glass of wine.

After dinner Gudrún opened the front door, and stood for a moment in the night air. There was a layer of ice in the pail Freyja had left next to the door, cracked and bubbled, and Gudrún stooped to see her reflection in it. She looked tired. She *was* tired; that was why.

The moon had risen in a green sky, and everywhere its light melted into colour: pinks and violets trapped in the icicles that hung from the roof, and in the snowflakes that blanketed the grass. It looked pretty, inviting even. When she turned to face the mountain, that too was alive, washed in the lightest of blues, its ridges and crevices smoothed over as if draped in cotton. Still, she felt a shiver catch hold of her spine at the unbroken landscape, the immensity of it. So easy to get lost out there, to fall into a crack and never get out. She wrapped her arms around herself even as she went back inside. Where, she wondered, had that come from?

*

On New Year's Eve they had another visitor. This time it was Freyja who answered the knock, and Gudrún heard her exclamation of surprise.

'Heaven preserve us from Father Fridrik,' Gudrún said, wiping her hands on her skirt.

Tomas, who had been keeping her company in the kitchen, ambled towards the door.

'I'll send him packing,' he said.

Gudrún hesitated, then followed him.

Freyja was in the badstofa with someone else; Gudrún heard a deep voice saying, 'Your badstofa is admirably clean,' and Freyja responding with a 'thank you.'

'That doesn't sound like your priest,' Tomas said.

'But then, what else should I expect from you?' the stranger said as Tomas and Gudrún entered.

Gudrún stopped in the doorway. Freyja was standing against the fireplace wall, her back pressed up against it, her chin tilted down to look at the floor. The stranger was standing about a foot away from her, his hat in his hands. He turned and looked from Gudrún to Tomas then back to Gudrún. His gaze was sharp and she found herself unable to break it. He looked to be in his mid-twenties, tall – much taller than any other man she'd seen – and broad, too. His eyes were green, his beard a dark brown. He was smiling, although at first glance she would have said he seemed wary, without knowing what gave her that impression.

'Please excuse my dropping in like this,' he said, and she felt his voice vibrating through her body. 'I came to bring Freyja a token of our appreciation, for all her hard work.'

'Your appreciation?'

'Yes – mine and Rósa's.'

So this was Magnús, Rósa's husband. Although he'd come to live at the Big Farm two years ago he didn't go out into the community often, and Gudrún realised with a start that this was the first time she'd seen him up close. She was taken aback by how masculine he was, and remembered, vaguely, some story from when he first arrived of how he'd got into a dispute with Skúli Skulisson about some sheep and smashed Skúli's plough to bits. She could imagine how easy it would have been for him.

She pulled herself together. 'Pleased to meet you,' she said. 'Will you stay for coffee?'

'Thank you, I will . . .'

'Gudrún.'

'Gudrún,' he murmured to himself. 'After Gudrún from the *Laxdæla*?'

'Yes.'

'And Freyja, Goddess of the Hearth. Your parents must have been fond of the sagas.'

'Our mother's favourite character was Gudrún. And any household looked after by Freyja is a lucky one, of course.'

'Of course,' he said, and turned his smile on Freyja, who ducked her gaze again.

Gudrún felt her stomach twist in sympathy. She would have found Magnús intimidating as an employer, too, she thought.

'And this must be your guest from Denmark?' Magnús said, looking at Tomas.

Tomas made a half-bow but didn't introduce himself.

There was an uneasy silence, during which Magnús smiled at the ceiling.

'Let me make the coffee,' Gudrún said, and escaped to the kitchen.

When she brought it through, the three of them were sitting down: Freyja and Tomas on the seat and arm of Freyja's chair, and Magnús in Papi's chair. Gudrún handed out the cups and took a seat herself.

'Is that a wedding ring you wear around your neck?' Magnús asked.

'Yes.' She brought her hand up to it. 'It was our mother's.'

'Gudrún married four times, is that right?'

'Excuse me?'

'In the *Laxdæla*.'

'Yes.'

'And had one of her suitors killed?'

'Yes.'

'Rather a bloodthirsty namesake, don't you think?' he said.

'All our literature is pretty bloodthirsty.'

'You wouldn't rather be a goddess?'

'Not on balance, no,' Gudrún said.

He smiled. 'I see why they call you the strong-minded one.'

She felt her cheeks heat up. 'Is that how I'm known?'

53

'I've heard it said that if all Icelandic women were like you, we would have achieved independence by now.'

Her cheeks flushed for a different reason, and she drank her coffee to disguise them.

'And what do you young people have planned for tonight's celebrations?' Magnús asked.

'Nothing,' Freyja said.

'No dances?'

'No.'

'Will you be going out?' Gudrún asked.

'Under duress.' He raised his cup to his mouth. 'My wife is the dancer, not me.'

'I don't see the point in it, myself,' Gudrún said.

Magnús smiled. 'I'm sorry to miss your father – where did you say he was?'

'Preparing the boat,' Tomas answered.

'That's a shame. I'd hoped to get his advice on some farming matters.'

'He won't be back before dark,' Freyja said.

'I see.'

There was another silence. Gudrún cast around for some conversation.

'You said something about a gift?' she said, eventually. 'It's very generous of you.'

Magnús waved a large hand. 'It's nothing. A shell I found while riding – Freyja had mentioned to my wife how she loves the pink ones, and this was particularly lovely.' He reached into his pocket.

Freyja looked away.

He took out a small, whorled shell, a delicate rose-colour.

'We both commented on how alike your ear it was,' he said.

Freyja blushed, and Gudrún felt her heart pinch. Of course, that was it. Freyja had fallen in love with Magnús.

'Oh, and, of course, some cheese from our favourite ewe. For the whole family.' He withdrew a larger object wrapped in white cloth and placed it on the arm of Papi's chair.

'Thank you,' Gudrún said. 'We're very grateful for it.'

'Thank you,' Freyja said.

She was still looking away, but Gudrún saw her bring her hand up and quickly brush at her eyes with its heel. It must be true love, Gudrún thought, for her to cry over a shell, no matter how pretty it was.

Magnús smiled again. Gudrún drummed her fingers against the arm of her chair. Resentment churned through her stomach – she couldn't have both Tomas and Magnús, not even Freyja—

She checked herself. Nothing Magnús had done indicated that he felt the same way. He was married to Rósa, anyway; he was probably just trying to make amends for the dismissal. Now that she knew, she wondered if maybe Freyja's feelings were the real reason she'd been let go. It was no wonder Freyja hadn't wanted to discuss the matter.

She met Magnús's gaze. 'Would you like to share some cheese with us now?' she asked. 'I'm afraid we don't have anything to go with it – I haven't finished baking yet.'

'Please don't worry.' Magnús stood. 'Thank you for the coffee. I'm afraid I should go – Father Fridrik is paying us a visit this afternoon.'

'Well, perhaps you won't make the dance after all,' Gudrún said. 'If the old windbag gets going.'

He raised an eyebrow. 'You must not know we were raised together, Father Fridrik and myself?'

Out of the corner of her eye she saw Tomas grin.

'No, I didn't.'

'In the north. We were raised by the same farmer.'

'I see.'

'Of course, I find the best way to end his visits is to mention politics.' Magnús smiled at her. 'The old windbag hates politics.'

Had she ever felt more relieved? She inspected her fingernails carefully, too confused to look at him.

'We found another way,' Tomas said.

'Ah yes,' Magnús said. 'Are you the madman?'

Tomas grinned again.

'But you *are* a sailor?'

'Yes.'

'Will you be fishing with Einar this year? It's a stroke of luck for him, getting an extra pair of hands this way.'

Tomas frowned slightly. 'We haven't—'

'No, don't go,' Freyja interrupted. She took Tomas's hand. 'You nearly drowned last time you went to sea.'

Tomas looked down at her upturned face, then shook his head. 'I won't if you don't want me to.'

Gudrún bit her lip.

'I see,' Magnús said. 'Well, good day.' He waved Gudrún down when she rose from her chair. 'Thank you for the excellent coffee, Gudrún Einarsdóttir.'

He closed the door behind him. Gudrún could hear his footsteps crunching through the snow, hear the jangling of reins as he mounted his horse, then the sound of the animal trotting out of the garden and onto the path leading to the Big Farm. She rose and went into the pantry, where

56

she could watch the rider get smaller and further away, until eventually he disappeared.

Freyja was quiet after the visit, and Gudrún wondered if perhaps seeing Magnús again had reignited her feelings for him. It would be easily done, she thought.

She tried to talk about him to Freyja, but each time Freyja changed the subject. She seemed even closer to Tomas suddenly and after a few days Gudrún gave up, and the two of them drifted into silence around each other.

Then, on the fifth morning of the new year, Freyja looked around the cowshed as she was milking Margret and almost smiled.

'What is it?' Gudrún asked, pausing in her sweeping.

'I was thinking how uncomfortable it is in here,' Freyja said.

'Poor Tomas,' Gudrún said.

Freyja caught her eye and smiled properly. 'Poor Tomas.'

'He never complains, though.'

'So brave.'

They giggled. Gudrún leaned her broom against the wall and went over to the milking station. Freyja was still pulling at Margret's teats. Gudrún laid her hand on the cow's flank, feeling the softness and warmth underneath her fingers. Without warning she thought of Magnús, what it would feel like to touch his skin, and quickly lifted her hand away.

'I think maybe he'll stay,' she said. 'Tomas, I mean.'

'Yes.'

'Do you want him to?'

'I wouldn't want him to stay if he didn't want to.'

'You're not making sense.'

'You know what I mean.'

Gudrún drew her thumb down Freyja's cheek and pressed it gently against the middle of her chin. 'You should be careful, Freyja.'

'Careful of what?'

'You shouldn't make it so easy for him.'

Freyja blinked and looked away.

'I'm trying to protect you,' Gudrún said. 'Men don't respect anything they don't have to work for.'

'Thank you for the advice.'

'It's unfair, but it's life. Women have to be a million things and men only have to be one, because they're the ones in charge. It's better not to get involved at all.' She put her hand back on Margret. 'It's better to use our time fighting the rules they've laid down for us.'

Freyja sighed.

There was another silence. Gudrún stroked Margret.

'How is it? How is he?' she asked eventually, despite herself.

'It's nice – he's nice.'

'How did you cope with the pain?'

'The pain?'

'Didn't it hurt?'

'Why would it?'

'They say it does, the first time.'

Freyja looked down. 'I suppose so.'

'What did you do?'

'You can let it wash through you. Like water. It ends.'

There was a sadness in the air.

'I'm sorry,' Gudrún said.

'Don't be sorry.' Freyja stood and picked up the pail. 'I like him.'

1975

THE RED STOCKING MOVEMENT had organised a strike for October 24th, but people were wary of the term, so in the end they'd decided to call it the Women's Day Off. Women were supposed to avoid any work – either paid, or domestic if they were housewives like her mother – in order to underline the importance of their contribution to society. The rally would take place in Reykjavik, with speeches and singing and 'whatever moves us', one of the organisers had said at the last meeting. They were supposed to be handing out flyers detailing the programme downtown, but Sigga had left a few around the house in places she knew Mamma would find them. She'd circled the heading: *Why a Day Off for Women?* and reasons six and ten: *Because it's commonly said about a housewife 'she isn't working – just keeping house',* and: *Because the work experience of a housewife is not considered of any value on the labor market.*

Just before she was about to leave she felt a horrible dizziness, as if her brain were sliding backwards out of her skull. Her stomach rose up to meet it, and she only just made it to the bathroom in time before covering the inside of the toilet bowl with vomit. Afterwards, she brushed her teeth again, splashed some water on her cheeks and felt much better. Pétur, who was waiting outside the bathroom, wrinkled up his nose when she came out.

'What the hell have you done in there?' he asked, and she pushed past him without answering.

She felt better again once she was outside, with the cold air on her face, but even so, she half wished she could forget the flyers, the meetings, forget the other women, and go for a swim instead. Sundhöllin was the closest pool, and its main room, with its high ceiling and deep water, its shafts of light that fell through tall, narrow windows, and the quiet lapping sound she made as she ploughed up and down the lanes, brought her the same kind of stillness that spending time alone with Amma did. Maybe because it was Amma who had taught her to swim – really to swim – after she'd almost drowned when she was six and three-quarters.

The *incident*, her family called it. They'd been on holiday when it had happened, staying in the summer house near Akureyri. Amma was there too – she came every year to help Mamma. Mamma was always different on holiday, after a lie-in. No matter what Gabríel and Pétur broke, or lost, Mamma didn't care. 'Boys will be boys,' she'd say.

Sigga loved their holidays, loved the drive up through miles and miles of uninhabited countryside, past hillsides curtained in birch trees, past fjords glittering in the distance, and the swans that drifted over them like little specks of white. Then pulling up to the summer house – the smell of pine and turf hitting them as soon as they climbed out of the car – and running up the front path, throwing open the door.

Before the incident, all her memories of their holidays were of being outside, the sunshine pouring itself over their bare heads and running down their necks, and how the air smelled like summer: like warm earth and spicy thyme and sheep dung. The brightly coloured houses of Akureyri were always gleaming in the distance, the long, deep blue finger of its fjord pointing upwards towards the Arctic, to where small waves wrinkled a surface otherwise as smooth as silk.

And then that day – the green all around her – she remembered suddenly how it had been oily and heavy, which surprised her, because water was nothing, it ran through your fingers when you held your hand under the tap.

Boys will be boys. Mamma still believed that after the incident too. Even after Sigga had come back from the hospital, when she'd tried to tell Mamma that it was Pétur who was closest to her on the harbour wall, so when she'd felt the hand in her back, the sudden shove, it must have been his hand, him shoving her. She'd fallen spread-eagled, arms and legs wheeling as if she could stay in the air that way, and all the way down she could hear them laughing, Pétur and the friend he'd made that summer.

But she was still here. And Amma had taught her how to watch the surface and judge the tide, how it doesn't always show on the surface, how it draws out the water underneath instead.

'It's the most important thing I can teach you,' she'd said. 'How to survive in the sea.'

Amma was quiet on the short walk to Hlemmur bus station, where they were going to start. It was almost nine thirty, and the sun was only now palely visible in the sky, skimming the aerials on downtown rooftops. Down the hill, a flock of snow buntings perched on the back of a bench facing out onto a patch of grass and concrete, the remnants of a house that had burned down the previous summer. Farther away still, waves splashed against the harbour wall. There was a pinkness to the sky that was already fading to grey; Reykjavik looked cold beneath it.

'Are you okay?' Sigga asked as they reached the corner of Grettisgata and Snorrabraut.

'Hmm?' Amma said. 'Did you say something?'

'Are you okay?'

She took Sigga's hand and squeezed it. 'I was just thinking about my sister.'

Besides never mentioning Pabbi's father, Amma hardly ever talked about her sister. All Sigga knew about her great-aunt was that her favourite food had been kjötsúpa, like Sigga's.

'What about her?'

'These flyers – the point about the farmers' wives. We weren't wives, but we were daughters, and we were part of that community, never mind our sex. And now they're not accepted as full members of the Farmers' Union. Sometimes it feels like two steps forward, one step back.'

'Would your sister have joined the movement?'

'She would have.'

'I wish Mamma would.'

'At least she has strong opinions,' Amma said. 'No one could ever accuse your mother of not knowing her own mind.'

'I guess so.'

Amma let go of Sigga's hand and brushed a piece of fluff off her coat. 'We don't always understand the people we love. I didn't understand my sister.'

'How so?' Sigga asked.

'Once, when we were girls, our cat went missing, and she went out two nights in a row, walking through the wind and the rain to find him. She made a bargain – she said she would give three years of her life if he could have three more. At the time I thought she must be very unhappy if she was willing to do that. Now I understand she was just more generous than anyone else.'

'Like Pabbi,' Sigga said.

'Anyway.' Amma tapped the stack in her hands. 'It's too much to hope everyone will come to the rally. But enough about us women – how's the aspiring gynaecology student?'

'Olafur? He sends his love. And he still wants to know what's wrong with gynaecology?'

'It's ridiculous that a man can think he knows more about a woman's body than she does. But apart from that – nothing.'

'Do you trust Pabbi to know more about your body?'

'He's a trauma surgeon. He doesn't mess around with women's reproductive systems.'

'Gynaecologists do train for years, you know,' Sigga said.

Amma shifted the stack from one arm to the other. 'That's how they want us to think.' She smiled. 'It's all part of a bid to mystify us and our sexuality so they can control it.'

'Olafur isn't trying to control me.'

'No?'

'Why don't you like him?'

'What's to like?'

'Amma.' Sigga tried to look stern.

'Oh, well,' Amma said. 'As long as you're happy, I suppose. You don't have to stay with him forever.' She frowned slightly. 'What's happening there?'

Hlemmur – a squat glass building covered in the bright red and yellow signage for *Stræto* bus company – sat in the middle of a large concrete island surrounded by three main roads. As they waited to cross Laugavegur, Sigga caught sight of two women arguing. The older one was trying to take away a stack of flyers from the other, who was clutching them to her chest. The second was Sigga's age, or slightly older, small and brunette with short bangs, wearing blue dungarees over a red woollen jumper.

The older woman tapped the flyer that had already been pasted onto Hlemmur's side and said something that was lost among the cars. The paper was plain white, with a red slogan in the middle. Sigga squinted to read: 'Our bodies, our choice'.

Amma shook her head, making tutting noises. 'Poor girl,' she said. 'She won't get anywhere with that.'

'Mamma would say she should be locked up just for talking about it.'

'Would she now?'

'Sometimes I think she'd have "If you make your bed, you lie in it" on her tombstone.'

Amma smiled. 'Some people talk a hard talk,' she said. 'But when push comes to shove, they're not so hard.'

'Well—'

The lights changed and she and Amma crossed.

Sigga caught sight of another figure, wrapped abundantly in colourful scarves, waving at them.

'Is Ava meeting us?'

'She offered,' Amma said. 'It's good for her to get out.'

'Oh,' Sigga said, and tried to keep the disappointment from her voice.

'You don't mind, do you?' Amma asked.

'Of course not.'

They stopped in front of Ava, whose eyes were the only things visible in the small gap left by the scarves.

'Hi, Ava,' Sigga said. 'Nice to see you again.'

'How's school, Sigga?' Ava asked, muffled. 'I didn't get a chance to ask you at the meeting.'

'Sigga won a writing competition,' Amma said, handing over a pile of flyers.

'Good for *you*,' Ava said. 'What's it about?'

'It's based on the Bárdur saga,' Sigga said. 'Of course.'

'Of course.'

'Tell her the title,' Amma prompted.

'*The Other*,' Sigga said. 'It's about Helga more than Bárdur.'

Ava's eyes crinkled. 'I can see why you won. It probably went right over their heads.'

Sigga laughed. She was feeling good again, kind of fizzy. She'd been pleased when she came up with the idea, no matter that Mamma had rolled her eyes at it.

'And now you know as much as me,' Amma said. 'I haven't been allowed to read it yet.'

'You didn't ask to,' Sigga said.

'Of course I want to read it – I want to know why you chose to write about her in the first place.'

Sigga blew out her cheeks. This was the part of the trip to London she was dreading, trying to come up with an answer to that *why*. On the face of it, the Bárdur Saga was about Bárdur Snæfellsás, who was descended from giants on his father's side, and trolls on his mother's, and brought up in the mountains of Norway. He'd sailed to Iceland with his wife and nine daughters, establishing a community on the peninsula with Bárdur as their leader. They lived peacefully for some time until Helga disappeared, pushed out to sea by his nephews. Bárdur murdered them in revenge and retreated to the mountains. Later, he learned that Helga was still alive and shacked up with a married lover. He forced her to come home with him, although she was never happy afterwards.

And then there was the son, Gestr, the result of Bárdur seducing Helga's lover's daughter; some sort of punishment for Helga's indiscretions. Helga had been made to bring the boy up until he was twelve or so, and then she'd disappeared from the narrative, which followed Gestr instead, until his grisly death at the hands of his father for converting to Christianity.

How could she *not* want to write Helga's side? It was more a matter of surprise that no one had done it before. It had always been plain to her that Helga was the link between the first and second halves of the saga, that her story precipitated Bárdur's reversion to the ways of his forefathers. The beginning of the saga, as it talked about his ancestors, and his childhood, was really telling readers who he *would* be, but it could only happen because of Helga. And his genealogy being laid out like that meant the family became an entity outside of time and Bárdur's fate became tied up in his ancestors' stories. Sigga knew history would repeat itself and the family's nature would stay the same, and she knew that was significant. But she didn't know *how* she knew that – it was just clear, in the way that it was clear that she liked skyr, and preferred John Lennon to Paul McCartney, and Gabríel to Pétur.

'Keeping up the suspense?' Ava said.

'Something like that,' Sigga said.

'Anyway, let's make a start,' Amma said. She drew her thumb down Sigga's cheek and pressed it gently against the middle of her chin. 'Sigga has to get to class by ten-thirty, so we get as far as we can before then.'

The flyering was a success, Sigga thought. Nearly everyone they approached seemed interested, with the exception of one middle-aged woman walking with a slightly over-weight, balding man, who put her hands behind her back rather than take the sheet, staring over Sigga's shoulder as if she wasn't even there. The man snorted and said something about baby-killers, and Sigga thought briefly of the other flyers from earlier and the girl in the dungarees, and wondered what had happened to her.

They got as far down as Prikid before Sigga had to run to her Literature class.

She arrived hot and breathless, hoping to sneak in, but her teacher, Mr Finnbogi, must have been waiting for her, because he launched into a speech about the story, and the prestige of the competition, and the rich heritage of Icelandic folklore, while she slid into her seat, wishing she could hide under her desk, instead. Then, after the class, he kept her back to talk about what she wanted to study at university, and how he thought she could get into the Literature course, while she fidgeted and nodded. She couldn't even think of applying for a course while she didn't know what would come out of London. If she *did* go abroad to study, she'd be the first in her family to leave Iceland. That would be something.

'Is everything all right?' he asked, at one point, and she realised she'd been nodding even though he'd stopped talking.

'I'm sorry,' she said. 'I'm just a little distracted.'

He clicked his fingers. 'You're helping organise the Women's Day Off, aren't you?'

She nodded again.

'My wife's quite excited about it. She works in local government, you know, and her boss won't hear anything about day nurseries. We're just lucky her mother moved to be near us to take care of the children.'

Beads of sweat bloomed around her hairline, and one trickled down her forehead. She wiped it away quickly, wondering why she suddenly felt jumpy and nervous. 'Very lucky,' she said.

When she got home that evening, the flyers she'd left for Mamma were waiting for her on the desk in her bedroom, neatly folded up.

*

Something was wrong, the strange pitching in her stomach again. She tried breathing slowly, looking at a fixed point, at the half-light – why was she waking so early these days? – seeping through the window, but the feeling grew more and more insistent, and then suddenly she had to scramble to the bathroom to throw up. Brown and orange chunks, brown liquid – last night's kjötsúpa.

When it was over, she sat back against the bath and let her head hang down. Mamma had been ill; maybe they were all getting it. Except now she felt absolutely fine, as she had before. Purged.

Otherwise – although it was a crazy thought – when had she last had her period?

Don't be stupid, she told herself, although she couldn't remember the date, couldn't remember it being since she'd gone back to school after the summer holiday. In fact, now she thought about it, she could remember buying a pack of sanitary napkins from the drugstore as far back as August, and then hastily shoving it into her wardrobe, where it lay unopened. Why hadn't she realised before now?

She stood up, wobbling, and made her way back to the bedroom. Olafur opened his eyes as she climbed in beside him. 'Is it eight already?'

'No.' She arranged herself so she was covered by the duvet from the chin down. 'I needed to pee.'

'You drink too much water,' he said, and rolled over.

Sigga looked out the window. It couldn't be a baby; she was always careful with Olafur when they did occasionally have sex. But still, she was hardly ever sick either.

She felt her pulse quicken, a tightness around her chest, and closed her eyes. No. It wasn't a baby, she wouldn't even think it.

She was feeling sick again, but an empty-sick. No chance of going back to sleep. She was due to meet Amma at Mokka, their favourite café, before school anyway. Amma would reassure her; she'd say, 'Oh, that doesn't mean a baby. You had too much salt, or not enough salt,' or something like that, and Sigga would feel better. And if it *was* a baby – Amma would know what to say then too.

'I'm getting up,' she told Olafur. 'Do you want the first shower?'

He opened his eyes, looked at her blurrily. 'No,' he said after a while. 'I've left some books at home. I'll go back there and shower.'

She got up, showered and dressed hurriedly in the bathroom. By the time she got downstairs, Olafur was sitting in his car – his father's taxi, really, a brown Plymouth Chrysler – outside the house next to Sigga's. As she walked towards the car, she looked up at the window on the top floor and saw a blur of movement, as if someone had drawn back the blind to look out and quickly dropped it.

She knocked on the passenger window and Olafur leaned over and wound it down.

'My neighbour's spying on you again,' she said.

'Which one?'

'The upstairs apartment.'

'I meant him or her?'

'Probably her. He's normally gone by this time.'

Olafur was fiddling with the radio. 'Don't tell me it's busted again,' he said.

'About tonight . . .' she said. 'Maybe I should spend some time with my parents. Mamma's still giving me a hard time.'

'That's a mother's job, isn't it?'

'Your mother's never like that with you,' Sigga said.

'That's different – I'm not her only daughter. Are you getting in or not?'

Sigga looked at her hands, gripping the open window. 'Can I ask you a question?'

'What?'

'Do you want kids?'

'Sure.'

'When were you thinking?'

'Better to have them while we're young, I guess.'

'That's what Karen says.'

Karen was Sigga's best friend at school.

Olafur looked at her briefly, then back at the radio. 'What else does Karen say?'

'She wants at least eight kids. Two triplets and one set of twins.'

'Any more than three and she's asking for trouble.'

'Why three?'

'After that there's no coming back, elasticity-wise.'

'Oh, right.'

Sigga had pictured the household – the screaming, the laughing, the half-eaten biscuits underfoot. And Karen adoring them, worshipping her husband who dropped by in the evenings, after the children were in bed, in search of a hot meal before leaving for a bar with his friends. She'd felt a wave of pity for this future Karen, then a wave of shame for her condescension. She didn't know where it came from. Only that sometimes people seemed so blind, so *contented*, never striving for anything beyond that. And there must be more, Sigga felt, existence couldn't be so colourless as contentment.

'Got it,' Olafur said, and turned up the volume.

'*. . . And now to recap our story from Botswana, where Elizabeth Taylor and Richard Burton just remarried,*' the newsreader was saying, and she couldn't breathe. Just for a second, but all the same, she suddenly couldn't bear the thought of being cooped up.

'Why are you still standing out there?'

'You know what, I'll walk. I want the fresh air.'

He eyed the bare stretch of leg between her boots and her skirt. 'Don't be stupid.'

'Thanks a lot.'

'Sigga – I don't want to fight.'

'Then don't pick one.'

'Okay, sorry. But you've been really weird with me lately.'

She straightened up, irritated. 'You said you weren't going to pressure me.'

'No, I don't mean the . . . intimate stuff.'

'Then how have I been weird?'

'It's ever since you won that story prize. It's like you think you're better than me all of a sudden.'

She looked away. *You could just be proud of me.* But maybe she *was* acting differently.

'Do you?'

She forced herself to smile. 'Of course not. We're fine, Olafur.'

'Really?'

'See you later.'

She heard him sigh as she walked away.

She got to the café five minutes early, pushed open the door and stepped into the cool room, with its mosaic pillars and copper, pendant lighting, its red carpet and leatherette booths. At the back, a waitress leaned against the glass counter that held show plates from the menu.

There was one other customer, sitting near the head of the stairs. Sigga ordered a waffle, paid, then sat in the booth closest to the door. While she waited she took out her notebook and pen. The café was always quiet this time of day – one of the reasons she loved it. And when she and Amma had started hanging out by themselves, it had been one of the only spots in the city they could be guaranteed not to run into the rest of the family.

The waitress brought over her plate, then returned to the counter. Sigga tore off a corner of her waffle and dipped it in the cream, then in the jam. Amma was late, which she never normally was.

She turned back to her notebook. She could use the time to write up her speech for the ceremony. But it all seemed kind of far away and unimportant now – the ceremony, her story. Why had she even written about Helga? So what if she'd been dragged away from the man she loved, compelled to act as de-facto mother to her half-brother but never had any children of her own. Was that really the greatest tragedy for a woman – not having children of her own?

She capped her pen again. What about having children and not being able to love them? But that was ridiculous. What mother didn't love her children?

She finished the waffle and pushed the plate away. Amma was almost twenty minutes late now. She gathered her things together and left, practically running past the jail, and onto Grettisgata, and all the way to Amma's.

Amma was standing outside, chatting to her upstairs neighbour. As Sigga got closer she heard the woman say: ' . . . must be a tourist,' and Amma say: 'Could be anything. Sometimes people got lost deliberately.'

'But think how *selfish* – all those people searching for you, putting their own lives at risk . . .'

Amma saw Sigga and her eyes opened wide. She touched her neighbour's sleeve and the woman stopped mid-flow.

'I'm so sorry,' Amma said. 'I completely forgot. We were going to Mokka, weren't we?'

'It's fine,' Sigga said, although it wasn't. *I was worried,* she wanted to say, but now that she was here, she found she was almost angry instead. *You forgot me because you were too busy gossiping?*

'My brain must be full,' Amma said, and her neighbour nodded vigorously.

'That's my fault,' she said.

'Did someone get lost?' Sigga asked, trying to keep her voice neutral.

'Not recently,' the neighbour said. 'It's the body in the news. I remembered your amma came from that part of the country.'

Amma gave Sigga a look. 'Do you want to come in for coffee?'

Sigga checked her watch. 'I've got class.'

'Tomorrow, then?'

'All right.'

Amma looked like she wanted to say more, but her neighbour started up again, and Sigga gave her a small wave then turned back in the other direction. It was better to go, she told herself, than stay and fight, which they never did. Amma hadn't meant to forget her, she knew, and by the time she reached school, she was almost not annoyed anymore.

1911

THE NEXT TIME GUDRÚN saw Magnús was on the seventeenth of January. Her mother's birthday. Around noon, on a whim, she left Freyja and Tomas making soap – boiling down sheep fat with soda ash, to Tomas's amusement – and walked to Hellnar Church in the biting wind. On the way she saw two crowberry bushes still bearing their fruit – almost like an omen – and picked some branches to take with her.

The church was deserted when she arrived. In good weather the setting was warm and inviting: sunlight cascading down the spire, the soft, green hills of the graves dotted around, the deep blue of the Atlantic lying at the bottom of the cliff. On a bad day the graveyard seemed lumpy and cold, the church desolate, the view unrelentingly grey: grey sky, grey tombstones, grey sea whipping itself into a frenzy. Still, she thought, on a bad day Father Fridrik was unlikely to be around.

Gudrún knelt at the foot of her mother's grave and laid the branches down in the shape of a cross. The snow in the graveyard was like sifted sugar, and already she could feel her joints creaking in protest at the cold. 'Happy birthday, Mamma,' she said, drawing her new scarf around her shoulders.

She was still kneeling when she heard her name being called. She looked around. Magnús was sitting on his horse at the entrance to the church. She lifted her hand in greeting and he returned the wave, then jumped off and came towards her.

'Why are you out in this godawful weather?' he asked, blowing on his hands.

Gudrún stood up. 'I could ask you the same question.'

'I've come to see Father Fridrik, but it looks as if he isn't here.'

'I've come to see my mother.'

'I'm sorry.' He was next to her now, and he rested a hand on her shoulder. 'Freyja said she died when you were quite young?'

She had to swallow once, before managing to speak. 'Very young.'

He took his hand away. 'It's hard growing up without a mother.'

'Did your mother die, too?'

'She may have.'

'You didn't know her?'

'No.' He smiled at her, then looked back at the church. 'Come inside, I want to show you something.'

She followed him, picking their way through the graves until they were at the church doors. Magnús pushed them open and they went into the gloom.

Gudrún hadn't been inside for years, but the smell of must was as strong as she remembered it, the domed roof as blue, if a bit lower.

There were four wooden pews on each side of the aisle, leading up to a plain pulpit on the right, a small organ on the left, and the altar straight ahead. Four windows along the two long walls let in what little light came through on such an overcast day.

'What did you want to show me?' Gudrún asked.

Magnús walked up the aisle and stopped at the pulpit, tapped a finger on the book lying open on it.

'This bible was donated by the family who owned most of the land before my father-in-law,' he said. 'Beautiful, isn't it?'

Gudrún looked down at the book – larger than any other bible she'd come across, and bound in a dark brown calfskin. The type was finer than she'd come across, too, and when Magnús shut the book, she saw gold-leaf ornamentation on the cover.

'Father Fridrik has told me how much it's worth,' Magnús said.

'How much?'

'More than either of us, anyway.' He smiled at her.

'Why does he leave it lying around, then?'

'He doesn't think anyone around here will take it.' He shrugged. 'Where would they be able to hide it?'

'The whole country is a hiding place,' Gudrún said.

'Hmm.'

He looked down at the book for a moment in silence, then patted it once and smiled at her. They turned back to the entrance.

'I hope you enjoyed the cheese?' Magnús asked.

'Yes, thank you,' Gudrún said.

'Good.'

'Is Rósa well?'

'Very well.'

'And did you enjoy the viki-vaki on New Year?'

'Not terribly.' He looked at her with his eyes crinkled up a little. 'I'd rather spend time in interesting conversation, but I'm told dancing is more fashionable.'

Gudrún laughed, feeling strangely light-headed.

'Although, as a matter of fact, I did meet one interesting person that night.' They'd come to the last of the pews and he stopped and leaned against the edge of the one on the right. 'Does your guest have any plans for working, if he's not going to join in the fishing?'

'I don't know,' Gudrún said.

'One of the farmers I spoke to owns a farm about the size of my father-in-law's. He's looking for someone to run it on a day-to-day basis, take charge of the labourers. I said I'd look for someone suitable.'

Gudrún smiled. 'I don't think Tomas has any experience in running a farm.'

'Oh, I'm sure Einar's a good teacher.'

'Still—'

'The money would be good, I've been told.'

'Where's the farm?'

'Near Glaumbær.'

Gudrún felt a throb in her chest. 'That's almost three days north of here.'

'It is.'

'He won't go.'

Magnús put his hand in his pocket and drew out a pocket watch, rubbed it with the heel of his palm. 'Because you'd miss him?'

'No, it's . . . I mean, yes, we're fond of him. I don't think he'd want to be that far away.'

'Why not?'

'Well . . .' She cast around for a reason. 'We're the only people he knows in Iceland.'

'Of course. Well . . .' He slipped the watch back into his pocket. 'It doesn't matter, anyway. We were just thinking we'd like to help.'

'We?' Gudrún asked.

'Rósa and I.'

Of course Rósa's trying to help, Gudrún thought. *She's heard there's someone in Snæfellsnes whose life she isn't running.*

'We just want to make sure your hospitality isn't being taken advantage of.'

'What do you mean?'

He looked embarrassed. 'I'm sorry – I didn't mean to offend you. I just wondered how he would pay his way now farming season is over.'

'He's no burden to us.'

'I'm glad to hear it,' Magnús said, and looked down the road. 'Are you headed home now?'

'Yes.'

'Let me offer you a ride back on Maria.'

She hesitated, and Magnús smiled.

'Please,' he said.

Gudrún ducked her face so he wouldn't see her cheeks flare up. 'Yes, thank you.'

Outside, it had stopped squalling and they smiled at each other and at the change: the startlingly clear blue of the sky, gossamer drifting past in a breeze, sunlight glinting off the dewdrops that still clung to it. A starling, whistling and trilling in the rowan tree. They left the church and went over to Maria, who was grazing a few yards away. Magnús helped Gudrún onto the horse, then swung himself on behind her.

'Are you sure she can carry us both?' Gudrún asked.

He patted her flank. 'Of course she can.'

He made a clicking sound and Maria started forwards, picking her way carefully along the road.

Gudrún sat up straight and kept her eyes facing forward. Everything seemed magnified somehow – the supple, rolling motion of the horse underneath her, the heat of Magnús's body at her back – and she was glad when the house finally came into view. Freyja and Tomas were in the garden, faces turned to Gudrún, a tub of laundry at their feet. They were standing so close together Gudrún thought they could almost be holding hands.

Magnús stopped Maria at the gate and jumped down from the horse, then put his hands on Gudrún's waist and lifted her down as lightly as if she were a child.

'Thank you,' she said.

He smiled.

'Would you like to come in for a coffee?'

'I'd like that very much.'

Freyja and Tomas had disappeared inside, leaving the front door open. Gudrún led Magnús through to the badstofa, then made her way to the kitchen. Freyja was filling the kettle.

'You invited him in for coffee,' she said, without looking around.

'Yes.' Gudrún took off her coat and scarf. 'I can make it.'

Freyja stepped back.

'I'll see to our guest,' Tomas said.

Gudrún turned back to the kettle. She heard him leave, whistling, heard muffled greetings from the badstofa. She drummed her fingers on the side, waiting for bubbles to appear in the water. Jules Verne emerged from some nook or other and rubbed hopefully against her legs and she shooed him away. Freyja moved aimlessly around the kitchen, picking up jars and putting them down again.

'Did you finish the soap?' Gudrún asked.

'No,' Freyja said, 'we got distracted.' She smiled to herself.

'Hmm.'

'Tomas wants to write another letter tonight. It takes half a page just to address them all. Can you imagine being in a family that big, Gunna?'

'No woman should ever have to go through that, let alone imagine it.'

Freyja smiled again.

Finally, the water boiled. Gudrún made the coffee and carried it to the badstofa.

Tomas was sitting in there alone, seemingly far away.

'Where's Magnús?' Gudrún asked.

'He had to leave,' Tomas said, looking up at her. 'He said goodbye.'

'Oh.' Gudrún tried to smile, but it felt stretched and odd. 'More coffee for us then. Freyja, help me.'

Freyja handed out the coffee cups and Gudrún went back for cream and sugar.

This time Tomas stood when she came into the badstofa. He held out his hand for the sugar.

'Let me,' he said, and turned to Freyja. 'Sugar first, of course.' He heaped a spoonful of sugar into Freyja's coffee. 'There you go.'

He sounded so serious Gudrún almost laughed, thinking he was mocking them, then she caught sight of his expression and realised that he wasn't. She looked away.

'I'd like to see Freyja's mountain up close,' Tomas said, when they were seated. 'Would you take me?'

'We'll go the next morning the sun shines,' Freyja said. 'You'll love it.'

'I'm sure I will.'

Freyja smiled. 'It makes me feel like dying isn't so bad,' she said. 'Not if it happened there.'

'Don't be so dramatic,' Gudrún said. 'You're sounding like Bjartur.'

Tomas raised an eyebrow. 'I thought you said he killed himself?'

'That's what I heard,' Gudrún said. 'He left a note for his brother.'

'What did it say?'

'"*Sorry, I have to.*"' Gudrún shrugged. 'He wasn't a great writer.'

'What was he like?'

'He seemed simple enough. He had a drink or two at the viki-vaki; he loved his wife; he played manni.' She saw Tomas open his mouth. 'An Icelandic card game. He was happy, until he wasn't. And now his brother will probably have to sell the farm.'

'He doesn't sound like Freyja at all,' Tomas said.

'No.' Freyja balanced her cup on her knee. 'And I mean it. Can't you imagine being part of the mountain forever?'

'I can't imagine forever,' Gudrún said, sharper than she was intending. 'No one can.'

Freyja looked stubborn. 'I can when I'm up there.'

'You and God.'

'I'm not talking about with my mind—'

'How else can you imagine?'

'With your body.'

'That's true,' Tomas said. 'My sisters' babies understood hunger and loneliness before their minds knew how to form ideas.'

'Well if we're looking to babies for answers . . .' Gudrún said and Freyja laughed, her stubborn expression melting away.

'Tell me a story from the Bárdur saga,' Tomas said suddenly. 'Where he helps someone.'

Gudrún sighed. 'Now?'

'Please.'

'One man who came from Norway with Bárdur – Ingjaldur, he was called – had settled near Mount Ennisfjall, where the giantess, Hetta, lived. Hetta kept killing his sheep, and when he confronted her she tried to trick him and told him she would give him the secret of a good fishing spot in exchange for the sheep she'd already taken.'

'Then what?'

'Then, when he rowed out, she brewed up a storm and he nearly drowned. He called on Bárdur, and just as he was about to freeze to death, a boat approached him with a single rower in it. He saw the rower was dressed in a grey cowl, and realised it was Bárdur come to save him.'

'How did he know?'

'Bárdur always wore a grey cowl after he went into the mountains, remember,' Freyja said.

'Oh yes.'

'He wasn't as heroic as you're thinking,' Gudrún said. 'He only came to people's rescue when they called on him and then they were grateful.'

'I suppose so,' Tomas said. He leaned forwards and squeezed her hand. 'How do you know so much, Gunna?'

'I just do.' She stood up, trying not to let them see her flustered. Tomas never called her Gunna, and he hadn't touched her since laying his head on her shoulder on the walk from Dritvik. 'I'll have another coffee, I think,' she said, and left the room.

*

The invitation came the next day after breakfast, when Freyja was washing dishes in the kitchen. Gudrún read it out to the other two. Rósa Gudmundsdóttir cordially invited them to a dance at the Big Farm held in honour of her husband's birthday.

'It's this Saturday,' Gudrún said, turning the card over in her hands. 'The twenty-first of January.'

'Does that mean something?' Tomas asked.

'She won't have left the planning until now,' Gudrún said. 'She didn't think to invite us before.'

'I don't know why we've been invited at all,' Papi said, and tugged at the sleeves of his jumper. 'Now we have to go.'

'No,' Gudrún said. 'We don't need her charity.'

'We're going,' Papi said.

'*Someone* wants you there,' Tomas said, and Gudrún felt her cheeks catch fire.

'If we must, then,' she said.

The morning of the party dawned clear and mild.

'Now will you take me to your mountain?' Tomas asked Freyja.

'Make sure you're back in time,' Gudrún said as if she didn't mind staying back with Papi and his book.

Freyja smiled and took Tomas's hand and pulled him out of the gate, her plait bouncing from shoulder to shoulder.

They only returned home shortly before five o'clock. Papi was waiting for them by the garden gate, a dark, shapeless figure, with the orange glow from his pipe making him look like a distant volcano.

'We leave in half an hour,' was all he said as they passed by him.

Gudrún hurried to the kitchen where she'd placed a large pot of water on the range, ready for boiling. She lit it and, while she was waiting, took a candle into her bedroom. Papi had laid their good dresses neatly on the bed, and she felt a catch in her throat at the idea of him handling them so carefully, all the while keeping an eye and an ear out for Freyja's return. They could have gone to the mountain any other day, she told herself. Why had Tomas suggested it today?

She brought through the pot of warm water, washed herself quickly, changed into the dress and ran a comb through her hair. Freyja was changing behind her in the shadows; Gudrún didn't look at her when she spoke.

'We're going to be late.'

'It won't start properly for hours,' Freyja said. 'They had plenty of parties when I was working there.'

'What will it be like?'

'There'll be music and dancing and food. They use the silverware for parties; it was always my job to polish it beforehand. Rósa said I did it best.'

'And only the best will do for her.'

'She likes people to think she has a nice life,' Freyja said. 'Sometimes I felt sorry for her.' She stepped into the circle of light cast by the candle and Gudrún felt her stomach swoop and settle inside her. She was wearing a white dress of their mother's, her golden hair pulled back from her face and tied up with a dark blue ribbon. It seemed even thicker and shinier than usual, her lips seemed fuller and redder, the skin on her arms and face glowing.

'Did you?' Gudrún said, and for a moment she saw that Rósa had been eclipsed as the most beautiful woman on the peninsula and could almost pity her too. She felt almost shy, then she shook herself. This was Freyja, her younger sister, whose hair she'd combed for lice, whose snotty nose she'd wiped as a child.

'Sometimes,' Freyja said. She was twisting her hands together, almost as if she felt shy too, and Gudrún took her by the wrists to calm her down.

'We should go,' she said.

The Big Farm was at the edge of the lava fields, and in the light from the swaying lantern, Gudrún could see the black rock tumbling up hills and down gullies, draped over with the thick, soft, greenish-grey moss that always followed the cooling. They were silent as they approached, their breath forming cloud-like wreaths around their faces, but already there was music on the air, and light shining out from the large building that sat in the middle of a flowery lawn bordered by birches. Gudrún could smell heather and wintergreen and hear the bubbling of a little stream coming out of the lava nearby. She turned her head to search for it, and Freyja pointed somewhere off to the left.

'It ends in a big pool over there,' she said. 'It must be twenty feet deep at least. When it's sunny, the bottom looks as blue as the sky.'

'Well,' Papi said, uncertainly, 'here we are.'

'I recognise that tune,' Tomas said.

They'd gathered outside the front door and for a moment no one moved or spoke. Gudrún looked around.

'Perhaps if we think loud enough they'll hear us,' she said.

Papi cleared his throat and knocked, and the door was opened immediately, letting out a fug of warmth. Gudmundur, Rósa's father, stood framed in the doorway. He was shorter than all of them, but broad-shouldered, with a bright red beard and round, silver-framed spectacles.

'Einar,' he said, and stuck out his hand.

Papi shook his hand, and Gudmundur clapped him on the back.

'Come in,' he said. 'We have more of that wine you enjoyed on Yule's Eve.'

Papi muttered something, but stepped inside, and the others followed him.

The badstofa was much bigger than theirs, with pine wood panelling on the walls and several ornamented chests placed around the room, their shadows flickering in the candlelight. The chairs and normal furniture had been moved out to make space for the thirty or so people already there, talking and laughing with each other so loudly it was barely possible to hear the trio of musicians in the far left corner, playing 'Krummavísur' on the accordion, langspil and fiddle. On the other side of the room, four young girls were lined up next to a serving table, their aprons uniformly crisp white, their hands a raw pink. Rósa and Magnús stood in front of the blazing fireplace in the middle of the far wall, both wearing a dark red colour that Gudrún was irritated to see set off Rósa's copper-coloured hair. Next to Magnús she looked even smaller and more delicate than usual. The two of them were speaking to Doctor Jóhann, but when Einar herded Gudrún and her family into the middle of the room, she saw they'd been noticed; Rósa pursed her mouth, as if she'd just tasted curdled milk, and Magnús's eyes widened for a second, then he smiled and came forwards.

'I didn't realise we would have the pleasure this evening,' he said, and shook Papi's hand too.

'You didn't invite us?' Gudrún asked, through the lump of disappointment in her throat. *Who then?* she asked herself. *Rósa?* It made no sense.

Magnús smiled again, unrestrained, if a little distracted. 'But what a charming surprise.' He took Gudrún's hand and kissed it, in a courtly manner, then did the same to Freyja, who gasped, and caught her right hand as soon as Magnús had released it, and cradled it to her chest as if it were something delicate.

There was a momentary hesitation among the group. Papi shuffled his feet and cleared his throat. Gudrún silently cursed Freyja's lack of subtlety.

'Well, I'll let you catch up with your guests,' Gudmundur said, finally, and joined the doctor and Rósa, who were still deep in conversation, although Gudrún had the feeling that the other woman was watching her from out of the corner of her eye.

As she looked at the little group, another man sidled up to them and Gudrún recognised Palli, who had lost an eye to a fish hook when he was young, and who had been in love with Rósa since before that, even.

'Please, have something to drink.' Magnús signalled to one of the girls lining the wall, and she brought over a tray of filled wine glasses.

'Thank you,' Papi said, and took the glass.

They all followed suit, except for Freyja, who shook her head.

'No thank you, Lauga,' she said, and the girl started as if she hadn't recognised her.

'You can take some to the musicians,' Magnús said to Lauga, and she bobbed her head and made off through the crowd.

'Are these parties always so loud?' Gudrún asked, raising her voice.

Magnús bent his head closer, until his mouth was level with her ear. 'Always,' he said, and she felt his hot breath like a blanket on her skin.

'The good Father Fridrik is here,' Tomas said.

Gudrún looked up and saw Father Fridrik bearing down on them, a plate laden with bread and cheese and tongue in his hands.

'Einar,' he said as he got closer. 'I have been meaning to speak with you. Why is it that every time I've spied you lately you turn and walk in the opposite direction?'

'I've been working hard,' Papi said. 'Perhaps I've been preoccupied each time.'

Gudrún took a sip of her wine. Of course Rósa was serving wine rather than brennivín at her party; did anyone here prefer it? The wine itself was earthy and dusty, with a note of cherry and she swirled it around in her mouth, irritated. It would be incredibly tedious to be stuck with Father Fridrik all night, although there was a slight tremble in the air, and it suddenly struck her that Papi found the priest as distasteful as she did. But then why not? Where had her opinions of her fellow countrymen come from if not from him?

'You must not let your head be so filled with worldly matters,' Father Fridrik said. He placed a hand on Magnús's arm and a strange expression crossed his face, almost eager, Gudrún thought. 'Your host understands the importance of carving out time for theological examination.'

'The unwise man weens all who smile and flatter him are his friends,' Papi said.

Father Fridrik sucked in a sharp breath and Gudrún paused, mid-swallow. Without meaning to she met Magnús's eyes and saw them crinkle almost imperceptibly.

'From the *Edda*,' Tomas said as if they'd been playing a guessing game all along. For a moment Gudrún wondered how he knew, then realised Freyja must have been reading it to him.

'I'm glad to see you're taking an interest in our national literature,' Father Fridrik said, stiffly. 'Excuse me.'

'*Papi*,' Gudrún said as they watched him leave.

Papi shrugged.

Gudrún looked to Freyja for support, but she was staring at a ladder in the far right corner that Gudrún guessed led up to the common sleeping room.

'I see Halldór,' Papi said, nodding at a group of older men standing close to the serving table. 'I need to speak with him about a wall.'

He disappeared into the crowd.

'You mustn't pay him any attention,' Gudrún said to Magnús, who opened his mouth to speak, then, behind her, someone stumbled and elbowed her in the small of her back and she jerked forwards, splashing some of her wine on the floorboards. She turned around and recognised the stumbler as Skúli, her old playmate. 'Goddamit. May the trolls take all your friends, Skúli Skúlason.'

Skúli took her face in two hands and kissed her mouth sloppily. He was running to fat now. 'Gudrún Einarsdóttir, the flower of Snæfellsnes.'

She pushed him off, cheeks burning, and he returned to his friends, laughing.

'There now.' Magnús produced a handkerchief and mopped up the spill. 'You've done us all a favour. The dirtier the floor, the better the party.' He signalled to a different girl, who hurried to them with her tray.

Gudrún exchanged her empty glass for a full one and took a long drink. She couldn't decide if Magnús's attention made her feel uncomfortable, or interesting, or a little of both.

'Do you play an instrument?' Magnús asked.

'No,' Gudrún said. 'I don't have any accomplishments.'

'That's not true,' Magnús said.

'Why do you ask?'

'I know your sister sings.' He caught Tomas's gaze. 'Have you had the pleasure, yet?'

Tomas shifted from one foot to the other and ran a hand through his hair. To Gudrún, comparing them, he looked suddenly, painfully childlike, and if she hadn't still been feeling sore, her heart would have gone out to him. 'Once or twice,' he said.

'I hope you know how lucky you are.' Magnús raised his glass. 'We used to enjoy listening to her as she went about the house.'

The musicians came to the end of their song and lay down their instruments and picked up their glasses. Someone nearby, whom Gudrún didn't recognise, started singing 'Ólafur Liljurós' and was quickly joined by his companions.

Olaf rode along the cliffs,
He's led astray,
He stills himself,
He comes across an elf-dwelling before him,
There's a red flame burned.
Gentle was the breeze beneath the cliffs,
Gentle was the breeze beneath the cliffs ahead.

Rósa was at Magnús's elbow now, and put her hand on his shoulder as if she were Gudrún the Far-Traveller herself, staking claim to Vinland.

'And how are you enjoying our little gathering?' she asked. She looked at Gudrún, and briefly at Tomas, but Gudrún saw she purposely avoided Freyja, who was still staring off into the distance. It was up to her to respond, she supposed, and gritted her teeth.

'Very much. We're glad to be invited.'

'I'm so pleased,' Rósa said. 'And how about you, my love?'

'How could I not enjoy my own birthday party?' Magnús said, and for a moment Gudrún thought she heard a faint note of irritation in his voice. 'You're too good to me.'

Rósa simpered. Gudrún finished her wine. She must have imagined it – or her ears were playing tricks on her with all the noise around them.

The singer switched to falsetto to sing the elf maiden's part:

'Welcome, Olaf Lilyrose!'
He's led astray,
He stills himself,
'Come to the cliffs and live with us.'

92

There a red flame burned.
Gentle was the breeze beneath the cliffs,
Gentle was the breeze beneath the cliffs ahead.

Behind Gudrún, Skúli Skúlason raised his voice. 'You're the ugliest elf-maiden *I've* ever seen.'

Rósa, facing him, looked disapproving.

'Skúli Skúlason has seen elf-maidens before then?' Tomas said.

'Sadly, none of them have fallen for his charms and spirited him away,' Gudrún said.

Magnús laughed.

Rósa's expression had changed from disapproving to sullen, but when Magnús looked down at her she smiled, showing perfect white teeth. Gudrún pressed her lips together so her own teeth were hidden.

'Don't be so severe, all of you,' she said. 'Skúli's just full of the party spirit.' She tapped Magnús on the nose.

'As always, I defer to you on all party matters,' he said.

She stabbed the sword into his side,
He's led astray,
He stills himself,
Olaf is hurt,
There a red flame burned.
Gentle was the breeze beneath the cliffs,
Gentle was the breeze beneath the cliffs ahead.

'Excuse me,' Gudrún said, and walked towards the serving table. She exchanged glasses again and drank this one in two swallows. Her stomach rose to meet it, and she realised she hadn't eaten anything since breakfast.

She picked up a smoked sausage with her fingers and ate it quickly, then a slice of rye bread, also with her fingers, then a spoonful of soft cheese. She could sense the serving girls staring at her, although no one tried to stop her.

'I'll have another wine,' she said to the nearest one, who poured her a glass and handed it over with her eyes cast down to the floor.

'Are you Lauga?' Gudrún asked.

'Yes.'

'You know my younger sister, Freyja.'

'Yes.'

Gudrún took another sip. 'Do you know why Rósa let her go?'

Lauga looked up, her eyes wide, and shook her head.

'Was it because of how Freyja felt about Magnús?'

Lauga's eyes widened even further. 'She never said anything,' she said, a little breathlessly. 'But they would go for walks together, sometimes all the way to Snæfellsjökull. And he could always make her laugh—'

'I wouldn't have thought Rósa would be jealous,' Gudrún said. 'But I suppose she feels entitled to control people's inner lives, too.'

Lauga looked anxious and said something Gudrún didn't quite catch. She could feel the buzz of the wine in her blood now, and her heart was starting to thump in her chest.

'Is it hot in here?' she asked.

Rósa's voice cut through the din, asking for quiet. Gudrún turned and saw she was standing in front of the fireplace again, clutching Palli's arm. He was staring at her with a mix of shyness and pride.

Gudrún snorted. 'She keeps him around like an old dog,' she said to Lauga, who looked around, as if for support.

'I thought we could play a game,' Rósa said, when everyone was quiet. 'How about Witch Hunt?'

There were a few scattered cheers.

Rósa smiled. 'Just because my darling husband is turning twenty-seven, it doesn't mean we can't enjoy a little childish fun.' She started scanning the room. 'Now, who should be our witch?'

Gudrún took another spoonful of cheese. She couldn't imagine Magnús wanting to play children's games and felt a little burn of satisfaction that his wife might not know him so well after all.

'I have the perfect person,' Rósa said, and Gudrún's neck prickled as she looked up and saw Rósa's eyes locked on her. 'Gudrún Einarsdóttir.'

'Perfect,' Palli said, and Gudrún silently cursed his remaining eye.

'You remember how to play, don't you?' Rósa said.

Half the room had turned to face her now. Gudrún replaced the cheese spoon as carefully as she could, and wiped her mouth with the back of her hand.

'A little,' she said.

'You hide somewhere in the house, and we turn out the lamps and try to find you. You can move about if you like, but if we call out "Where are you, witch?" you have to cackle.'

'I remember.'

'We'll count to sixty,' Rósa said. 'Palli, you douse the fire. Everyone else start blowing out candles then close your eyes.'

There was a sudden flurry of movement and Gudrún paused for a moment until the room was in darkness, then started moving, her heart thumping painfully against her ribs. With all the lights out it was black as tar; the game suddenly seemed more serious, and she realised she really did want to hide.

Almost immediately she banged her thigh against the serving table, and heard a ripple of laughter from the guests closest to her.

'Twenty,' Rósa was chanting. 'Twenty-one, twenty-two.'

She moved off again, feeling the space in front of her with her hands until she came to a wall. Out of nowhere she felt a hand take her own and tug her to the right, where she'd seen a doorway earlier.

'Lauga?' she whispered, and felt a little pressure where the girl was squeezing.

The pressure stopped, and her hand was dropped, and when she shuffled forwards, she felt nothing but air in front of her.

'Forty-three, forty-four . . .'

She slipped out of the badstofa and into the corridor, trailing her right hand out to the side along the wall until she came to another opening. She moved into it slowly. It was even darker in the new room, but from the smell – coffee beans, and oats and a faint hint of apples – she guessed she was in the pantry. She took another step, stumbled over a sack of something and sat down hard on the floor, biting down on her tongue so she didn't cry out.

From the main room she heard Rósa call out 'sixty', and another cheer go up. Someone called out, 'Let's find ourselves a witch,' and for a moment she was filled with an unreasonable sense of terror, wondering what they would do to her when they found her. She huddled back against the sack, listening as they started searching for her. There were footsteps, and crashes, laughter, and the occasional swearing, until, after a few minutes, someone remembered to call out 'Where are you, witch?'

She wet her lips and let out a little cackle, and heard a yelp of excitement nearby. A man's yelp. Then someone else was in the pantry with her – she couldn't see them, but she heard heavy breathing from the direction of the doorway, and then the scrape of shoes on floorboards. She rolled onto her hands and knees and crawled towards the doorway. Her head was pounding and she half wondered if she was going to be sick, but then she was out of the room, and pushed herself to stand and immediately bumped into someone.

'Palli?' the someone (Skúli again?) said and she gave a deep grunt, and pushed off the wall and started walking away from them as quickly as she could.

'Where are you, witch?' Rósa's voice came from the badstofa, and she cackled as quietly as she could.

'She's in the corridor with me,' Skúli called. 'I'll get her.'

Gudrún dropped back down onto her hands and knees and entered the badstofa that way. If she could just get to the ladder, she told herself, maybe she could wait it out until they got bored.

'Find the witch,' someone nearby started chanting, then more people joined in, and Rósa's laughter sounded above them all. Someone trod on her hand and tears came to her eyes, but still she stayed silent. She scrambled away instead, and back onto her feet.

'Where are you, witch?'

Another quiet cackle, then a gasp, as she felt a hand lifting her skirt. Her pulse doubled, and she took a long, shuddering breath, even as her feet refused to move. Then there was another hand – someone new? Or simply the free hand not holding her skirt? – running its finger up her leg. It tickled, and the tickle felt good, but it was wrong, she knew, and surely it would stop, she told herself, even in the darkness no one could feel such impunity, but still it went up, up until it had almost reached—

'No,' she screamed, so that everyone would hear, and finally tore herself away from the hands.

'What's wrong?' someone said from nearby, almost exactly the spot she'd just run from. Tomas's voice.

No, she said again, but silently this time. *Surely not him?*

She pressed her hands against her ears and shrank back against the wall, tried to keep it at her back and move around the room that way, but they were closing in on her, then someone had their hands on her waist, was drawing her gently towards them.

'Gudrún?' Magnús said, and she lowered her hands, relieved. 'Is it you?' he asked again, and she realised she hadn't answered.

'Yes.'

'I've found her,' he called, and someone groaned nearby, and someone else must have lit a candle, because she could see his face now and the worried expression on it.

'Is everything all right, Gudrún Einarsdóttir?'

'Yes.' She wet her lips again. 'Of course.'

Tomas and Freyja were nearby too, and Rósa, and about ten other people who must have all been playing.

Rósa pouted. 'You didn't make it very difficult for us,' she said. 'Oh well – light the candles again, everyone. The musicians have rested long enough.'

She moved off, and after a moment the music started again and flames sprang up all over the room.

'You look pale,' Freyja said, coming forwards and putting her hand on Gudrún's arm.

Gudrún shook her off, embarrassed that Magnús might notice too now. Tomas hadn't looked at her since the candles were lit, but she could tell he was listening. She wanted to confront him, hear him deny it, but then Freyja would be upset. 'Someone stepped on my hand,' she said. 'It hurts.'

'Have another glass of wine,' Magnús said. 'You deserve it.' He signalled to Lauga, who brought a glass.

'I can look at your hand,' Tomas said, holding his out.

'It's nothing,' Gudrún said, hiding it behind her back. 'I don't need your help, thank you.'

'All right,' Tomas said, shrugging.

If it was him, how could he be so calm? Maybe he'd thought she was Freyja, although they were distinguishable enough, even in the dark.

Freyja, who had been standing in front of Gudrún, her hand still hovering where it had been shaken off, turned to him. 'I want to dance,' she said.

'Let's dance then,' Tomas said. Gudrún saw him look sideways at Magnús, who smiled indifferently.

They disappeared into the crowd, and Gudrún was left alone with Magnús.

'So,' she said, then realised she had nothing to follow up with, so sipped at the wine.

Magnús looked down at her, waiting.

'If you need to talk to your other guests ...'

'Yes?'

'I give you permission,' she said, suddenly very tired, wishing she hadn't come.

Someone had opened the door and Gudrún turned her head as she felt a slight breeze on her cheek. It carried the sweet smell of woodsmoke and cooked fat and the sourness of sweat with it, and she breathed in deeply. Outside, a ripple went through a lawn that was the same, soft shade of blue as everything else in the darkness, and she could faintly hear the sound of waves washing against rock. She could almost imagine that she and Magnús were on an island. An island in the middle of an island.

'I didn't like that game,' she said, after a while.

'I'm sorry to hear it.'

'She didn't need to choose me.'

'Ah well. A witch is just a different name for an interesting woman, don't you think?'

'Why are you kind to me?' she asked, before she could stop herself, then bit down on her tongue.

He didn't answer her at first, but when she dared to look at him she was glad to see a slight crinkle around his eyes, and the glimpse of white teeth.

'Magnús,' Rósa called, impatiently. 'Come and settle this argument, my love.'

'Coming,' Magnús called back, without looking away. He placed his hand on Gudrún's shoulder and squeezed, gently. 'If you ever need my kindness, or help, I'll be only too happy to oblige.'

She was drenched in sweat, and too weak to speak, but she nodded, once.

'Remember that,' he said, and left.

1975

'SIGGA, YOU'LL PAIR WITH the new girl,' her history teacher said. 'I want you to do a presentation on the 1940 invasion, due back in two weeks.'

'New girl?'

'New student from Akureyri.' Mr Kristján looked up from the paper on his desk. 'Sitting towards the back. Maybe you can show her around a bit too.'

Another responsibility, she thought, but she said: 'Sure,' and smiled at him.

She started towards the back. Halfway there, her hip knocked into a desk she was trying to squeeze past and the occupant looked up at her.

'Hi there,' the girl said.

'Sorry, sorry,' Sigga said automatically, then, 'Oh. It's you.'

The girl with the flyers.

'Yes, it's me.' She cocked her head. 'I recognise you. Were you there, the other day at Hlemmur? When I was fighting with that old bat.'

'Yeah.' Sigga sat down in the empty chair next to her. 'What happened?'

'Couldn't face them after they wouldn't listen about the flyers. Fucking hypocrites. As if it isn't the same issue.'

From the front of the room, Mr Kristján raised his head and fixed them with a disapproving look.

'I guess so,' Sigga said, lowering her voice to a whisper.

The girl lowered hers to match Sigga's. 'It's their fucking priests telling the women to go home, make it up with the husband who tried to kill them.' She drummed her fingers on the desk. 'Sorry. You're not religious, are you?'

'No, it's fine.'

'I'm Sóley, by the way.'

'Sigga.' She tucked a loose strand of hair behind her ear. 'So, I came over to say we've been paired up for this presentation.'

'Okay, cool.'

'Do you want to come to mine to talk it through? I've got a couple of free periods today and tomorrow.'

'Why not.'

Mr Kristján got up and started writing something on the board at the front of the class. The two boys – Haukur and Daníel – sitting directly in front of Sigga and Sóley turned around.

'New girl. Did you come from Snæfellsnes?' Haukur asked, pointing at Sóley.

'Nope.'

'Oh, I heard you had. My uncle moved out there, to Arnarstapi. He's chief of police. He said he wanted to retire and still get paid a salary, and now he's got dead bodies to deal with. He never had that in Reykjavik.'

Sóley shrugged. 'Never been to Arnarstapi.'

'The body in the ice? What are they doing with it now?' Sigga asked.

'They're moving it here for tests. Then probably burn it.'

'Really?'

Haukur leaned back, resting his elbows on the desk behind him. His jumper rode up slightly, revealing the trail of fine, dark hairs that led down from his abdomen, and Sigga had to look away in case he caught her staring. He'd always been slightly overweight, until he'd come back from the last summer holiday suddenly lean and made it onto the football team. The rumour was he'd been sent to fat camp in America, but whatever the reason, there was something about him now, a certain swagger, that she found both repulsive and appealing.

'It's not like anyone's going to claim it, anyway,' he said, and she tried to meet his gaze nonchalantly. 'It's more than fifty years old.' He nudged Daníel. 'If it's a chick, you could always use it for practice. Maybe you'll get past first base.'

'Shut up, idiot. What about Audur?'

'She doesn't count, man, she's been with everyone.'

Sóley raised an eyebrow. 'What are you all talking about?'

'The dead body they found in the ice,' Sigga said. 'There was a report about it and then they kind of dropped it.'

'The news got it wrong, anyway,' Haukur said. 'It was in an ice cave. Foot all smashed up, or something like that.'

'Ice cave then,' Sigga said. 'Whatever.' She shifted in her chair and felt a sudden jolt of pain on her left-hand side. A stitch? Was that because she'd been skipping her swimming sessions lately? Or maybe her oxygen was already being diverted elsewhere. She'd flicked through Pabbi's old medical textbooks the previous night, reading up on the early stages of pregnancy, what her body might be doing under the surface.

'Sigga, you okay?' Sóley asked.

She took a deep breath, pushed her hand against the pain. Was it just her imagination or was her belly slightly rounder than usual? Just the tiniest little swell.

'Is it listening to these morons?' Sóley said. 'They making you want to barf?'

Haukur snapped upright. 'Excuse me?'

'Go on, shoo,' Sóley said and waved her hand at them.

They agreed to meet by the main entrance after the first afternoon bell. As soon as they were out of the school grounds, Sóley lit a cigarette, sucked on it, paused, then blew out a cloud of smoke. Her shoulders seemed to relax, her face too, and she smiled, openly this time.

'Your school is fucking intense,' she said. 'There's so many of you. There were about fifteen of us in my last school.'

'My mother's from Akureyri,' Sigga said. 'Her sisters are still there. They all say we're too soft down here.'

'Sounds about right,' Sóley said. 'Our new house has an electric kettle. None of us knew what it was at first.'

'Where are you living?' Sigga asked, and Sóley waved a hand in the direction of the pond.

'Other side,' she said. 'It's temporary. The university found it for us – my parents teach there now.'

They turned left and started walking up Spitalastigur. A little way up on the south side was a three-storey-plus-basement house in green corrugated iron with black window mullions and a black roof. A white picket fence ran along the edge of the garden. The windows on the raised ground floor were open, and a ginger cat sat in the middle of the windowsill. Sóley stopped and held her hand out, making little kissing noises; the cat ignored her.

'I'll know a guy's right for me when he likes cats,' she said. 'That's my new rule. All the boys in Akureyri liked dogs.'

'What's wrong with that?' Sigga asked.

'Dogs love you no matter how badly you treat them. And they wanted their girlfriends to be the same.'

On the other side of the road, a red and yellow pick-up truck was parked half-on, half-off the sidewalk. It had a Coca-Cola sign on the side and crates of empty bottles in the back. The driver was sitting on the roof of his cab, reading a newspaper. The left-hand page facing outward was a full-page advertisement for a Brewmatic coffee-maker. Sigga had seen it before: it showed a young, pretty woman, in faded colours, holding a cup and saucer in bold. Above the picture, the message read: 'Hey! I just got a promotion . . . I'll bet you it was my coffee!'

She thought of Olafur. 'What if they're not interested in animals at all?'

'Psychopaths,' Sóley said cheerfully.

The house was quiet when Sigga opened the door. 'Mamma?' she called. 'Pabbi? Are you in?'

There was a noise from the living room of someone getting off the sofa and feet padding towards the hallway. Mamma must have been reading her cooking magazines.

'This is Sóley,' Sigga started, then stopped when she saw Pétur in the doorway. 'Oh. It's you.'

'Hi,' Sóley said, looking at Pétur, who was looking back at her.

'Hey,' he said. 'We haven't met before, have we?'

'Leave her alone,' Sigga said. 'Do you want a coffee, Sóley?'

'Sure,' Sóley said.

They went into the kitchen and Sigga turned on the kettle, took out two mugs and rinsed them under the tap, then turned around and started, almost dropping the mugs. Pétur was standing in the doorway.

'Sorry,' he said, smirking. 'I thought you heard me. Is there enough water for me, too?'

'No,' she said, turning away. 'Make your own coffee. Where's Mamma?'

'She went to borrow some kind of pie dish from Amma.'

'Were your legs not working?'

He shrugged. 'She said I wouldn't know what to look for.' He brought his thumb up to his mouth and chewed on the nail, like he used to do when they were kids. 'She's dieting again.'

'Oh good,' Sigga said, 'she'll be extra moody then.'

Sóley pulled a face. 'God, I can't imagine anything worse than not being able to eat what I wanted.'

'Just wait until we're older and our bodies don't do what they're supposed to do anymore,' Sigga said.

Pétur smirked again. 'You sound just like her.'

Sigga's chest constricted. 'No I don't.'

The kettle clicked and whistled. She poured the water over the grounds in the French press, placed the plunger next to it, waiting, fetched milk from the fridge, a tray from the cupboard. And what would happen to her body if there was a baby in there, taking it over? Would she never look the same again? Ragga hadn't changed, but Ragga was different. Nothing ever went wrong for her.

'Did you hear me?' Pétur asked.

'We're going upstairs,' Sigga said. She plunged the coffee. 'So you can go back to the job you don't have, or whatever.'

His face contracted with something that looked like irritation, then he shrugged and went back into the living room. Sigga led Sóley up to her room.

'Who was that?' Sóley asked when they were behind the closed door.

'My middle brother. You can ignore him.' She pointed to a photo above her desk. 'This is my older brother and my nephew. They're the good ones.'

Sóley peered at the photo. 'Cute.'

Girls had always flocked to Pétur, but Sigga thought Gabríel was the better looking of the two. He and Ragga made a striking couple, anyway. Gabríel was six foot four, with dirty blond hair and beard, and the only one of the three of them with Amma's blue eyes. And Ragga looked like a goddess.

In the photo, Gabríel was wearing eighteen-month-old Tóti in a sling on his back. Tóti's arms were draped over Gabríel's shoulders, his head lolling forwards in sleep. Sigga felt a rush of love for her brother and nephew and then a wrench of envy, of how sure Gabríel and Ragga were of what they wanted, how tight they were as a family. But just because it worked for them didn't mean it would be the right thing for her.

She pressed her hand against her abdomen again. Little vests and coats, bibs for milk-vomit, gurgles, smiles. How great if that was all babies were.

'How much older are they?' Sóley asked. 'Your brothers, I mean.'

'Pétur's three and a half years older than me, so he's twenty-two and Gabríel's just turned twenty-five. He works on his father-in-law's fishing crew in Heimaey. And Pétur does nothing. He was supposed to go to university but he can't decide what to study, apparently.'

Sóley adjusted one of the straps on her dungarees. 'I don't really care about that stuff. I don't think people's jobs tell us who they are, anyway.'

'Never?'

'Sometimes, maybe.'

Sigga sat down on the bed and Sóley sat next to her and crossed her legs at the ankle. She had nice ankles, Sigga thought. 'What do you want to do, then?'

'Me? I want to be in charge.' Sóley pulled a face. 'Can you imagine a female Prime Minister in this country? And I'll make my future husband do all those stupid coffee mornings, and visit the sick kids, and give interviews about what he cooks when the ambassadors are round for dinner.'

'Future husband as in you haven't met him yet?'

'Yep. He's going to be really handsome, and really smart. So he'll hate all the crap he has to do, but at least he won't mind earning less than me.'

'My boyfriend would.' Sigga looked out the window. 'He thinks that's a man's job, like giving is masculine and receiving is feminine. Except for oral sex, obviously.'

Sóley raised her right eyebrow so high it was lost underneath her bangs. 'So your boyfriend doesn't like licking you out?'

Sigga blushed. 'I didn't say that.'

'You kind of did.'

'I mean . . .' She looked down. 'He's going to spend all day looking at them. I guess they won't be that special to him.'

'*What?*'

'He's a gynaecologist. Not yet – he's still in medical school, but he wants to specialise.'

'See, I thought maybe gynaecologists were just doing what they love.' Sóley pulled a face. 'Is the sex even any good?'

'It's all right.'

'Sigga, Jesus. We're too young for all right sex, don't you think?'

'It's just . . . is it that important?' Sigga asked. 'Don't the other things matter more?'

'You haven't slept with too many guys, have you?' Sóley said.

'Two.'

'Well – when you do find someone who loves you *and* is a great fuck, then you'll get what all the fuss was about.' She lay back on the bed and grinned at Sigga.

'Whatever,' Sigga said. 'You're the one with the imaginary perfect boyfriend. Who doesn't exist, by the way.'

'Of course he does.' She pulled a pack of cigarettes out of her dungarees. 'Can I smoke in here, by the way?'

'Sure. I'll open a window.' Sigga got up and crossed over to it and Sóley followed her.

She pushed the sash open and when she turned around Sóley was riffling through the pages that lay on the desk to the right of the window.

'What's this? It's not for school, right?'

'Oh that.' Sigga examined her nails. 'It's something I wrote. It won a story competition recently. The prize-giving's in London. Not that that means anything, obviously, but I keep thinking maybe it'll lead to something.'

'What's the story about?'

'You know the Bárdur saga? I rewrote it from the daughter's perspective. Helga.'

'Sounds interesting,' Sóley said. 'Congrats, man.' She put the papers down and slid a cigarette out of its packet, leaned against the windowsill.

'Now I think I should have made Bárdur a woman, or something like that. I mean, why not? Helga goes off and lives in the mountain too, after Bárdur brings her back from Skeggi's house. She could have saved people too.' Sóley was looking at her intently and Sigga felt her cheeks heat up. 'Anyway – like I said, it's not exactly a scholarship. It probably won't change my life or anything.'

'Tell me more.'

'No, really. There's nothing to tell right now.'

'Okay, then tell me more about the boyfriend.'

Sóley patted the windowsill next to her and Sigga leaned against it. 'How did you guys meet, anyway?'

'It's a long story.'

'Tell me.' She smiled winningly. 'I know I'm kind of prickly, but I don't judge.'

Sigga looked at the ceiling, then the floor, then at Sóley. She could still remember the party that night, or maybe it was just blurring with all the other parties in the basements of schoolfriends' houses: a mass of teenagers sharing bottles of brennivín, smoking, listening to the Who, the Stones, Led Zeppelin, discussing the merits of each band at length.

'I went to a party,' she said, 'and I left kind of late and I missed the night bus, so I thought I'd walk home.'

'Okay.'

'Then, when I was around Tjörnin, I noticed someone was following me, this guy. When I looked back at him, he sped up.'

'Shit.'

'He put his arm around me – no one else was around, by the way.' Sigga's mouth was getting dry and she swallowed. 'He said "hi", and I said "hi", because—'

'Because you had to,' Sóley said.

'Then he asked where I'd been, and I said out with friends, and he asked if I'd been out with my boyfriend, and I said no, but then I got the sense that that was a mistake, so I said I had a boyfriend, and he was coming to meet me, and I'd just started walking because I was cold, and the whole time he was smiling.' She felt sick. 'It was horrible. And he was really . . . big – big arms, big chest. Not that tall, but I knew he was stronger than me. So I just kept talking, about anything, trying to distract him, and looking around, like I was expecting my boyfriend to show up at any moment.'

'Yeah.'

'And then, just as we got to Bankastræti, he tried to pull me down this alleyway, but then I saw this guy coming down the street towards us, and he was really tall, and I said "That's my boyfriend," and the first guy kind of went loose, and I pulled away from him and started running towards this new guy, and I was calling out, "Hi baby, I thought I'd missed you," yada yada. Trying to signal that I needed help just using my eyes or something.' She gave Sóley half a smile, then looked down at the floor. 'And the thing is, he got it straight away. He put his arms around me and asked me how my night had been, really loudly, so the other guy could hear.'

'And the tall guy is now your boyfriend?'

'Yeah.'

They were quiet for a moment, then Sóley reached across and tapped her hand. Sigga looked up and met her gaze. It was sympathetic, a little weary.

'No one else knows. I just told my family we met at the party. I knew they'd all just say I was an idiot for walking around alone at night. Or Mamma would, at least.'

'Your mamma shouldn't make you feel like that.'

The comment caught Sigga by surprise. 'Mamma's fine,' she said after a moment. 'She's kind of hard-assed, but you know, Akureyri.'

'Well. We're not all nuts up there.'

'No.' Sigga clasped her hands together. 'I think it's because life's harder for women. That's why Mamma pushes me more.'

Sóley took another drag. 'You know her better, I guess.'

'Yeah.'

'Anyway.' She turned her body slightly to face Sigga. 'So you want to be a writer?'

'I don't know,' Sigga said. 'I think so.' She rearranged the stationery on the desk. The previous summer, Gabríel and Ragga had gone away with Ragga's parents, and Pabbi had been busy at the hospital, and Sigga had decided not to join Mamma and Pétur at the cabin. She'd stayed up most nights reading, and napped in the afternoons, and eaten nothing but hot dogs from the Bæjarins beztu stand on Tryggvagata. Sometimes she'd gone swimming in the evening, but mostly she'd sat at the desk they were standing by now, and written. Pages and pages. Not just the Helga story, but others too. If her life could be like that summer, then everyone had been lying, she thought, when they went on about the seriousness and the responsibility of being grown-up.

'Cool,' Sóley said, and grinned at her.

Sigga felt a little flutter in her stomach. *You're being ridiculous*, she told herself, but there was something so different about Sóley, and also so familiar, like they'd known each other for years. 'Yeah,' she said. 'It would be cool.'

*

Somehow, four days had gone by since she'd been sick, and Sigga had managed to avoid Olafur the whole time, so she didn't have to tell him. When he called up she made excuses to get off the telephone after only a few minutes – homework, or meetings, or dinner – and when he wanted to come over she pretended she had a headache. After the second day, she realised she actually did have a headache: a throbbing around her temples, and a light-headedness when she stood up too quickly.

'You look terrible,' Mamma said when she came down for dinner on the Monday. 'Here, let me feel you.' She placed the back of her hand against Sigga's forehead. 'You're not hot at least.'

'I'm fine,' Sigga said. 'Just tired.'

'Are you staying up late doing homework?'

'I suppose so.'

Mamma clicked her tongue against her teeth. 'You need some rest. And wear a little more make-up.'

'Thanks, Mamma.'

'I'm only saying it for your sake. You need to keep looking good, or Olafur might lose interest.'

'*Mamma.*'

Mamma turned back to the stove. 'I'm older than you, Sigrídur. I know how it works.'

The throbbing got worse and Sigga rubbed her fingers against her temples. The kitchen was too stuffy, and the smell of fish and onions was almost too much to bear.

'Is that what they told you when you were at dancing school?' she asked Mamma.

'I was never at dancing school,' Mamma said. 'We didn't have the money for that. I went to a local dancing class in Akureyri.'

'But you were good,' Sigga said. 'Pabbi said you auditioned for a company here, before you two got married, and they picked you.'

'Yes.'

'And you could have gone with them when they took it to Norway.'

'They offered.'

'Why didn't you go?'

'I had a life here,' Mamma said.

'But you could have tried it.'

Mamma turned to look at Sigga for a moment, as if she was weighing up what to say. 'If I'd gone then you three wouldn't have been born,' she said eventually, and went back to stirring the food.

Sigga paused too. 'What are we having?' she asked, and it seemed like such a nothing question, but she couldn't think of anything else to say.

'Plokkfiskur. Pabbi should be home in a minute. We'll eat then.'

'You mean me and Pabbi will eat.'

Mamma waved a hand at her, dismissively. 'You know how small my stomach is.'

Sigga looked over at the grey mass inside the pot and felt her own stomach protest. A bubble formed and burst in the béchamel and she turned away.

'I just need the bathroom,' she said, and ran upstairs.

She threw open the windows in her bedroom – both the street-facing ones and the one above the front door at the side of the house – and sat on the windowsill of the former, sucking in great lungfuls of fresh air. October tasted different, she thought, like mist and damp earth and grilled lamb fat. She leaned her upper body out, enjoying the feel of cold air, the faint light slipping over her skin. To the right, the sky changed from apricot to pink to burnt red. Stars came out and twinkled prettily above the painted houses.

Footsteps came briskly along the sidewalk, and Sigga saw Pabbi's shape materialise through the dusk. She was suddenly overcome with the desire to stop him, like she used to do when she was younger. Back then, she would keep him there for five, ten minutes at a time, talking about their days, before he came in and her brothers claimed him.

She scrambled to the other window and opened it wider, leaning out just as he turned in through their gate. Out of the corner of her eye, she saw a light flicker on in the room opposite, and heard the scrape of a casement window opening.

Pabbi looked up and called out a soft hello, but not to Sigga, to their neighbour, who was also leaning out.

'Hello, Thórfinnur,' she said, then caught sight of Sigga. 'Oh,' she said, and her face crumpled for a moment – less than a moment – then she rallied and smiled. 'It's Sigga, isn't it?'

Pabbi swung round to look up at Sigga, and she thought he looked almost guilty.

'Yes,' she said. Her mouth was dry, like she'd been eating sand. 'How did you know?'

'Oh, well.' The woman laughed; it was a nice laugh, musical. 'I hear your boyfriend calling you from the street when he comes to pick you up.'

'Well, goodnight, Ísafold,' Pabbi said. 'Have a good weekend.'

'Goodnight,' the woman said. She lingered for a moment, then fluttered her fingers at both of them. 'Very nice to see you.'

Pabbi smiled at her, then at Sigga, then opened the front door and came into the house. Sigga could hear him taking off his coat and shoes, going into the kitchen, saying something to Mamma. She closed her bedroom window, a little harder than she'd meant to, and descended the stairs. Loki was lying on the bottom step and she sat down two above him, bending to tickle his ears.

Pabbi came out into the hallway.

'How are you feeling?' he asked. 'Mamma said you're working too hard.'

'I'm not,' she said. 'I'm working a normal amount.'

Pabbi held out his hand and she hesitated for a second, then took it, and stepped over Loki and into his hug.

'I told you how proud I am about the competition, didn't I?' he said into her hair.

'You did.' She burrowed her face into his armpit, relishing the scratch of his woollen jumper, the musky, rosemary and citrus smell of his cologne. This was Pabbi – it was ridiculous to think he'd looked guilty; he'd never do anything to feel guilty about.

'I had a friend, growing up, who loved the Bárdur saga as much as you,' he said. 'Mamma was trying to educate us all about Snæfellsnes even back then.'

'Which friend?' she asked. 'Örn or Gústaf?'

'Neither of them.' He was quiet for a moment. 'We used to pretend to be Bárdur and Helga.'

'Oh,' Sigga said. A girl, then. 'I can't imagine you being that young. Who were you like? What did you like doing?'

'Normal stuff, I suppose,' Pabbi said. 'Before I was ten I spent most of my time fishing and drawing.'

'Oh yeah.'

'Did I ever tell you I used to make up my own version of my father? He was a soldier sometimes, and sometimes a famous actor. Douglas Fairbanks, I think it was. And he always loved fishing and drawing too, and when he came for me I thought we would all go to a cabin near a stream. And he and I would get up early to draw landscapes, then we'd sit and catch salmon.'

'But he never came?' Sigga asked. As soon as she'd said it, she regretted it; Pabbi shook his head, and his expression turned opaque.

'What else did you like?' she asked, before he could turn away.

'Other than fishing – I liked building rafts – that reminds me of Gabríel. He was always good with his hands. I used to hang around the harbour and help the dockhands unload the cargo, make a króna or two that way, then I'd always spend it at the cinema. So I liked stories, and films, like you.'

'Nothing like Pétur?'

'Not really. I used to wonder if he was actually a changeling. Except they were always unnaturally good – in your grandmother's stories, anyway.'

Sigga laughed, like she knew he was expecting her to, and he smiled, then shook his head again. 'Don't tell your mother I said that. You're all wonderful, in your own ways. But it's nice to have a genius in the family.'

Mamma came to the kitchen doorway. 'Does a genius know how to lay the table?'

'I was just going to drop my story off at Amma's,' Sigga said. 'I'll only be five minutes.'

'I'll set the table,' Pabbi said, releasing Sigga. He went forwards and kissed Mamma on the cheek. 'Dinner smells delicious, Eva.'

'You've been at work all day,' Mamma said. 'Sigríður can do it and drop off the poem after dinner.'

Count to ten, Sigga told herself. *Or maybe twenty.*

'Where's Pétur?' Pabbi asked.

'On a date.' Mamma untied her apron. 'I don't know when that boy's going to settle down – he seems to have a different girl each week.'

She looked pleased, Sigga thought.

'I'm going to wash then,' Pabbi said.

'Hurry up,' Mamma said. 'I'll pour you a glass of wine.'

Sigga went into the kitchen and took the cutlery from the drawer and started to lay the table.

That night, when Olafur called, Sigga came to the telephone. They talked for a few minutes about his studies, about the chess tournament he was in. Olafur was losing to a player he said was cheating. Sigga half listened, half thought about her father: with his absent-minded smile, his love of *Njáll's Saga* and the *Edda*, his long pianist's fingers that could drop any cup and burn any cake, his moon-shaped glasses that he would fall asleep wearing, and in the morning wake with them standing proud above his head. The thought that he could be keeping a secret from her was physically painful. But then, wasn't she keeping a secret from him? From all of them, in fact.

'So what do you think?' Olafur asked.

'Is it possible, to cheat at chess?' she asked, wrapping the telephone cord around her little finger until the tip turned a waxy, yellowish-white.

'Haven't you been listening to my story?'

'Not properly, sorry.'

'Why not?'

'I've been thinking about something else.'

She would tell him now, she thought. If he asked her in the right way then she would tell him.

'I'm sorry to bore you,' Olafur said.

'I didn't say that.'

'All right, I'm sorry if what I'm saying isn't important enough for you.' He waited for a moment, then burst out, 'I'm doing all the talking here, you know. All the guys I know would have given up by now.'

Not tonight, then, she thought.

'I'm going to bed,' she said. 'We'll speak later, okay?'

'Will we?'

'Of course. Goodnight, Olafur.'

1911

IN THE WEEK AFTER the party, Freyja and Tomas went to the mountain almost every day. They didn't invite Gudrún, and she didn't ask to join them. There had been another time in her life when Freyja had gone to the mountain every day, just after her monthly bleeding had first started. Gudrún had tried to go after her once, to make sure she was safe, but it was she who had got lost, and fallen and scraped her shin and banged her elbow. She'd hobbled home after a while to find Freyja already in front of the fire.

'You shouldn't follow me,' Freyja had said, solemnly, when Gudrún scolded her. 'I go up there to be alone. It helps me think.'

'Talk to me,' Gudrún had said. 'I'll do the thinking for us.'

Freyja had shaken her head.

Gudrún had the same sense of separation and frustration now, watching the other two heading out of the garden gate; Freyja might not be going up there alone, but she wasn't sharing her thoughts with Gudrún when she came back down.

'She reminds me more and more of your mother,' Papi said to Gudrún one time.

'But Tomas is nothing like you,' Gudrún said, and he grunted.

Whenever she looked at Tomas she thought of the hand creeping under her skirt and wished she hadn't been so quick to reject Magnús's offer to find him a job elsewhere. What would he do, after all, once Pabbi was out at sea?

Then, on the Saturday, Tomas came to find her while she was in the pantry lining the sieve for skyr. She used cheesecloth, which would let the excess whey soak through from the milk curds; afterwards, she would use what collected in the jug for preserving food, or mix it with water to drink. It was a calm chore, quiet, and methodical, and she wasn't necessarily pleased to be interrupted.

'I want to cook the meal for tonight,' Tomas said. 'Will you let me use your kitchen?'

'It's not *my* kitchen,' Gudrún said, stiffly.

'Is there a special cake that Icelanders make for celebrations?'

'Vínarterta.'

'Will you show me how to make it?'

She looked at him. His cheeks were a slight pink and his eyes shiny, and she felt herself unbending a little. 'It's a layered cake,' she said. 'We should probably start on it now if you want to eat it tonight.'

'Thank you, Gunna.'

'What are you making for the main course?'

'Kjötsúpa?' he suggested, and she gathered carrots, potatoes, lamb, butter, almonds, flour, eggs, prunes, cardamom, sugar and a little bit of skyr and took them to the kitchen.

Tomas helped her peel the potatoes and carrots, and grind the almonds and cardamom seeds for the biscuit layers in the cake. After a while he started singing, and Gudrún kept time with her chopping. The sun came out and lit all the dust motes and she grumbled that she was always dusting and it never made any difference, and Tomas said it looked like the kitchen was decked out with jewels.

'Do you always find something to admire?' Gudrún asked.

'Yes.'

'You must have been a very happy boy,' she said, and he rested his cheek on her shoulder for a moment, as he had done that time they'd walked along the cliff.

'I was,' he said 'But I'm happier now.'

The memory of the straying hand tugged at her and she shifted away slightly and he straightened up. *You don't* know *it was him*, she told herself. Or that he hadn't meant his touch for Freyja. He hadn't so much as looked in Gudrún's direction since the party; that must mean something.

'Did you always want to be a sailor?' she asked.

'I didn't think about it much,' he said. 'Life happens even when you don't plan it, don't you think?'

'And a philosopher to boot.' She rubbed at her cheek with flour-dusted fingers and he laughed at her. She rolled her eyes, and tipped the prunes into a pan of boiling water. 'For the jam filling,' she said, 'soak these, then mix them with sugar and cardamom.'

'We have a cake like this in Denmark,' he said.

'We eat it at weddings here.'

'So it's very special,' Tomas said. 'Good.'

'Why . . .' she started, then stopped.

Outside, hoofbeats could be heard. The church bells chimed the quarter hour in the distance; a hand knocked against the front door.

Gudrún went to answer. Surely it would be Magnús, she told herself, her heart banging wildly against her ribcage

She opened the door. Father Fridrik was standing right outside, so close that without the door between them their faces were practically touching. He smiled widely, and she noticed his teeth were all a strange shade of yellowish-grey.

'My child,' he said. 'You see, I've not given up on you or your sister. I'll come as often as it takes to coax you back to church.'

'Come in,' Gudrún said. 'I'm cooking with Tomas, but you can stand in the kitchen and talk while we work if you wish.'

She turned on her heel and went back towards the kitchen, and after a moment she heard him follow her.

'Where *is* your sister?' he asked, when he came into the room, carrying his hat in his hands.

'Sleeping,' Tomas said.

The priest tutted. 'In the middle of the day?'

'We've been walking since early morning,' Tomas said. He turned down the heat underneath the prunes and put the lamb, carrots and potatoes into another pot waiting on the side.

'Goodness me,' Father Fridrik said, 'what do the women in Denmark do with their time if their men take on all their work?' He held up his hand as Gudrún opened her mouth to respond, and smiled sweetly at them. 'I'll go wake your sister.'

He was back a few minutes later with Freyja. Gudrún and Tomas stopped what they were doing for the moment, and faced them.

'Now,' Father Fridrik said, 'I've also come with a special mission. A member of our congregation, Birta Jóhansdóttir of Arnarstapi, died two nights ago.'

'I'm sorry to hear that,' Gudrún said. 'How did she die?'

'The Lord called her to him.'

'I see,' Gudrún said, 'and was it a surprise that he called, or had he given prior warning?'

Father Fridrik narrowed his eyes. 'Your father has certainly raised you ladies to be very light-hearted.'

'I knew Birta,' Freyja said suddenly. 'She worked at the Big Farm before I did. She married the harbour master.'

Father Fridrik bowed in assent.

'I saw her not long ago,' Freyja said. Her eyes were bright, Gudrún noticed. 'She was perfectly healthy.'

'She died giving birth to a daughter,' Father Fridrik said.

'But her aunt was a midwife,' Freyja said.

Fridrik waved one hand dismissively. 'She wanted her aunt there, but I managed to dissuade her. God has a plan for all of us, I told her, and it's human vanity that causes us to interfere. And there was no reason to assume there would be any complications.'

'She didn't have *anyone* there to help her with the pain?'

Gudrún heard the anger in Freyja's voice and felt her own anger rising in sympathy. She looked over at her sister and saw her mouth was pinched and white.

'At the very least she could have had some ergot,' Gudrún said. 'Surely you're not against that. God makes that grow, doesn't he?'

'Women are obliged to experience pain during childbirth to atone for original sin,' Fridrik said, running his free hand through his hair.

'And how do you know God's plan so intimately?' Tomas asked. 'Maybe it was for the midwife to be there after all.'

The priest turned red. 'And what business is it of yours? This is a community issue.'

'My mother was a midwife,' Tomas said. 'And my grandmother too. I'll bet they've saved more lives than you, Father.'

'More bodies perhaps. I'm more concerned with souls, of course.'

'You said you had a mission,' Gudrún interrupted. 'It can't possibly have anything to do with Birta Jóhansdóttir, since we barely knew her.'

'The widower has no female relatives,' Father Fridrik said. 'I suggested that Freyja come and look after the babe since she is currently without employment. He was more than happy with the suggestion.'

Gudrún felt her mouth fall open. 'You're not being serious, of course. *Freyja?*' Out of the corner of her eye, she saw Freyja walk over to stand next to the pot on the range. 'I'm sure the child's father will be adequate.'

Tomas joined Freyja, and they turned their backs on the rest of the room.

'What are you making?' Freyja asked.

'A surprise,' Tomas said.

Father Fridrik turned even redder. 'I see I'll have my work cut out for me here,' he said.

'I'm sorry, Father,' Gudrún said. 'But, as you can tell, we're very busy.'

He jammed his hat back on his head and left.

Gudrún went to stand behind the other two. 'You can take the prunes off now,' she said. 'Drain them, chop them,

126

stir in the other ingredients, then back onto the fire until it's sticky.'

'You're making vínarterta?' Freyja asked.

'I hope so,' Tomas said, picking up the pot and carrying it to the sink.

'It was Mamma's favourite,' Freyja said. 'Papi said she would take the layers apart and eat the jam first, then dip the biscuits in the coffee.'

'I didn't know that,' Gudrún said.

Freyja turned and smiled at something just over Gudrún's shoulder and Gudrún had to resist the urge to look behind her.

'Why did you react that way to his suggestion?' Freyja asked.

'Did you *want* to look after the baby?'

'No.'

'Well then—'

'She's not saying you couldn't do it,' Tomas said. 'Are you, Gunna?' He poured the contents of the pot into the colander and the plummy, blossomy smell filled the kitchen. 'This smells good already. What other cakes do you make here?'

Freyja looked at the floor.

'There's skúffukaka,' Gudrún said, after a moment.

'Will you make that for me?'

'All right.'

Tomas smiled at them both. He tipped the drained prunes onto a board and began chopping them up. When Freyja walked past he reached out and touched her lightly on the back with his free hand.

'I've got prune juice on you.'

'I don't mind prune juice,' Freyja said. She turned pale suddenly, and Gudrún rushed forwards, but Tomas already had an arm around her.

'What is it?' Gudrún asked.

'I just . . .' She looked at Tomas. 'It's nothing, I think. I just couldn't see you for a moment.'

'Are you ill?' Tomas asked. 'Is it a headache?'

'It's not a headache.' She touched his face. 'I'm fine now.'

*

A few days later, Gudrún was stirring flour, sugar and cocoa together when Freyja came into the kitchen, rubbing her eyes.

'Where's Tomas?' Freyja asked.

Gudrún laid down her spoon. 'He went for a walk, I think. Didn't he find you?'

'I was sleeping.'

'Again?' Gudrún asked.

Freyja peered out the window. 'It's almost dark.'

'I'm sure he'll be back soon. Come help me make the batter for the skúffukaka.'

Freyja knotted her fingers together. 'They had skúffukaka a lot at Rósa's. The men did, anyway. Rósa always said it was too rich. She called it sinful.'

'Nothing nice is a sin,' Gudrún said. 'Here – put on that apron.'

'I'll take a lantern out to the gate first.'

'Suit yourself.'

Freyja took a lantern and went out. Gudrún added milk, eggs and melted butter into the bowl and stirred until the batter was smooth, then stirred some more, waiting for Freyja to return. Outside, the sky was purple turning soft and black. She strained her ears; there was no movement to the side of the house, but from the front she could just hear a steady *clip-clop,* far away but getting closer.

Her chest tightened. Not Father Fridrik again, so soon after his last visit. Which would mean—

She leaned the spoon against the edge of the bowl and washed her hands thoroughly, as if to prove she was in no hurry, then walked along the corridor to stand with Freyja in the doorway.

'Who is it?' she asked.

Freyja was staring at a figure on the road ahead. 'It's not Tomas.'

'Of course not. Unless he found a horse on his walk.'

Freyja looked at her silently.

'We should go back inside,' Gudrún said, but neither of them moved.

She could tell it was Magnús from a hundred feet away or more, even in the dark. No one else would have reared up from the saddle in quite the same way.

The horse was walking slowly; Gudrún adjusted her skirt and smoothed back her hair and still it seemed hours before the pair reached the circle of light from the lantern hanging on the gate.

'Good evening,' he called, shielding his eyes.

'Good evening,' Gudrún said.

'I've been riding Maria all day – do you think I could tie her up here for an hour and let her drink?'

'You're very welcome,' Gudrún said.

Freyja turned and disappeared inside the house. Gudrún waited while Magnús tied up the horse, then remembered the water and ran to the kitchen to find a pot. She filled it and carried it out to him, letting some spill over the side in her haste.

'Thank you.'

He followed her into the badstofa and removed his coat and gloves.

'It's a cold night,' she said.

'But very cheerful in here.'

'Oh, well.' She looked around. 'Anything seems cosy if it's small enough.'

'It's not so small.'

'You're stooping now.'

He smiled. 'I am. But you never saw the room I grew up in.'

'Would you like some coffee?'

'Thank you,' he said. 'Although you mustn't think I come especially for it.' He smiled again. 'It's true, of course, but you mustn't think it.'

She didn't know how to answer that, so she went into the kitchen and made the coffee.

He was standing in the middle of the room when she came back, one hand in his pocket.

'Did I see Freyja in the doorway with you?' he asked.

'Yes.' Gudrún handed him a cup. 'She's . . . she had to finish some chores.'

They sat and drank.

'I also came to say – I'm sorry you didn't seem to have a good time at the party. Sometimes it's easiest to let Rósa organise things the way she thinks best.'

Gudrún shrugged. 'You didn't need to come all the way here to explain yourself.'

'So you forgive me?'

'Of course.'

Magnús smiled. They drank some more.

'Tell me about yourself, Gudrún Einarsdóttir,' he said, eventually.

'What do you want to know?'

'Let's see.' He balanced his cup on his knee. 'So far, I know you're well versed in our national literature. I know you make good coffee. I know your reputation of being fearless, and outspoken. What else should I know, as a friend?'

'Are we becoming friends?'

'I'd like that.'

Beads of sweat sprang up along her upper lip, and she fought the urge to wipe them away.

'I don't know what else to tell you,' she said. 'I've never been asked to put myself into words.'

'I find that hard to believe.'

'I'm not everyone's favourite sister.'

'Ah,' he said, and looked at her intently for a moment. 'I can help you start off. What do you want?'

'Want?'

'Yes. What do you want from life?'

'I want to be a human.'

His eyes crinkled. 'Surely that matter has already been decided.'

'I want to be recognised as a human, then. I want to be allowed to make mistakes and decisions for myself. I want to earn my own living, and own the roof above my head.'

'This is revolutionary talk.'

'Don't tell me you're afraid of it,' she said without thinking, then bit her tongue.

'Not afraid, no.' He moved his cup from his knee to the floor. 'Although I think you'll find a few people who are.' He met her eye. 'But you haven't mentioned your husband – what he'll do in all this.'

She hesitated; Magnús raised an eyebrow.

'Do I have to have a husband?' she said slowly. 'Can't I be a human without one?'

'You don't want to marry some poor soul and rule over him with a rod of iron?'

'I don't want to marry anyone I can rule, in the same way I don't want to be ruled over myself.'

'You're quite a novelty,' he murmured.

'I don't think so.'

Gudrún caught a flash of movement out of the corner of her eye and turned to see Freyja had entered the room. She was twisting her hands together.

'He's still not back,' she said, looking at Gudrún. 'What if he's fallen?'

'I'm sure he hasn't.'

'But if he *did* fall – in the lava field – we'd never find him.'

'I'm sure he's fine, Freyja.'

There was the sound of boots stamping outside and Freyja flew to open the door.

'Papi,' she said. 'Have you seen Tomas?'

Papi came in to the house rubbing his hands together for warmth. He caught sight of Magnús and started.

'Good evening,' Magnús said, rising from his chair.

'Good evening,' Papi said. 'Did Gudmundur send you after me?'

'Papi?' Freyja said. 'Have you seen Tomas?'

Papi waved his hand at her. 'He didn't come with me,' he said. 'I'm sure he'll be home in time for dinner.' He looked back at Magnús before she could answer. 'Was there a problem with the rent?'

'No, no,' Magnús said. 'I called in on my way back from Arnarstapi.' He shifted awkwardly. 'I didn't realise it was your guest you were missing.'

'Why?' Freyja asked, frantically. 'Have you seen him?'

'I'm afraid so.' He looked from one to the other of them. 'In Arnarstapi. I didn't know he was acting without your knowledge or I would have kept him.'

'What are you saying?' Gudrún asked. 'Kept him where?'

Magnús wearily ran a hand over his face. 'In Iceland,' he said. 'He bought passage on one of the boats leaving for Denmark.' His voice was apologetic. 'It sailed this evening.'

There was a stunned silence for a moment, then, '*No*,' Freyja said loudly.

'Freyja, shush,' Gudrún said.

'It's not true,' Freyja said.

Papi cleared his throat.

'I'm afraid I saw him board,' Magnús said.

Freyja turned and walked out of the house.

'I'm so sorry, Magnús,' Gudrún said, but he shook his head.

'It's a shock – I understand.'

She clasped her hands together and looked down. She didn't know what to feel: gratitude to Magnús for his calmness, his graciousness; pity for Freyja; anger at Tomas. Perhaps that finger at the party *hadn't* been him mistaking her for Freyja. He was a swine after all, she thought, although a tiny part of her remembered his smile, and didn't want to believe it.

'Let me speak to Freyja for a moment,' Magnús said. 'She seems to have taken it badly.'

'Thank you,' Gudrún said.

Papi gestured to the door, then sat in his armchair and took out his pipe and started cleaning it. 'Good riddance, then,' he said.

Magnús put on his hat. Outside, the grass was tipped with frost, and his shoes made a crunching sound as he followed Freyja out to the gate. The moon was up now and everything its light touched glowed like Papi's fish-gutting knife. Gudrún could see Magnús place a hand on Freyja's shoulder and bend down as if to say something into her ear. Freyja didn't move, not even to look at him, and he straightened up after a moment wearing a sympathetic expression. He looked back at Gudrún, standing in the doorway, and she felt her pulse quicken, her cheeks burst into flames.

She raised a hand in goodbye, and he lifted his hand from Freyja's shoulder to wave back, then turned and unhitched Maria, mounted her, and rode away.

*

In the days after Tomas's departure Freyja withdrew again. She and Gudrún milked the cow in silence, cured meat in silence, spun wool in silence, washed floors in silence. Gudrún felt an ache at how little she could help.

Papi was busy getting everything ready for the fishing season to begin later that month. Gudrún half wished he was gone already; maybe Freyja would talk if it was just the two of them. She knew why Freyja had reacted the way she did to the news, knew what had happened;

towards the end of Tomas's stay, Freyja hadn't bothered to hide from Gudrún when she got up in the night and went to the cowshed, or when she came back in the early morning, before Papi woke up. She knew, and Freyja knew she knew, but they didn't talk. Gudrún could have shaken her for her carelessness, but she knew it would be no use; Freyja could be stubborn when it pleased her.

Now, though, Freyja stopped coming to bed altogether. Sometimes, Gudrún would wake up in the morning and find her dozing in her chair before a burnt-out fire. Other times, she would be in the cowshed with Margret already, hair pulled back from her face as she bent over the milk pail. Dark smudges appeared underneath her eyes and bloomed.

She picked at her food, too. Jules Verne had never eaten so well, until Gudrún was forced to shut him out during mealtimes. And they never knew whether they would find Freyja irritable or miserable, only that it would be one of those two; Papi took to staying out of her way.

The day before he left for the fishing outstation, Gudrún spent hours in the kitchen baking skúffukaka for Papi to take with him. The air was ripe with the smell of the cakes – butter and malt – and she felt a sense of stillness within herself and in the house itself. She heard Papi whistling in the badstofa as he finished mending his nets, and Jules Verne padding in and out of the larder on the hunt for scraps. Outside, the rain fell relentlessly, but inside, the only signs were the pattering against the walls, and the way the drops on the windowpane glittered in the candlelight.

Gudrún laid out the last batch on the wire rack to cool and wiped her hands on her apron before going in to Papi.

'Will you be finished soon?' she asked.

'Another hour or so.' He threaded a needle, squinting.

'We can eat early, if you like?'

'Hmm.'

Gudrún sat on the edge of her chair, resting her elbows on her knees and cupping her chin in her hands. She watched Papi for a moment, listened to the crackle of the fire and the soft *thunk* of the needle as Papi pushed it through the fishing net. Every so often he glanced at something on the arm of his chair, and it took her a little while to realise it was a compass, inlaid with gold.

'What's that?'

'A compass.'

'I know – I meant, where did you get it?'

'The boy gave it to me.' Papi coughed, seeming embarrassed. 'Said he had it in his pocket when we saved him.'

'Is he not going to sail anymore then?'

'Maybe not.' He glanced at it shyly. 'Worth a good bit of money, I reckon.'

'Did he say anything to you about leaving, Papi?'

'No.'

'I thought he'd stay.'

Papi shrugged. 'His family's in Denmark.'

'I know. But he could have said goodbye, then, not run off like a coward.'

'That's Danes for you.'

'Hmm.' She leaned back against her chair. 'Well, it was hard on Magnús having to tell us.'

'Rósa's husband?' Papi asked, sounding surprised.

'Of course.'

'He didn't seem to find it too upsetting that I saw. Why would he?'

'He said he felt responsible for letting him go.'

'Well, who knows what those northerners think and feel,' Papi said. 'They're not like us.'

'Papi – not everyone can come from Snæfellsnes.'

'Didn't I hear something about him when he first moved here?' Papi asked, half to himself. 'He broke Skúli Skulisson's plough over some sheep that kept grazing on their land.'

'Are you sure Skúli didn't smash it up himself?' Gudrún said.

Skúli had played with Gudrún and Freyja when he was a red-headed boy of ten and Gudrún was nine. At one time she'd thought she would marry him, but Skúli's father had died shortly afterwards and his mother had gone mad and he had been left looking after his brothers and sisters and had no time to play anymore. The more she thought about it, the more she could imagine the responsibility might have got to him in the end.

'Why would he do that?' Papi asked.

'It doesn't seem like something Magnús would do, anyway.'

'Half wild, northern folk,' Papi said. 'This one looks like he's half giant, too.'

'Like Bárdur.'

'He's no Bárdur.'

'Oh Papi.' She shook her head. 'Where's Freyja?'

He went back to his mending. 'Isn't she in the kitchen with you?'

'No.'

'I saw her go that way.'

'She's not in there.'

'She'll be in bed then,' he said, nodding towards the corner of the room, where the curtain was pulled around Gudrún and Freyja's bed.

Gudrún left him and went to look. There was nobody in it, but the window above it was open, the curtain flapping inwards and rain soaking the pillows. She closed the window with a bang and the curtain shuddered still.

'Freyja?' she called.

There was no answer.

She hurried back to the kitchen. Freyja was standing at the table in front of the candle Gudrún had lit earlier. She was holding her right hand palm-down over the flame, close enough that Gudrún saw yellow lick her skin.

She took a step forwards and knocked Freyja's arm away. 'What are you doing?'

'Nothing.'

'Where have you been?' Freyja's hair was wet, and drops of water stood out on her forehead. 'Were you sleeping with the window open?'

'I lay down for a little while.'

'Give me your hand.'

Freyja raised it slowly. There was a small black mark in the crease of her palm.

'We need to wash it.'

She got together a bowl of water and a cloth and dabbed at the hand until the black was gone. Freyja let her do it, her arm limp.

'Doesn't it hurt?' she asked.

'No.'

'Don't do it again.'

Freyja's eyes flashed. 'You think I'm crazy, don't you?'

'Do you blame me?'

'I'm not crazy.'

'Look . . .' Gudrún wrung the cloth above the bowl until the water stopped dripping out of it. 'I know you miss Tomas—'

'You *don't* know,' Freyja said.

'So tell me.'

'He wouldn't have left like that, Gunna. It doesn't make sense.'

'Men don't think the same way as us,' Gudrún said. 'They don't have to.' She didn't need to mention their conversation in the cowshed, how she'd tried to warn Freyja against giving herself away; it hung between them even now. She watched Freyja's frown deepen, her eyes cloud. 'Darling—'

'No, I can't talk about it, Gunna.'

Gudrún went to her and took Freyja's hands in her own. 'I'm sorry, Freyja.'

'I know.'

'Let's sit with Papi until dinner.'

They walked to the badstofa hand-in-hand but Freyja pulled up short in the doorway, her face pale. Gudrún looked past her to where Papi was sitting with the compass in one hand, polishing it with the other. He looked up at them and opened his mouth to speak but Freyja cut in first.

'Put it away,' she cried.

Papi's face creased in bewilderment. 'Are we back to last summer again?' he said. 'I thought you'd got over your moping?'

Freyja wrenched her hand from Gudrún's and turned and fled. Papi looked to Gudrún, who bit her lip. How to tell Papi that Tomas's things were dangerous around Freyja? She was sure he must have known *something* had gone on, but you never knew with Papi what he might pick up on, or what he might choose to turn a blind eye to. Twice she started to say something, and twice she held back, not wanting to reveal too much.

'How are you feeling about tomorrow?' she asked eventually.

'I'll take my chances on the open sea,' Papi muttered.

'I'll go and check on dinner,' Gudrún said, and left hastily.

*

Gudrún realised about the baby when Freyja dropped the skyr and cried.

It happened at breakfast the week after Papi went down to the outstation. Gudrún helped pick up fragments of the bowl and wipe the floor, running through a timeline in her head as she did.

Afterwards, they stayed kneeling on the kitchen floor, facing each other.

'It's going to be fine,' she told Freyja, and nodded at her sister's stomach.

Freyja's eyes widened. 'How did you know?'

'I don't know how I missed it for so long. You've been so dreamy, and weepy. And your fingers are swelling up.'

'They are, aren't they?' Freyja looked down at her hands. 'It won't be fine, really.'

'I'll think of something.'

'Gunna, don't—'

'Papi won't be back until April. But if you don't want him to know—'

'I don't. Oh God – he can't find out.'

'He won't throw you out, Freyja.'

'I don't know what he'll think,' Freyja said quietly.

'You're not showing yet. It won't be here before midsummer. If you stay away until August, he won't need to find out.' Gudrún looked at Freyja's stomach. 'Would you go back to Rósa, if she'd take you? You could do needlework, or something less strenuous. And she might not let on, if we begged her.'

'I'm not going back there – don't make me, Gunna. Please.'

Her voice was shrill, verging on hysterical, and Gudrún's heart contracted. It occurred to her that Freyja might actually not be strong enough to cope with her situation.

'Shush, shush,' she said soothingly. 'I won't make you. We can think of something else.'

Freyja ground the heels of her palms into her eyes. 'Gunna—'

'Don't cry, Frey.'

'I'm just so tired.'

Gudrún took Freyja's hands and kissed them. 'Let's get you to bed then.'

She put Freyja to bed and went to sit in front of the fire. Jules Verne was cleaning himself on the hearth and she nudged him with her foot. 'Good judge of character, aren't you?'

Jules Verne glared at her, then went back to his wash.

She picked up her book, but her mind wouldn't focus, and it was a relief when she heard the hoof-beats. She went quickly into the kitchen and snatched up a pail, then pulled on her coat and boots and slipped out the front door.

Magnús was almost at the gate by the time she reached it.

'Hello again,' he said.

'Hello.'

'I've been meaning to call in on you – I was sorry to be the bearer of bad news last time.'

'It wasn't your fault.'

'How are you all feeling now?'

'Angry, mostly,' Gudrún said.

He dismounted and leaned against the fence post, wearing a sympathetic look. 'I can imagine – it seems to me as if he treated you all very poorly.'

'You don't know the half of it,' Gudrún said, and felt a sudden yearning to tell him everything. He talked so easily, so calmly. And then there was that affable smile, those eyes—

She suddenly realised what their green colour reminded her of. It was the pond Papi had dug in their garden when they were younger. It must have been a rocky part of the garden because it had never looked muddy, as other ponds did; sometimes it was aquamarine, sometimes emerald, but always a pure green, except during sunset, when an orange light ran through the water. Papi had filled it in after wild animals kept falling in and drowning at night.

'And where are you off to with your pail?' he asked.

'Oh this.' She looked down. 'Freyja's not feeling well and we're out of lava moss.' She thought of the pile in the pantry and quickly tried to put the image away, as if he could read her mind.

'I'm sorry to hear that,' he said. 'She was always in such good spirits at the farm and lately she's seemed rather down.'

'It's nothing,' Gudrún said quickly. 'She'll get better.'

'I'm glad.'

He held out his hand and Gudrún looked at it stupidly for a moment before realising he was asking for her own. She gave it to him and he squeezed it, staring into her eyes the whole time.

'It's always a pleasure to see you, Gudrún Einarsdóttir.'

He released her hand and she pulled it back as if from a flame. A smile touched the corners of his mouth then was gone again as quickly. He raised one foot into the stirrups and hoisted himself onto Maria.

'Are you leaving?' Gudrún asked.

'I shouldn't trouble you while you have someone to take care of.' He touched his heels against Maria's flank and she started and wheeled around. 'Besides, I've been sent to Hellnar on business and my wife takes any delay on my part very seriously.'

Damn Rósa, she thought. *Why doesn't she do the considerate thing and contract some awful disease?*

'I'm sure I'll see you shortly,' he said.

'You're welcome any time.'

He touched his hand to the brim of his hat and trotted off.

Freyja slept until mid-afternoon, only appearing when the ruddy daylight was already in retreat. Gudrún didn't hear her footsteps, and was startled at the shadow that fell across her book. She looked up at Freyja, framed by the setting sun.

'Are you hungry?'

Freyja shook her head. She sat at the table, running her fingers lightly over its surface, looking at the fireplace and something much farther away. Gudrún watched her.

She couldn't explain it, but she felt suddenly, overwhelmingly, shy.

Freyja spoke first, still looking into the distance. 'I need to find Tomas.'

Gudrún frowned. 'We don't know if he's home yet. You could write to his address, if you remember it—'

Freyja shook her head quickly. 'He's still here.'

'Here? In Iceland? Have you seen him?'

'No, but I can feel it.'

Gudrún carefully closed her book. 'So you haven't seen him?'

'No, I already said no.'

'All right, darling. Where do you think he is, then?'

'I don't know.' Freyja closed her eyes. 'I can't tell.'

Gudrún crossed over and knelt before her. 'Freyja, listen to me. You're not the first woman to have a baby without a husband. Hekla has three now, all with different fathers they say, and she's the cook for Father Fridrik. They get in the way while she's baking, of course, but it's not such a bad thing.'

Freyja was silent.

'Papi's a good man, if you're thinking of him. Maybe he'll worry that it'll be harder for you, but he wouldn't throw you out.'

'I just need to find him,' Freyja murmured. 'And he's not in Arnarstapi.'

Gudrún raised her voice. 'Papi earned his tenancy working for Rósa's family – they won't take that away from him. And eventually we'll inherit from him. And if we're over twenty-five' – she tapped her chest twice – 'we won't need guardians either.' She tried to sound cheerful. 'See – sometimes it's lucky to be unmarried.'

Freyja drew back and looked at her; her expression was hard to read, but Gudrún saw her hands trembling in her lap, and felt her own heart thud in response.

'Gunna, I need to find him,' she said. 'I need to know what happened.'

'Freyja.' Gudrún felt herself sinking under the weight of Freyja's obsession, felt the hopelessness of fighting against it. 'What's wrong? Is it more than the baby? Even Magnús noticed you've been down recently.'

'Was Magnús here?'

'Only for a moment – he was on his way to Hellnar and I was outside.' Gudrún ducked her head to hide the flush on her cheeks.

Freyja pushed her away, catching her off guard, and Gudrún fell backwards with a thump. 'You won't help me, will you?' she said, and burst into tears.

Gudrún felt a sharp pain in her elbow as it hit the floor, and another, different pain in her head. 'I don't know what I'm supposed to do,' she said, and heard the anger in her voice. 'Tomas is gone, and I warned you, so what am I supposed to do now?'

Freyja stopped crying and stared at her.

Gudrún rubbed her elbow, looking away. She remembered how she'd felt when they'd told her Mamma was dead. After the shock she'd felt angry for some reason, and run away from them into the kitchen, where Freyja was playing with bottle tops on the floor. Seeing her come in, Freyja had smiled from ear to ear and held out her arms to be picked up. And Gudrún had known, even at four, that she would always be responsible for her sister now.

It was then. That was the moment that had solidified Gudrún-the-little-girl, with all her life opening up like a flower, into Gudrún as she was now, her flower long gone. She'd let it slip into the river of time, let the water carry her onwards with no thought of deciding the current herself. Freyja, Freyja, Freyja. Every day the same all-consuming worry for her sister, the same thankfulness, the same piercing love. But for what? Had she been born to be subordinate to another soul, to tamp herself down completely?

'Maybe this will be good for you,' she said, with all the righteousness she felt right then. 'You've never had to face the consequences of your actions before. Maybe now you'll grow up.'

Freyja shook her head, as if to clear her ears. 'What did you say?'

Gudrún climbed to her feet. 'I said I won't look after you this time.'

'Are you *glad* that it's turned out this way? Do you want me to feel desperate?'

'Don't be ridiculous.'

Freyja's eyes were shiny again. 'All this time I wondered how Bjartur could do it, but maybe he had a sister like you.'

'I've done the best I can,' Gudrún said, trying to keep her voice level. 'Maybe now I can choose my own life before it's too late. And you – you're on your own.' She suddenly couldn't bear it anymore, any of it. She turned and walked out, leaving Freyja sitting alone in front of the fire.

*

Gudrún found the note in the kitchen the next morning. Freyja had left it on the windowsill, held in place by the butter dish. *I had to do it*, it said, and that was it.

Half an hour later she was in the badstofa at the Big Farm, sitting in front of Rósa Gudmundsdóttir.

'I need to see Magnús,' she told her, for the fifth time.

'I still don't understand. Why has Freyja gone?'

'She's just gone.' She clasped her hands together and squeezed, crushed them until she felt a white-hot pain. 'She's been ill. She must have been confused when she left.'

'*Where* do you think she's gone?' Rósa asked.

'She loves the mountain. She goes for walks there in the summer.'

Rósa looked unconvinced. 'And you think she's gone for a walk there now?'

'She can't have left long before I got up,' Gudrún lied. 'She was in bed with me until at least a few hours ago. If we leave soon we've got a good chance of catching up with her. Especially since she's . . .' She caught herself just in time. 'Ill.'

'Gudrún, I know you're worried about Freyja,' Rósa said slowly. 'But you don't even know she's gone in that direction. Going into the mountains in February is dangerous. The cold—'

'I know,' Gudrún said. 'But she'll die.'

Rósa bit her lip. It was a nice lip; all of Rósa Gudmundsdóttir was nice. Her hair was nice, her face was nice. Her ankles were nice. Her badstofa was nice. Gudrún tried to picture Freyja sewing by the window, or cleaning the hearth, and felt a clawing inside her chest. How could she tell Rósa she knew that was where Freyja had gone? *It's her mountain,* she could say, and Rósa would think she was mad. *And she's desperate. She told us once she wanted to die there. And I drove her away.*

'She spoke very highly of you,' she said. 'Please.'

'I liked her. But—'

'But you won't help.' Gudrún clenched her fists in her lap.

'I'm not convinced she'll be there. Surely we should start looking closer to home.'

'But I *know* she's there.'

Rósa paused again, and when she next spoke her voice was harder. 'Is it Magnús?'

'What?'

'I'm asking if you're looking for an excuse to spend time with my husband. Everyone around here knows how good a climber he is. Of course you'd run straight to him, if Freyja was really up there.'

'Goddamn it, Rósa—'

'What's going on?'

He was in the doorway. Gudrún rose, buzzing with a rush of blood, and held out her hand unthinkingly. He looked at it, looked at her, for what seemed like an eternity, then came into the room and took it.

'Sit,' he said. 'Please.'

She sat, suddenly embarrassed at how forward she'd been.

'What's going on?' he asked again.

'Gudrún Einarsdóttir is here,' Rósa said. 'You two seem to cross paths quite often these days.'

'Rósa,' he said gently, and went to stand behind his wife. 'What's happened?'

'Freyja's missing.'

'God.' His expression changed instantly. 'How long for?'

'Sometime early this morning.'

'What are we waiting for then? I'll get some men together.'

Rósa gave Gudrún a sidelong glance. 'We don't know where—'

'She's on the jökull,' Gudrún said.

She heard Rósa's intake of breath and wondered if it was dislike or merely impatience. 'There's no proof.'

'That's where she'll be.'

Magnús paused, looking down at his wife's head, then at Gudrún, meeting her eye. 'Are you sure?'

'Yes. She's sick, maybe even delirious. She'll have gone somewhere familiar to her. And she has something on her mind – she used to say it helped her think, going up there.'

'All right then.'

'My love—' Rósa said.

He put a hand on Rósa's shoulder. 'We should trust Gudrún.'

Something passed over Rósa's expression; it was so fleeting Gudrún almost didn't catch it, but she thought it was irritation, and felt a sense of triumph that he'd taken her side against his wife. She met his eye and sent him a silent prayer of thanks. He smiled as if he knew, and his whole face altered, seemed softer.

Rósa paused for a moment, then stood up. 'Will you wait here then?'

'Thank you,' Gudrún said, and looked away so they wouldn't see her eyes fill up.

With Rósa gone the clock on the wall seemed louder. Gudrún could hear creaks coming from above and the murmur of female voices. Freyja would have slept up there.

Magnús cleared his throat. 'You must excuse my wife's reluctance,' he said. 'She's always been a pragmatist. She does care for Freyja really.'

'Thank you, for believing me.'

'It's nothing.'

'It's not nothing.'

Her voice caught in her throat, and he looked taken aback and left the room abruptly. Gudrún pressed the backs of her hands to her cheeks, to cool the burning skin there.

He came back in with a glass of water. 'Here,' he said in a low voice.

'Thank you,' she said, and felt like crying again.

He took out a pocket watch and consulted it. 'I myself prefer something with more kick. It's not quite noon, but if we're to brave the mountain weather today – do you mind?'

'Of course not.'

He smiled. 'Thank you.'

He poured himself a large glass of brandy and knocked it back. 'Excuse me – I'm going to help my father-in-law send word to the neighbours.'

'Can I help?'

'No, no. I won't be long.'

Gudrún waited in the parlour while people came and went around her. Eventually, Rósa appeared again, pulling on a pair of gloves.

'I have to visit a sick tenant,' she said. 'Good luck with your search.'

'Thank you,' Gudrún said.

Rósa gathered her lips together in a wry smile. 'I hope you're right about Freyja's whereabouts – you certainly seem to have convinced my husband.'

'He's been very kind,' Gudrún said, copying her expression.

'I can imagine.' Rósa let the smile drop. 'I'm very fortunate.'

'I'm glad for you.' Then, because she couldn't help herself, 'How long have you two been married now?'

'Five years. When I first met Magnús he was lodging in Reykjavik with an older woman. Well-off, but lonely, you know the type.' She put a hand up to pat her hair. 'Then, after a few years, he began courting me. He said it took him that long to work up the courage to ask me out.' She met Gudrún's gaze with her own and Gudrún could read the challenge in it.

'You're right,' Gudrún said. 'You have been fortunate.'

Rósa gave her one last half-smile, then turned and left.

Not long after Magnús reappeared with Gúdmundur. Several other men turned up too, and skulked in the doorway until a maid took their coats and found chairs for everyone. There was Palli, and Einar, who could cure any sick animal just by laying his hand on its head. They were older, perhaps thirty. Then Gudmundur's friend, Haraldur, who was older than Papi, even, and served as parish clerk. Then a boy she didn't know, who seemed to work for Haraldur. Then there was Skúli, who gave Gudrún a nod when he came in. She returned it.

Eventually there were ten of them in total, including Gudrún, lined up in the parlour. Gudmundur made Gudrún retell the story.

Freyja was ill, she said. She'd been half-aware of her getting up that morning, but by the time she got up herself, Freyja was gone. She often went for walks, but in her state, who knew what she was wearing, and if she'd get lost. They should start soon.

'You're not going to come, are you?' Skúli said.

'Of course I am.'

He opened his mouth again, but Gudmundur cut him off.

'Anywhere in particular she likes to visit on these walks?'

'Snæfellsjökull.'

She waited for the muttering to subside.

'I know it's dangerous—'

'You came to us in time,' Magnús said. 'It's still a rescue mission; that's worth the risk.'

Gudrún clasped her hands together so the others wouldn't see them tremble. Magnús's meaning hung over the room.

'There's a storm due this afternoon,' Gudmundur said, and Haraldur nodded. 'There'll be no visibility on the mountain, and the ground will be hard, slippery. Chances are, we'll all break our necks.'

'What are you saying?' Gudrún asked.

'It's more than two hours to the base, and we'd have to descend before the storm hit. There's no way we'll make it up there today.'

'Aren't we even going to try?' Magnús said.

'It's no use,' Haraldur said, lighting his pipe. 'Better that we start out tomorrow when the skies are clear all day.'

'Please,' Gudrún said. '*Please.*'

They shook their heads, not meeting her eye, not even Skúli.

'I'm sorry,' Haraldur said, and puffs of smoke escaped from his mouth as he spoke.

She took a deep breath, and then another. 'I'll go alone then,' she said, and saw Gudmundur shake his head sadly.

'I'll go with you,' Magnús said.

'Then we'll come for three bodies tomorrow,' Gudmundur said.

Gudrún felt sick. She looked at Magnús, who smiled encouragingly at her.

'Rósa told the girls to get some provisions together,' he said. 'We'll set off as soon as they're ready.'

'Thank you,' she said again, and wished the others were far away so she could put her arms around him. Thank God for him, thank God for Magnús, the best man in all of Iceland.

'I hope I'm wrong.' Gudmundur handed Gudrún two flashlights and a flask of coffee. He looked out of the window. 'And wrap up warm. The snow's started to melt, but it'll still be freezing up there.'

The men stood and anxiously stamped their feet, lit cigarettes. Gudrún waited by the front door, watching them. There was a low hum as they spoke to one another, comparing reports about the success or failure of the hay this year. No one complained; the most they allowed themselves was a slight ruefulness as they recounted having an entire flock of sheep swept out to sea, or all the cows mysteriously drying up. Once or twice, a man would look her way and give her a sympathetic look. She didn't blame them, not really. It was madness, what she was asking. But Magnús thought nothing of taking time away from work, from his family, to help her, and she let herself give thanks again for him. She couldn't bear to think of what he would say if he found out Freyja meant to kill herself, as Gudrún was sickeningly sure she did, and was comforted that Papi wasn't here to know about it.

A small, yellow-haired maid appeared and handed the two of them pouches of dried fish, bread and cheese. Gudmundur left the room, then came back with a pair of trousers.

'Here,' he said to Gudrún. 'They'll keep you warmer than that skirt you're wearing.'

Gudrún took them. They were dark green, and heavy, and smelled off-puttingly sweet.

'They belonged to one of the farmhands who died last year,' Gudmundur said. 'Good thing you're tall.'

'Thank you.' She fought back revulsion at the thought that he might have died wearing them, and pulled them on under her skirt. There was a piece of cord around the top that she used as a belt and with that the fit was perfect. She slipped her skirt off and turned to face the room.

Magnús was looking at her; his pocket watch was out again and he was turning it slowly in his hand. The expression on his face was amused, although this time he wasn't smiling exactly; she caught his eye and for a moment they stared at each other while Gudrún felt her knees wobble and sweat gather at the base of her spine.

'Let's go,' he said.

1975

SHE WAS HAVING STRANGE dreams, although they were more memories than dreams. The summer she was seven and a half – she recognised that one straight away. She'd been helping Mamma clean the house, and Mamma had promised to take her shopping for a new dress for Karen's birthday party, but just before they were leaving, Pétur had come back with a scuffed elbow and blood on his T-shirt and a bust-up bike. Mamma had pulled him in for a hug and sent Sigga off for the holtasóley. And then when she'd come back with the jar of ointment, Mamma was sitting on the sofa, with Pétur resting his head on her shoulder.

'Good girl,' she'd said. She'd started dabbing it on Pétur's cut. 'Sigga, there's been a change of plan.'

'What?' Sigga had asked, sitting on the arm of Pabbi's chair.

'There's a film on at Nýa bío that Pétur wants to see – *Dr. No.*'

Sigga had swung her leg back and forth so it hit the side of the chair. 'What about my dress?'

'You don't really need a new one – you must have at least five or six you could wear.'

'They're all too small for me – I had that growth spurt last Christmas, remember?'

'Well, anyway' – Mamma had finished with Pétur's elbow – 'you can do something nice for your brother today, then you can get a dress another day.'

Sigga swung her leg harder against the chair.

'*Stop* that,' Mamma said. 'Go and get your shoes on.'

Sigga looked at Pétur, who smirked at her. She slid off the arm of the chair and went into the lobby. She sat on the bottom step of the staircase and pinched herself: on the cheek, on the neck, in between her thumb and forefinger. Mamma seemed to get irritated with her more often now, after the incident, and sometimes when her voice changed, Sigga imagined how her lungs were expanding, filling up with dead air, and the blood was crashing around inside her skull, just like when she'd been in the water. But if she pinched hard enough, she could forget the burning feeling in her chest and after a while everything went away.

After a minute or two she stopped and put her shoes on.

'I'm going to Amma's,' she called.

Mamma came out and stood over her, frowning. 'You're being very selfish, young lady,' she said.

'I never get to do what I want to do,' Sigga said.

Mamma looked down at her some more, then turned around. 'If you want to believe that, fine,' she said. 'Go find Amma.'

She woke up shivering and got out of bed, sat at her desk. A few months ago she would have been grateful to wake and find Olafur there, would have burrowed into him for comfort. Now the thought made her feel prickly and impatient. Was it really the story competition that had changed everything? Of course Olafur would think so – that would make it her fault. Everything was always because of her. But people changed. You couldn't get with someone and hope they never grew, or wanted new things. Still, she should talk to him.

After a moment or two, she switched on her lamp, picked up her pen and continued the presentation notes that she'd been taking before bed. Anything was better than going back to sleep.

She was exhausted the next day. For the first time, she skipped school, staying in bed for another few hours, then headed to Amma's house around midday and knocked urgently on the door.

'What is it?' Amma asked, yanking the door open so quickly, Sigga almost fell in. 'What's happened?'

'Nothing's happened,' she said, 'but—'

'Sigga.' Amma put a hand on her chest. 'Don't hammer on my door like that.'

'Sorry.'

Amma looked at her then back over her shoulder, as if she couldn't help it. Sigga peered over her and saw the kitchen in its usual state, a plate of garlic sausage and a hunk of bread half-eaten on the table, the radio on in the background. A few pages lay in a pile by the food. Amma had underlined a paragraph from the top page:

Helga could see that change was coming, like a tide, and she felt sorry for her father, spending all his time and energy trying to retreat from it, but he was her father, so she held her tongue, even after he found the ships and gathered together a ragtag bunch of folk – mostly men but some women too. She stood on the prow of the ship as they sailed to distant Iceland, away from Norway, the shoreline vividly clear, down to every crack, every niche in the rocks, the midnight air already brightening although the sun had only just dipped below the horizon. She watched the coast recede, felt the invisible rope that linked her to it stretching until it snapped, and only then did she go below to try to sleep. If there was moisture on her cheeks it could have been from the spray.

'That's my story,' Sigga said. 'Have you read it already?'

'I have. It's wonderful.'

'Thanks.' She paused for a moment, in case Amma was going to say more, but she already seemed distracted, looking at something over Sigga's shoulder. 'What did you—'

'Let me just . . .' Amma said, and walked over to the radio and snapped it off. She clasped her hands together, let them go, then seemed to make up her mind about something. 'Would you like to go for a walk?'

'Are you having lunch?' Sigga said. 'I can wait.'

Amma shrugged. 'What about school?'

'I don't have classes this afternoon,' she said. Another lie.

She waited for Amma to put on scarf and coat and they went out again, into the dim afternoon. Thick white clouds had gathered across the sun, and the water at the bottom of the hill looked strangely dull. After the last few, mild weeks, it felt like they'd suddenly started tumbling towards winter, and Sigga wrapped her arms around herself as if to ward it off. She thought about confessing, about the sickness, the late period, but Amma's gaze kept wandering away from Sigga, and Sigga had a sudden fear of her disappointment, of driving something between them.

'So,' Amma said, after a few minutes. 'Are you coming to Ava's on Thursday to make the banners?'

'Ava won't mind if I bring someone, will she?'

'Of course not.' Amma drew her coat more tightly around herself. 'Who are you thinking of?'

'Sóley,' Sigga said. 'She's a new friend.'

Amma raised an eyebrow. 'Have you fallen out with Karen?'

'No. Why?' Sigga heard the defensiveness in her voice. 'I can have more than one friend, can't I?'

'Of course,' Amma said. 'You've just never really mentioned anyone else. Like your father. He had Gustav and Örn and that was enough. Although I suppose . . .'

'Yes?' Sigga said after a moment.

Amma waved her hand dismissively. 'There was Ava's great-niece. They were the same age. But that was long ago. I'm not saying you can't make new friends, of course. But you were never like your brothers. They seemed to run around with whole armies of boys. Especially Pétur. That made your father feel a little better when you were all young.'

'Better about Pétur?'

'He wasn't as close as you and Gabríel,' Amma said. 'And Pétur worried him in general. He was so touchy, flying into rages when he couldn't keep up with Gabríel.' She stopped for a moment to peer into the window of the bookshop they were passing. 'It was difficult for Eva. Thórfinnur thought she didn't feel she could spend all her time with you because Pétur needed her so much.'

'What's her excuse now?'

Amma didn't turn her head from the window display. 'You don't feel like your mother spends enough time with you?'

Her eyes prickled, strangely. 'I don't know.'

'Can I ask you something?'

'Yes?'

'You make Gestr nearly drown in your story – why?'

'I don't know. It just came out.'

'Do you think about what happened to you much?'

'Not much. More since I started writing the story, putting myself in Helga's head, that kind of thing. I don't know why.'

'That's interesting,' Amma said. 'Do you feel there's some similarity between you two?'

'I don't know.'

'Something connected to nearly drowning?'

'I don't really remember everything that happened.' Sigga fidgeted. She wasn't lying, exactly, because she could make herself forget. At least, she could if she wasn't talking about it. 'Amma – were you two poor? You and Pabbi, I mean.'

'*That's* a change of topic.' Amma smiled. 'We weren't well-off, anyway.'

They started walking again.

'The attic above Ava's, where you used to live,' Sigga said. 'It was tiny, wasn't it? He says he didn't really know you were poor until he was an adult. He always had food, I guess, and he said you made the apartment nice.'

'Thank you for the vote of confidence.'

'You didn't mind that it was just the two of you?'

Amma cleared her throat. 'Have you spoken to your father about this?'

160

'No. Why?'

'There was a time when he minded,' she said. 'I just wondered . . .'

'What?'

'Why the sudden interest?'

'I don't know.'

They were silent for a while; Amma was the first to break it. 'I tried to raise Thórfinnur without my past,' she said. 'I thought that if I showed him how *much* I loved him that would be enough.' She lifted her shoulders in a shrug. 'But the older I get, the more I think what happens to our family shapes us, even if we aren't born when it happens.'

'I hope so,' Sigga said. She smiled at Amma. 'Otherwise my story is meaningless.'

Amma didn't smile back. 'You know, I think Helga's the saddest character of all time. And you got that so right, in your story. How could you?'

'Well, she never gets to choose for herself – that's always going to be sad.' She shrugged. 'Gestr has it pretty bad too. At least Helga's eyes aren't clawed out by her father in a dream.'

'That's just melodrama,' Amma said. 'Helga's lonely. And the worst of it is she isn't allowed to be with the man she loves.'

Just ask her, Sigga told herself. *She might tell you.* 'What didn't you want Pabbi to know about your past?'

'It wasn't just that I didn't want him to know. *I* didn't want to think about it. I'd come here for a fresh start.'

'Fresh start from what?'

Amma blinked rapidly a couple of times; Sigga waited.

'You know my sister died when we were young – around your age?'

'Yes?'

'And my father not long after. I didn't want to live in our home without them. We could see Snæfellsnes from our windows, and it was . . . important to our family. And then, when they were gone, I felt like I couldn't get away from its shadow.'

'You moved because of the mountain?' Sigga asked.

'Yes and no.'

'I don't understand,' Sigga said. 'What's it got to do with Pabbi's father?'

Amma stopped walking abruptly. 'We weren't talking about his father.'

'No,' Sigga said. 'But—' She bit her lip. 'Pabbi said once you never dated anyone after you came to Reykjavik, so I thought maybe you were still in love with Pabbi's father, or maybe not, maybe you were angry with him . . .'

Amma stroked a gloved thumb down Sigga's cheek and pressed it gently against the middle of her chin. 'Part of the reason I told Thórfinnur that the past was nothing to do with him was because I wanted him to think he could be his own person, that he didn't have to look for traits from me or his father. I didn't want him to feel bound to a stranger.'

'So his father was a stranger?'

'I didn't know him for long,' Amma said, and let her hand drop. 'But the time I did know him for felt very intense.'

'Will you tell me more about him?'

Amma started walking again. 'Maybe,' she said eventually.

'What about your family?'

'I can tell you how much you would have loved them. And they would have loved you. Especially my sister.'

Sigga felt her cheeks glowing with pleasure. 'Really?'

They'd looped around and reached the junction where Laugavegur turned into Bankastræti. Before them, the road dipped sharply, the buildings on either side thinning out at the edge of the old town. Sigga could see familiar landmarks: the tiny, wooden Reykjavik Cathedral, the Art-Deco Hótel Borg. The Grand Old Lady, people called it. Sigga had heard the stories about its heyday. Building had begun on it in the 1920s, when people still rode on ponies through the streets of Reykjavik; when women ran laundries at hot springs around the city; when the country had recently been declared an independent state under the Danish crown. When Pabbi was a teenager, living with Amma.

Sometimes she was jealous of Pabbi, that he'd had Amma all to himself all those years. Twenty-five years, in fact, before he moved out to live by himself. Then four years later, he'd met twenty-year-old Mamma. A mutual friend had set them up, although Sigga couldn't imagine why. Mamma and Pabbi were so different.

They were passing the corner of Bankastræti and Ingólfsstraeti, and Sigga glanced to the left automatically as she stepped onto the road. A couple were climbing the steps from a basement apartment a few houses up, and she saw them reach the sidewalk, saw the man gently touch the woman's elbow, the woman nod and look at her feet. There was something about them that seemed so intimate, even though they weren't kissing, or embracing. Had Pabbi and Mamma been like that? The man reminded her a little of Pabbi, his height, the colour of his hair, his coat—

She stopped suddenly, and Amma looked back at her.

'That's Pabbi,' Sigga said.

The couple were walking towards them now, and Sigga saw the woman was their next-door neighbour, although she couldn't remember her name. Amma waved to them and the woman's face turned as white as the sky. Then she noticed Sigga and she seemed to relax, broke into a slow smile.

'Hello,' she said when she reached them. 'I didn't see you at first.'

'What are you doing?' Sigga asked Pabbi.

She saw the look that passed between them and knew they were about to lie to her.

'Your father's been helping me look at temporary properties,' the woman said.

'Ísafold's apartment has damp,' Pabbi said. He stuck his hands in his pockets, rocked back on his heels and smiled at the ground.

'Don't they live on the top two floors?' Sigga asked.

'There's a leak in the roof,' Pabbi said, like it was perfectly natural for Sigga to be probing them. He nodded at Amma. 'Have you met my mother?'

'I haven't,' Ísafold said. 'Nice to meet you.'

'Likewise.' Amma smiled at her.

They talked a little about the weather, about the rally, three days away. Ísafold looked wistful and said it sounded important, and Amma made encouraging noises and told her about the banner painting evening at Ava's. Pabbi stood around awkwardly, and Sigga stared at him. It was too unbelievable, she thought, that Pabbi would be friends with this woman. Or more than friends. But then what was happening? Ísafold had been waiting until he came home, looking forward to talking to him – that's what her crumpled face had meant, Sigga was sure. But what about the way she'd looked today? More terrified than disappointed. Was she in love with Pabbi? He must know. But then why was he encouraging her? What had they been doing in that basement?

'Can I bring anything?' Ísafold asked

'Ava will have wine, and I'm making skúffukaka,' Amma said.

'The best in Iceland,' Pabbi said.

A sense of loyalty and resentment swelled in Sigga. 'Mamma's is just as good,' she said.

Pabbi coughed, and Amma raised an eyebrow.

'It always smells amazing, whatever your mother cooks,' Ísafold said.

Pabbi met Sigga's gaze and quickly turned away.

*

By October 24th the sun was already dimmer – as if someone had turned down its wick – and lower in the sky. Sigga spent the morning looking out of her classroom windows, tapping her pen against her notebook. She was called upon to read a few pages from *Independent People* and took so long to find her place in the book that Mr Finnbogi waved at some other student to take over.

After class, she found Sóley in the girls' toilets on the ground floor, running her fingers through her bangs.

'Do you want to come over to mine for lunch?' Sigga asked.

'Always,' Sóley said, and linked her arm through Sigga's. She was wearing perfume that was a mix of muskiness and vanilla, and Sigga had a strange prophetic flash that she would be able to pick out the smell for the rest of her life now.

Pétur was at home again when they got back, bringing a dirty plate through into the kitchen.

'You again,' he said, and Sóley dipped her head in agreement.

'We're here for lunch,' Sigga said.

'I made myself a sandwich,' he said. 'Do you want me to do some for you?'

'What kind?' Sóley asked, at the same time as Sigga said, '*You* made it?'

'It's just grilled cheese and pickles.' He seemed almost embarrassed.

'My favourite,' Sóley said, sitting down at the kitchen table.

'Do you want some wine?' he asked. 'There's a bottle open in the fridge and our parents won't finish it.'

'We've got afternoon classes,' Sigga said.

'Yeah, of course.'

'I'll have a glass,' Sóley said.

'Okay.' He went to the fridge and brought out the bottle and some blocks of cheese and the pickles. 'Sigga, are you sure you won't have any?'

Sóley grinned at her and she felt a wave of irritation at them, and the sudden conspiracy that seemed to have sprung up between them. *You're being paranoid.*

'I'll have a sandwich,' she said, and sat down too. 'Just to check it's not poisoned. For my guest.'

He rolled his eyes at her and poured out two glasses of wine. He handed one to Sóley, took a sip from the other, then fetched the bread from the bread bin and started sawing it into slices. Sigga took out her pencil case and History exercise book.

'So, how much do you know about the 1940 invasion?' Sóley asked.

'You're doing the World War Two module?' Pétur asked. 'Easy, just ask Mamma and Pabbi.'

All of them knew the story. Pabbi had taken Mamma out for their first dinner, and Iceland had been invaded the same night by Britain, hoping to keep Hitler and Germany out. Around four in the morning on May 10th, 1940, Sigga knew, Pabbi's friend Gústaf had called, to say that a reconnaissance plane had been spotted overhead a few hours before and warships were approaching the harbour. Half the town had turned out to watch the destroyer dock.

Pabbi had told her about it so often she could picture it almost as if she'd been there. It would have been cold at that hour, and quiet, with all the people lined up on the harbour watching in silence as the marines disembarked, and even the seagulls wheeled overhead without calling to each other. The marines seemed to pick up on it, Pabbi said, because they were quiet too, and didn't look people in the face, just marched down the gangplank and stood in rows at the bottom, then fiddled around with their rifles and seemed anxious. A few of them looked a little green around the gills.

The Chief of Police turned to the crowd, smiling affably.

'Everyone make room,' he said. 'There's four hundred of them to fit down here.'

Then there was the sudden roar of the plane overhead, and Pabbi said Mamma had flinched, and he'd put his arms around her. The crowd turned to look as it swept low over the roofs of the city and circled back again.

'A British plane,' Pabbi said, 'and the soldiers were from Britain too, standing on Icelandic soil. They'd asked to come, we'd said no, and they came anyway. And we had to pretend we didn't mind.'

The plane banked sharply, with everyone in the crowd watching, and Pabbi and his friends, Örn and Gústaf, looked at each other, then Örn took his sons' hands in each of his own and Gústaf said: 'I suppose we're in the fight now.'

Maybe it was no wonder Pabbi and Mamma had clung to each other after that, Sigga thought. But the war had finished long before Gabríel had come along.

'The real question is,' Pétur said, 'whether they went down to the docks together. Dinner was surely over by then.'

'You're sick,' Sigga said, and threw a pencil at him. She turned back to Sóley. 'I haven't done anything on the present-ation. Sorry – I'll have more time after the rally, I guess.'

'No worries,' Sóley said. 'I can give you my notes.'

'You've done them?' Sigga heard the surprise in her voice and winced. 'Sorry, I mean—'

'Sigga normally does all the work for these things,' Pétur said, his back to them, and Sigga was surprised again, almost grateful. 'She's kind of the teacher's pet, you know.'

'Yes, I did them,' Sóley said, and took a sip of her wine. 'I was the teacher's pet back in my old school.' She smiled at Sigga, who smiled back.

'Has she told you about the competition?' Pétur asked.

'Yep.'

'You'll probably read about it in the newspaper too. Our family are one day away from taking out a full-page announcement. They've always liked to tell everyone there's at least *one* high-achiever in the mix.'

'Very funny,' Sigga said.

'Speaking of the competition,' Sóley said, 'how's that boyfriend of yours?'

'Olafur?' Sigga realised with a start that she hadn't even thought of him the last few days. He hadn't rung the house since Saturday. Maybe he'd given up on her. 'I haven't seen him for a while.'

'Don't tell me there's trouble in paradise,' Pétur said. 'How will we cope without his scintillating conversation over dinner?'

'Shut up, Pétur.'

But she suddenly couldn't remember whether Olafur had ever made her laugh or not. And what if their baby was boring? Or if it screamed as much as Mamma always said that she'd done?

You cried whenever you were in your pram. You cried when you were taken out again. There were days when it was raining and we just sat there in the living room and you cried the whole time. For hours. And I could see the way everyone looked at me. When they started tutting on the bus we would get off at the next stop, even if it was in the middle of nowhere.

Could she bear it?

But Amma had said Pétur was the one who flew into rages, and needed all Mamma's attention and Mamma didn't seem to mind that.

She stood up. 'I'm just going to the bathroom.'

She lingered in there, splashing her face with water over and over, hoping the sandwiches would be ready by the time she got back. Then they could take them up to her room and away from Pétur.

The ground floor was quiet when she came out and she deliberately made herself quiet too as she crossed the hallway to stand in the kitchen doorway. Pétur and Sóley were standing very close together, in front of the grill, drinking wine and smiling at each other. She had to catch her breath, as if someone had punched her in the gut, and a stupid little gasping noise escaped her and they turned around. Sóley looked neutral but Pétur's eyes slid away from her guiltily, and she stared at him, knowing he would be able to feel it, wanting him to squirm. *Why can't I have anything of my own?* she wanted to ask him, and then immediately wondered what she even meant by that.

'Are they done?' she asked, and Pétur shrugged.

'Yeah.'

'We can eat them upstairs,' she said to Sóley.

Pétur loaded them onto two plates and they took one each. He looked like he was wrestling with something, then as he handed the plate to Sigga, he leaned forwards. 'You know—'

She turned. 'Come on, Sóley.'

Sóley waited until they got upstairs, then took out a cigarette and tapped it against her hand, eyebrows raised.

'What's up with you and your brother?' she asked. 'You looked like you wanted to kill him down there.'

'You should probably stay away from him,' Sigga said, sitting on the bed. She sounded prim, even to her ears, and hated herself for it.

'Why?'

'He doesn't care about girls.'

Sóley opened the window. 'Oh, I'm not going to marry him.' She grinned at Sigga.

'God, don't.' Sigga took a bite of her sandwich. 'He'll fuck you over, and Mamma will say it was all your fault.'

'That doesn't sound very cool.'

'He's an idiot. Although his sandwich is kind of good, actually.'

Sóley lit her cigarette and took a long drag, held it, then released it. 'I meant your mother. You don't have to listen to her, you know.'

'Excuse me?' Her heart sped up for some reason, and her fingers pricked with the sudden rush of blood.

'Not to be rude, but it sounds like she's got her own issues and she's using you as some sort of scapegoat.' Sóley leaned her elbows on the windowsill, picked a piece of fluff from the tip of her tongue.

'It's not that simple.' Sigga looked past Sóley, out of the window.

'People always say that when it's very simple.'

'I mean – do you think motherhood comes naturally to some people and not others? Or do you think everyone has to learn? Or do you think it depends on the baby?'

Sóley hooted. 'I asked my mother once if she knew what to do as soon as I was born. She said her body knew what to do. She didn't know shit. But I started crying and there it was – milk everywhere. And then it got so the milk came for anything small and helpless. One day she found a puffling that had fallen from its nest and just started gushing. She said it was fucking hilarious, how useless that was as a response.'

It was hard to imagine Mamma making milk for a puffling. But maybe that was why Sigga's crying had bothered her so much. Maybe she'd just been dehydrated.

'Yeah, okay,' she said, and went back to her sandwich, heart still pounding.

*

When the hospital had allowed Sigga to go back to their summer house after the incident it was Pabbi, who'd driven up from Reykjavik especially, who'd picked up her and Gabríel.

'Amma wanted to come, but she had to go back to Reykjavik,' he'd said in the car. 'Her neighbour's having a baby and she's got to be around to look after the older kids.'

'Where's Mamma?' she'd asked, throat closing up with the urge to cry.

Gabríel and Pabbi had given each other a look.

'Mamma's making dinner,' Pabbi had said. 'We thought we should eat a nice meal together to celebrate you getting released. And I bet the food at the hospital was disgusting. I remember when I had my appendix out, I thought I was going to die – of starvation.' He looked at her in the rearview mirror, the skin around his eyes creased so she knew he was smiling.

'It was all right,' she said.

After Pabbi pulled into the drive and turned off the engine, Sigga sat for a moment in the car, looking up at the summer house. She'd always loved it, with its big main room with windows on three sides, kitchen in one corner, dining table in another, living area in another. The ceiling was high and the walls were made of an orangey wood, imported from Finland, Mamma had told them. Outside in the garden was a hill to roll down, a tree for climbing, a vegetable patch. The edge of the lawn frothed with flowers that wouldn't grow in Reykjavik. It had always felt magical before, but now it seemed almost sinister.

'Come on,' Pabbi said, opening her door, 'let's get you inside.'

Mamma wasn't making dinner when they walked in; she was playing 'pairs' with Pétur.

'Not now,' she said, when Sigga tried to climb onto her lap for a hug. 'I'm in the middle of something with your brother.'

Sigga felt a rash of heat on her cheeks. Pétur didn't look at her either; his skin was completely bloodless.

'Come on,' Gabríel said, and took her hand. 'I'll help you put your stuff away.'

Pabbi smiled at her in a tired way as Gabríel led her out of the room.

They stayed in Sigga's bedroom until Mamma called them for dinner. Sigga could smell kjötsúpa as they opened the door, and in the dining room corner someone had turned off the main light and lined altar candles along the window ledges. Outside, the sky was softening into evening.

They all sat at the table.

'Thanks for dinner, Mamma,' Sigga said.

'You're welcome.' She ladled an extra portion into Sigga's bowl and passed it down.

'Hey,' Pétur protested. 'I didn't get that much.'

'Pétur,' Pabbi said. 'We're celebrating because Sigga's all right, aren't we? We had a lucky escape.'

'Pass me your bowl, Pétur,' Mamma said.

'It's Sigga's night tonight,' Pabbi said, firmly.

'I don't see why,' Mamma said.

'Mamma,' Gabríel said. 'That's not fair.' He was almost thirteen, and he'd shot up recently, and Sigga saw the surprise on Mamma's face, as if she was suddenly seeing him differently.

'I don't see why,' she said again, louder. 'Sigrídur was the one who scared us half to death. Is that something we should be rewarding?'

Sigga froze, hand and spoon halfway to her mouth. Her ears were buzzing, her heart pounding.

'It's not the right time to talk about it now,' Pabbi said.

'I think it's exactly the right time,' Mamma said. 'Let's just get it over with.' She turned to Sigga. 'You almost got yourself drowned, Sigrídur.' She rearranged the cutlery in front of her. 'Thank God Amma was nearby, to jump in after you. And thank God Pétur called her over.'

Sigga put down her spoon. Her fingers felt odd as she uncurled them; she looked down at them and saw they were white from clutching it so tightly. 'It wasn't me,' she said. 'Pétur—'

'Stop right there,' Mamma said. 'Your brother told me what he did. Of course he shouldn't have been messing around like that, but you shouldn't have been standing on the edge in the first place. I've told you not to climb on the harbour wall, haven't I? It's asking for trouble.'

'Eva,' Pabbi said. 'I really don't think we should go into this now. Maybe Pétur can just apologise to Sigga.'

'He's ten,' Mamma said. 'He's just a boy. You're talking like he knew what was going to happen. Anyway . . .' She took a sip of her water. 'I've spoken my mind, so we can move on. I think Sigrídur knows to be careful in the future now, don't you?'

They were all looking at her now, other than Pétur, who was looking at the floor. She felt an overpowering sense of anger that suddenly disappeared and left her feeling strangely ashamed.

'I don't feel well,' she said.

'Go and lie down if you need to,' Pabbi said, and patted her hand as she stood up from the table.

*

Amma and Ava were standing on the corner of Njálsgata as she came home from school that afternoon.

'What are *you* doing here?' Sigga asked.

'Just ran into each other,' Ava said.

'Your mother asked to borrow a tin,' Amma said. She turned her cheek and Sigga dropped a kiss on it; the skin felt paper-soft under her lips – an old woman's skin – sending pangs through her.

'Are you staying for dinner?' Sigga asked.

'If I'm invited.'

'I want to hear more about your story,' Ava said. 'Are you getting excited about the ceremony?'

A breeze started up, skimming Sigga's exposed legs. She looked up at the sky and away again, blinking; it was grey, but a bright, almost blinding fall grey. 'Not really.'

'Oh?'

'I don't want to jinx it. Maybe I won't even get there.'

'I didn't think you were superstitious.' Ava took a cigarette out her purse.

Not superstitious. Pregnant, maybe.

'I remember coming to Reykjavik for the first time,' Amma said. 'Let alone travelling all the way to London. We got to our new lodgings at night, me and your father, Sigga. They'd left us bread and milk and a few rashers of bacon on the kitchen table. And apart from the table and two chairs and a cot in the corner, the place was completely bare.' Amma shrugged. 'I remember I had a lamp that I hung on a nail next to the front door and the room was completely dark, except for this little golden circle. And I stood there for ages just looking out the window. I hadn't been quite prepared for how much bigger the city would feel. And there was no one who knew me, and no one I knew, except for my land-lord, who I wouldn't have been able to pick out on the street. I was trying to picture the lives going on in the other rooms I could see, the families sitting down to a meal, or maybe young married couples calling to each other. It was exciting. I felt a little like my new self lay before me. Like snow before the world wakes up.'

'And you weren't much older than me, right?' Sigga asked and heard the waver in her voice.

'I was very young,' Amma said.

'A lifetime ago.' Ava smiled. She lit a cigarette and pointed it at Sigga. 'Have you done something different with your hair?'

'No,' Sigga said.

'You look very well. Glowing.'

'Don't say that,' Sigga said, without thinking, and they squinted at her.

'Youth is wasted on the young,' Amma said, after a moment.

'Amen to that,' Ava said.

Mamma cornered Sigga as soon as they came in, and handed her an apron. She'd bought lamb shoulder, potatoes, carrots and onions and she was full of plans to make roast lamb, with potatoes fried in butter.

'Sigríður, you help me with the cooking,' she said. 'Amma, make yourself comfortable in the living room. Thórfinnur should be home soon.'

They were crowded into the main landing, still shedding coats. Pétur came slowly down the stairs.

'Did you hear?' he said to them. 'There was a tremor earlier in Heimaey.'

'Another eruption?' Mamma asked.

'It's not due,' Amma said.

'Krafla will be next,' Sigga said.

She was busy hanging up her coat and when she turned back she saw they were all looking at her.

'What makes you say that?' Amma asked.

'I don't know,' she said, her cheeks heating up. 'It just makes sense.'

'She's making it up,' Mamma said.

'The Hekla eruption five years ago,' Pétur said, 'that was a proper one. Not the one Gabríel goes on about. He's always, "Look at me, I fought a volcano in Heimaey."'

'Don't do your brother down. It'd never been done before,' Mamma said. 'All the big-shot geologists around the world were watching to see if it worked.'

Pétur shrugged. 'I've seen the footage. The lava's barely moving.'

'I remember when Katla began erupting,' Amma said. 'Your father asked whether the world was ending.' She smiled. 'Of course, Vikings saw Katla erupt, and out of that they were able to describe Ragnarök, in "Völuspá".'

Sigga saw Mamma roll her eyes. Mamma thought that Amma pushed her education down everyone's throats, which wasn't fair, because Amma had never even gone to school.

'What did you tell him?' she asked, and heard Mamma barely suppress a sigh.

'I said the earth would be around long after us. We might wipe ourselves out, but she'll survive.'

'Anyway, I'm hungry,' Pétur said. 'What's to eat now, Mamma?'

Sigga looked at him, lolling against the bannister, smirking, and felt her irritation rising. 'Why don't you make yourself a fucking sandwich?' she said.

'*Sigrídur*,' Mamma said. 'Don't you dare use that language.'

'Sorry,' Sigga muttered.

'Pétur, Amma, you can wait in the living room. Sigrídur, come into the kitchen. Now.'

'Fine.' She followed Mamma into the kitchen, threw her satchel in the corner of the room, and poured herself some milk, slamming open the cupboard to find a glass, then slamming that down on the kitchen counter. It felt good to slam, she thought, to crash and kick and punch and rip. There was too much to think about right now. Maybe a baby, the ceremony, the rally, the weird distance with Amma, Sóley. If only someone would take her in their arms and hold her, tell her she didn't have to work it all out alone. If only she had someone she could call on, like the people of Snæfellsnes had Bárdur. But he hadn't been much good as a father to Helga, only helpful against witches and suchlike.

She slipped the apron over her head and tied the strings in a double knot. 'What do you need?'

'Peel these,' Mamma said, and handed her a sack of potatoes.

Sigga sat at the table and started to peel, dropping each potato in a bowl of cold water when it was done. After a while the bowl filled up, but she continued dropping the peeled ones in until the mound overbalanced and half the potatoes went rolling all over the table, leaving trails of water behind.

Mamma came over with a dishcloth in her hand and wiped the table, tutting.

'Sorry,' Sigga said.

'Now, I know it's only *cooking*,' Mamma said, 'and *keeping house*, but some of us like eating, and living in a nice, clean home.'

'What are you talking about?' Sigga asked.

'That leaflet you left out for me.'

'Mamma – that's not what I think. That's *why* we're marching on Friday.'

Mamma snorted. 'For me?'

'Not just for you.' Sigga gathered the loose potatoes and filled another bowl with water and dropped them inside. 'But yes, so everyone recognises how hard you work here.'

Mamma dropped the dishcloth in the sink and turned back to the dough she was rolling out.

'Mamma, we work, we raise our children, we pay taxes. We're just as human, so we want an equal share of representation and wages, of the world we live in. What's wrong with that?'

'It seems like there's a lot of whinging that goes on these days about how hard life is.'

'You want us to just ignore it?'

Mamma dusted her hands, and placed them on her hips. 'When I was growing up, there was a farmer who lived nearby. He lost his son in the war, and his back went in an accident. He could barely walk. He had to give up the farm, but there were no relatives to take him in. He couldn't afford to eat half the time. You're telling me that a good-looking woman with money is worse off than that man?'

'What good is money if you don't have a voice? If men are the ones writing the laws.'

'Don't be ridiculous, Sigrídur.'

'Think about abortion.' Sigga's heart was beating wildly, like Loki's when he saw a bird he couldn't get to, and she put her hand on her chest to calm it. Of course that was part of the decision, she'd known that all along, but saying the word made it suddenly real.

'That's going too far,' Mamma said.

'I mean God, Mamma. Don't you think there are people out there that shouldn't have been born? And maybe women who shouldn't really have been mothers?'

'Sigrídur, that's *enough*. Just go if you don't want to be here.'

Sigga felt a flash of anger that suddenly disappeared and left her feeling strangely ashamed. She untied her apron and hung it up, then lingered by the doorway. Mamma had gone back to kneading the dough and didn't look at her. The image of Pabbi and Ísafold coming out of the basement suddenly reared up before her. Mamma didn't deserve that, if it was anything; she'd only ever been totally devoted to Pabbi.

'Are you sure?'

'I've never understood you,' Mamma said, without looking up. 'But then you've never understood me either.'

She felt her eyes prickle and left before they spilled over. *Probably hormones.*

Amma and Pétur were playing chess when she came into the living room. Amma was winning; she could beat all of them except Gabríel. Gabríel was a natural chess player. And swimmer, footballer, photographer, musician. Sigga did well at school but she worked hard; Gabríel never seemed to struggle with anything. She couldn't understand how he was happy just working on the fishing boat, but when she'd raised it, Ragga had called her a snob, in a friendly way. '*This* is why the rest of my family think feminism is for city people,' she'd said. 'It's all about women getting educated, becoming businesswomen, lawyers. There *are* other jobs, you know.'

'How many moves to checkmate?' Sigga asked.

'Four,' Amma said.

'Good. I hate watching Pétur play. It's like watching a four-year-old.'

'That time of the month?' Pétur said. 'Because you're being a real bitch.'

Amma tutted. 'What did you do to your sister?' she asked.

Pétur turned red. 'I didn't do anything.'

'I know Sigga – she doesn't lash out for no reason.'

Sigga shrugged. 'It's fine,' she said. 'One day it'll be Pétur's body they find in an ice cave and there'll be too many suspects and they'll have to throw the case away.'

'What are you talking about?' Amma said, raising her eyes from the chessboard.

'About Pétur being annoying.'

'I meant about the body.'

'You know, Amma – the body on Snæfellsjökull,' Sigga said. 'It was on the news a week or so ago.'

'I didn't hear the part about the ice cave.'

'A boy at school told me. His uncle's the chief of police there.'

'Man or woman?'

Sigga shrugged. 'I can't remember. But the body's been preserved. There was a broken foot, or leg, or something like that. They probably crawled into the cave for shelter and froze to death.'

Amma had turned pale.

'Are you okay?' Sigga asked her.

'I just thought . . .' She brought a hand up to her mouth and looked at them both, wide-eyed. 'I thought—' She sagged forwards.

Sigga and Pétur caught her together, and there was a moment of confusion, with the chessboard overturning and all the pieces clattering to the floor. *It's a heart attack, oh God, it's a heart attack*, a voice in Sigga's head kept repeating, then Amma was suddenly straightening up again, pulling away from them.

'*Amma*,' she said, and took a deep breath.

'I'll get you a glass of water,' Pétur said, and disappeared.

'Fuck, Amma,' Sigga said. 'Have you done that before?'

Amma wiped the back of her hand over her eyes. 'Done what?'

Sigga's heartbeat was gradually slowing down to normal. 'You *fainted*, Amma.'

Pétur reappeared with the water.

'We should take you to a doctor,' Sigga said.

'Don't be ridiculous,' Amma said. 'It's just being on my feet a lot today. And old age, probably. I'm fine.'

'We should tell Pabbi at least.'

Amma waved a hand at her dismissively. 'There's no need.'

'*Amma*.'

'I said there's no need. Help me pick up these chess pieces. I suppose we'll have to start again.'

Pétur met Sigga's gaze and shook his head once and Sigga knew what he meant: Amma was too stubborn to budge right now. She knelt on the floor and started gathering the pieces.

'Do you need a lie-down?' she said. 'Dinner won't be ready for a while.'

'I'll be fine,' Amma said, and dropped her hand onto Sigga's. She left it there for a moment, and Sigga let herself relax, enjoying its solidity, then Amma smiled at her, moved it off and they went back to picking up the pieces.

PART TWO

The Mountain

1911

THEY PAUSED AT THE base of the mountain. As Gudmundur had said, the snow had started to melt, and the lower slopes were only streaked with white, but when Gudrún lifted her head she saw the peak was still completely covered; it blazed against the vivid blue of the sky and hurt her eyes to look at.

Freyja's mountain. On a summer's day, when they were children, they could climb to the saddle near the summit in around six hours, as long as they avoided the glacier's crevasses. Now, in winter, it would be almost nine hours to the saddle, but sunset would be sooner than that, giving them only five and a half hours from now. Unless a storm blew up, as the men had predicted, although there was no sign of one now and she wondered if perhaps Rósa had said something to discourage them—

But she had Magnús. And they had five and a half hours.

Then there was the true summit – to reach that required ice climbing.

Then Freyja won't be able to reach it either, Gudrún told herself. *Don't lose hope before you've started.*

From somewhere to their right there was a low rumbling that built quickly to a roar. A mass of snow – about the size of a house – was sliding down the mountainside, followed closely by a jumble of rocks bouncing madly against each other. All of it, snow and rocks, reached the bottom and scattered like waves. There was a ringing silence.

'We should go straight up,' Gudrún said.

Magnús indicated the slope with a sweep of his arm. 'Ladies first.'

Gudrún started walking, dislodging tiny stones that slid down behind her. She could hear Magnús crunching over them as he came up, then he was suddenly level with her.

'You look on our left and I'll look on our right?' she said.

'All right. And you mustn't worry about what my father-in-law said. I won't let you come to any harm up here – I'm not quite as useless as he makes out.'

'You don't get on?'

He inclined his head slightly. 'I live in his house. Don't think he lets me forget it.'

'I didn't know he was so petty.'

He looked at her with that familiar amused expression. 'You wouldn't be trying to get on my good side, would you?'

'Maybe.'

'Don't let me stop you.'

The slope was steep already, and sweat had darkened the hair on his brow. Gudrún concentrated on putting one foot directly in front of the other, eating up the black rock between her and the saddle. Beside her, Magnús was finding his own way, choosing different stones to step onto, skirt around. In a way climbing a mountain was like swimming, she thought; no climber could follow exactly the route that their companion had taken.

Freyja had always chosen the vertical route. Gudrún could see her beside them now, long legs shimmying up boulders, leaping over gullies. And always, always, Gudrún behind her, watching with her heart in her mouth. Had she always resented her responsibility?

She shivered. The trousers were warm, but the air was making its way inside nonetheless and her legs stung with the cold. Ahead of them, a shadow moved on the ground, and she looked up to see a white-tailed eagle gliding over them, so close she could discern each individual feather and the lift of its wings as it changed direction.

After a while Magnús cleared his throat. 'Why did Freyja come to work for us and not you?'

'I was needed at ours.'

'It had nothing to do with Rósa?'

'No.' She was too quick to answer, she thought. She should have sounded more surprised.

'Earlier, at the farm – it sounded like the two of you aren't friendly?'

'It's nothing.' Her heart boomed in her chest. 'I was worried about Freyja – I lost my temper, that's all.'

'I see.'

From out of the corner of her eye she saw him look at her, then quickly back at the mountain.

'I wonder if things would have been different, had it been you who came,' he said, but so quietly, she almost didn't catch it.

'In what way different?'

'Hmm?' He pointed to a boulder to their right. 'Did you know there's a church underneath that rock, for the Hidden People? One man was allowed inside once, to shelter from a storm, and he was never the same afterwards. Stopped talking to his family, and went to bed for the next ten years.'

'Because he brought something back that he shouldn't have,' Gudrún said. 'That was Freyja's favourite story when we were little.'

'Was it?'

She stopped and unscrewed her thermos and took a sip of coffee. 'I had to tell her stories before she could fall asleep.'

'And which one was your favourite?'

'I don't know.'

She put her coffee away and started walking uphill again. He walked behind her; she could feel his gaze on her back and tried to ignore it.

They didn't talk for another hour or so while they trudged upwards. Gudrún kept a lookout for any sign of Freyja to her right. Once or twice, she caught a flash of movement, but it was just an Arctic fox with a luxurious yellow-white pelt. It seemed to be shadowing them, skipping away whenever it caught her looking.

'Did you see that?' she asked after the fourth time she'd caught it out of the corner of her eye.

'See what?'

'There's a fox following us.'

'Pity I don't have my gun.'

'You don't like foxes?'

'They're vicious. And cunning, which makes them even worse.'

'I quite like them,' she said. 'When I was younger, there was one who lived at the end of our garden. I thought maybe it was our mother, come back to watch over us.'

'Was it?'

She looked at him, expecting to see his smile, but his expression was serious, gentle.

'If it was, she went away again,' she said.

'Perhaps she saw you could take care of yourself. And look after Freyja too.'

Gudrún thought of her last glimpse of Freyja, alone in front of the fire, hands clasped together as if in prayer. 'I don't know what I've done to give you that impression.'

'There are some women who carry the world on their backs,' he said, 'and I've learned to spot them, however easy they make it look.'

'Oh,' she said, and felt her whole body blush.

The mountain got steadily steeper, and soon they were leaning forwards to counterbalance the slope, almost scrambling up on all fours. Gudrún could feel her legs and lungs protesting, but she kept going until Magnús tapped her on the shoulder.

'We should eat,' he said.

They crouched down and unwrapped their food. For a while there was silence between them as they tore into the bread, and swallowed the dried fish with coffee. Gudrún looked back at how far they'd come. Beyond them, the volcano's foothills were dramatic, blue and soft with snow at their peaks, and black elsewhere. They hadn't climbed high enough yet that she could see the Eysteinsdalur valley on the other side of the foothills, a stretch of land that during the summer was covered in a springy, green moss, but now would be frosted over. The voices of elves could be heard among the rocks and in craters all over the region, but Gudrún had only heard them once and that was in Eysteinsdalur. They had been singing, and the sound had been so sweet, so gentle, it could almost have been the breeze passing through the valley.

A hundred feet or so above them, the snow began in earnest, and lay thickly on the mountainside, reaching all the way up to the glacial peak. Gudrún felt her heart sink at the thought of the two of them trying to make their way through it, then a faint twang of hope. If Freyja didn't want to be found up here, surely she would have looked for somewhere to hide rather than stuck it out in the snow, where she'd be far more visible.

'She can't have climbed much higher than this,' she said. 'Maybe she started up here and changed her mind.'

'Changed her mind?'

'I mean – came to. We should be looking for a cave, or something, at this level, rather than going up any further.'

Magnús rubbed the back of his neck. 'I haven't seen any.'

'Me neither.'

'Did she have a favourite spot? A cave, like you suggest?'

'I don't know.'

'Did she never spend the night up here?'

'In the summer, sometimes. But I didn't come up often with her.'

'No?' He let out a long breath. She was sure he was judging her, but when she looked over at him, his expression was neutral. 'I'll look around for one.'

'No.' She struggled to her feet. 'We shouldn't separate.'

'You look tired.'

'I'm fine.'

'Surely among all those bedtime stories, you told Freyja the story of Bjarna-Dísa?'

'They tried to make her stay behind because she was dressed inappropriately for the weather,' Gudrún said, 'whereas I'm dressed perfectly. And besides, if you don't leave me to die in the snow, I won't haunt you and try to strangle you in your sleep.'

'As comforting as that is—'

'I don't need to sit here like a lump of rock while you look for my sister.'

'Perhaps your parents were right with your name,' he said amiably. 'You do know your own mind.' He took out his pocket watch and began to rub it with his sleeve. 'You can come if you insist, but it's past two o'clock.'

'I won't slow you down. We'll find her before it gets dark.'

'I hope so.'

They pocketed the pouches and Gudrún started walking. Magnús put out his hand as she went past and lightly touched her right thigh, on the crease between cheek and leg. She whirled around and glared at him, but he held up a small, black object.

'It was hanging out of your back pocket,' he said.

'What the hell is that?'

She leaned closer; now she could make out a black, ridged leg, with four toes at the bottom, one facing the opposite direction from the others. At the top of the leg, the black silken feathers that would have continued up the bird's body were mutilated and cut short.

'A raven's foot,' he said. 'Jon – the farmhand – used to catch them and kill them. I didn't know he cut trophies off too.'

Gudrún felt sick.

'He was as stupid as he was ugly,' Magnús said.

'Please put it away.'

He put it into his pack with his thermos and flashlight. Gudrún turned and continued walking, trying not to pay attention to the prickle on her thigh, where he'd touched her. She was suddenly, painfully aware of her body. The throb of her heart, the burning of her lungs, the heaviness of her bones inside her. She was so conscious of her physical self it was almost as if she couldn't think anymore.

Just above them another flash of movement. But this time it was bigger, darker. She couldn't swear to it, but out of the corner of her eye she'd thought it was man-sized, and dressed in grey.

They walked on. There was no clear path to take around the mountain and Gudrún found they were still climbing upwards, diagonally now, rather than in a straight line. They got themselves into a crack filled with ice, and it took twenty minutes to move across and out of it. The effort of it all began to consume her – she knew Magnús was there, but she couldn't feel him. She was utterly focused on what she was doing, until she began to feel almost detached, floating above, watching herself scrabble and shift and work upward.

After a while, they switched positions so Magnús was in front; each time they encountered a larger boulder he stopped halfway over it to pull her up after him and each time she muttered a thank you.

The edge of the snow seemed to get closer and closer, until the rocks on her right were covered in a layer of ice-tissue. Another hour passed. The wind had died, and there was a stillness to the air that was broken only by the sound of their breathing and the crunch of their footsteps. Gudrún bowed her head, more tired than she'd ever felt in her life. She knew, again without being able to explain why, that Freyja wasn't outside anymore, and that there were entrances into the mountain all around them, tiny fissures and cracks that animals used to escape predators or to take shelter. They just needed to find one big enough.

She raised her head again and her eyes recoiled at the glittering whiteness pressing in on them. For a moment she saw the man in grey again. Not that she could tell if he was really a man, his face was too indistinct. He stood ahead of them, pale and slight against the landscape, seemingly unaware of the weather, while ice piled up around his feet and climbed his legs until he was half buried in it.

She blinked and the figure was gone.

'Wait.' Magnús stopped so abruptly she walked into his back.

'What is it?'

'They were right,' he said. 'The storm's coming.'

'No.' Panic filled her; she could hear it buzzing in her skull, growing louder until she had to put her hands over her ears to stop it.

Magnús pulled them away. 'Are you listening to me? I said we need to go down.'

'We can't leave Freyja up here.'

'We don't even know she's up here.'

'She's up here.'

'It's too dangerous, Gudrún.'

'We'll be fine,' she said. 'It'll pass quickly. We can wait it out then go on. It's perfectly safe.'

'I can't let you take that risk.'

Fear and frustration made her sharp. 'You can't *let* me do anything. I'm not your little wife.'

His face tightened. 'I think we can safely say that's true.'

He turned away and she took a step towards him, panicking.

'Magnús – wait—' She missed her footing and fell. A small shower of pebbles bounced in front of her and she put out her hands to break the fall but found Magnús's arms instead.

'I've got you,' he said.

He was holding her very close, and she could smell the burnt odour of chicory from the coffee, and the sweetness of ewe-milk cheese. And underneath that was a salty, musty smell that she found strangely pleasing. She tried to straighten up and felt a spurt of fire licking at her ankles and climbing her leg, and held on to him even tighter.

'Something's wrong with my ankle.'

'Let me look at it.' He bent down and peered at it. 'I can't see it properly. You need to sit down.'

'Here?'

'No. There must be somewhere more sheltered.'

She looked around. Everything was black rock and white crystals, looking exactly like foam on sand, and she felt a sudden aching to be by the sea and off this wretched mountain.

I'll bring Freyja home, she told herself, *then I'll go and stand on the shore and watch the waves.*

'Somewhere,' Magnús repeated.

There was a small gully, more blue than white, and Gudrún followed it with her eyes as it rose towards an arch about a hundred feet above them. Beyond the arch was a darkness that seemed soft and inviting against the dazzling snow. The arch was jagged and big – big enough for five men to stand in – and she wondered at how they hadn't seen it before, unless it had been overhung with snow and icicles from all other angles.

'There – I can see a cave.'

'Where?'

She pointed at the opening. Magnús opened his mouth to speak then stopped; a snowflake had landed on the tip of Gudrún's outstretched finger.

They looked up and saw the sky had transformed. Where before it was blue, now it was a yellow-grey, with a great dark wall of cloud rolling towards them from the south, swallowing everything in its path. It was swift and relentless, constantly swirling and changing; occasionally, a stack or peak burst through, as if coming up for air, then the cloud would close over it again, and Gudrún had the terrible sense that they were gone for good.

'It'll be here in less than five minutes.' Magnús's voice was urgent. 'Lean on me.'

Slowly, painfully, she pushed off her swollen ankle and they started to walk. Snow was falling faster and thicker already, making the faintest of ticking sounds as it landed on the rocks in front of them.

'Can you go any faster?'

Gudrún gritted her teeth and sped up, limping heavily. Icy blasts of air stung her ears and bit her hands. They snatched the strength and feeling from her good leg, until she could no longer tell if she was intact, or if she were some sort of Frankenstein's monster, sewn together in parts but unable to feel.

You're dreaming while awake, she told herself, and knew that was a bad sign.

The air was full of eddies, not so much falling as simply hanging there, gradually increasing. Snow landed on them but there was no time to shake it off. Ahead of them, the path was completely covered, and it was only a steepness underfoot that told them to start climbing. Gudrún dug her fingers into the snow, hoping to find a hold in the rocks underneath, but she was slipping, and looked behind her to see the snow had erased everything and turned the mountainside into a sheer drop. Panic rose in her chest, then Magnús had hold of both her wrists and was hauling her up after him, scraping her stomach and knees on the ground, until the floor levelled out and they were lying at the entrance to the cave, panting.

'We need to go inside,' Magnús said, and he pulled her up after him.

They hobbled further into the cavern and stopped. Where they stood resembled a rocky, unkempt porch, lit up by the snow outside, but a few feet further on the light petered out.

Gudrún looked over her shoulder and saw snow blowing in behind them.

'I'm going farther in,' she said.

She hopped forwards, and felt him move hesitantly along with her.

The cave narrowed into a small corridor. Gudrún's eyes adjusted to the gloom, and she saw the corridor end in a wall of rock, other than for a slit in the middle, just big enough for both of them. They squeezed through the slit and all of a sudden the cave opened out again, into a great domed room. The floor was still rocky and dark, but the walls were a glassy, azure blue with ice, and intricately patterned, almost like lacework. The ice climbed up and stretched across the ceiling too, like the ribs of a skeleton, and here and there stalactites hung down, winking with reflected light. Gudrún looked back and saw the outside world framed by the doorway in the rock; it seemed further away than it really was, and less significant somehow.

They shuffled on. The air was warmer than outside, and the snow began to melt on her clothes.

'This was a lucky find,' Magnús said. His voice echoed faintly. 'Although it certainly smells ripe, our sanctuary.'

'Can we stop?' Gudrún asked.

'Of course.' He found a slab of rock and guided her towards it and down, then crouched in front of her. 'This will do.'

He slipped her boot and sock off, and Gudrún looked away, embarrassed by her big foot with its rough skin underneath the toes. Rósa probably bathed her feet in milk to keep them soft.

'It's not too bad.'

His fingers were so gentle, it felt as if they were barely touching her, but all the same, a wave of heat ran through her.

'Wait here.'

'Do I have another choice?'

He smiled. 'I suppose not.'

He stood and started walking towards the mouth of the cave. She closed her eyes, suddenly overwhelmed by Freyja's disappearance, by their journey, by how much she wanted him to touch her again.

Stop it, she told herself. *You're not thinking straight. You haven't thought straight since you met him. You're confused because, apart from Papi, and Skúli-who's-now-fat, and that farmhand who you kissed once when you were seventeen, Tomas was the only man you spent real time with. And that was never alone. And he was only a boy, really, if you compare him to Magnús.*

She pressed the heels of her hands against her eyes, trying to make him disappear from her brain. Magnús, with his hidden strength, and his teasing conversation, with the directness of his gaze, that smile that wasn't quite a smile. She wondered what he had been doing when Rósa had first met him, then felt a hot prick of jealousy at the thought of how he'd loved her for years before he declared it, at the thought of their marriage, at how Rósa had everything she wanted without even seeming to try.

'Stop it,' she said again, but under her breath.

She didn't hear him return, but all at once he was kneeling down before her pressing a lump of snow against her ankle. She started and let out a small cry.

'I know it's cold, but it'll make the swelling go down quicker,' he said.

'It's fine.' She was thankful for the gloom, for hiding the redness of her cheeks. 'I know that.'

He sat back on his heels. 'What?'

'I know to put something cold on swellings.'

There was that amused expression again; she could feel a buzz of irritation at the sight of it.

'Do you have to argue about everything?' he asked.

'I'm not arguing.'

'Yes you are.' He slipped his free hand into the pocket with the watch. 'Women are just like the Hidden People. Some of you more than most.'

'How fortunate for me to be trapped in here with the only man who understands all women.'

He smiled. His teeth seemed whiter in the gloom, almost impossibly white. The colour of skyr, of the inside of a hen's egg, of a seashell. 'Quarrelsome,' he said. 'Cunning, headstrong. Beautiful. Doesn't that sound like them?' He looked away then, as if suddenly self-conscious. 'Not to mention a certain figure from the *Laxdæla*.'

She forgot what she was going to say. She had the strange feeling that he was in her mind, not reading her thoughts, but *in* it.

There was a silence between them. She held out her hand for the clump of snow and he passed it back, looking surprised, as if he'd forgotten he was holding it.

'How long will we have to wait in here?' she asked.

'Overnight at least.'

'What do we have?'

'Coffee.'

'That's all?'

'I can catch a rabbit if the blizzard dies down.'

'All right.' She could hear the flatness in her voice. He must have too, because he slipped off his coat, cleared a space on the floor, then laid it down.

'You should rest,' he said. 'Lie on this.'

'What about you?'

'It's not so cold in here.'

She didn't have the energy to argue, and shuffled off the rock and onto his coat. He started to say something to her, and she tried to listen, but her eyes were closing and everything was falling away.

'Don't worry, I'll look . . .' she heard, then his voice faded.

'I'm still here,' she said. She forced open her eyes and blinked in amazement. It was summer, after all. She and Freyja and Tomas were on their way around the coastline. The sky was a warm, wonderful pink – the same pink that Freyja's ears turned with the candlelight behind them. They would eat kleinur and their hands would smell of the dough. They would crawl on their bellies through the grass to find the eider ducks, nesting at the edge of the small cliff, where it shelved down to the beach. Maybe they would bring back an egg as a keepsake. No, they mustn't do that. The mother ducks would be frantic. Here they came now, in fact, a whole horde of them, wings locked together so they stretched out almost to the end of the bay. They were starting to take off, just skimming the water now, and as they passed overhead she felt webbed feet grasp her, and lift her into the air.

They're taking me home, she thought, and she slept for real.

*

When she woke he was gone. She looked to the mouth of the cave, and saw the sun had set, leaving a velvet darkness in its wake. The cave around her was blurred and softened, and for a moment, she wondered how she could see anything at all, until she realised the snow had piled up around the entrance and was reflecting the moonlight. The smell had changed from the damp, stale air of earlier, to a crisper, sweeter note, and that, too, would be the snow. It would be almost pleasant, she thought, if she wasn't so cold that her eyes felt heavy, and her fingers and toes numb.

She lay motionless for a moment, not wanting to find out if her ankle was still painful. She felt strangely apart from her body, as if she were something else entirely inside it. Then she sneezed and felt the jolt down her back and leg, and the throbbing in her ankle returned with a vengeance.

You're too fanciful these days, she told herself.

She pushed herself up and onto the rock again. For some reason, she didn't want to be lying down when Magnús came back.

She waited in silence for what seemed like hours. He was silent too when he returned; she sensed the light change at the entrance and looked up to see the outline of his form. He stood like that for a while, as if letting his eyes adjust. It seemed fitting somehow; he was so strange to her anyway that he might as well have been an outline.

She let him come halfway in before she called out softly, 'Where did you go?'

He stopped, looked around, and found her on her rock. He held out his hand and she saw a limp, furry body hanging from his fingers, one long ear flopping over the face.

'There are lots of them,' he said. 'We wouldn't starve if we had to be up here for more than one night.'

'Will we?'

'How's your ankle?'

'It hurts. Is the blizzard over?'

'Blew itself out after an hour or two.' He went to his haversack and started unpacking it. 'You slept well.'

'What's that?'

'Kindling.'

'You carried it all this way?'

'I told you – I'm not as useless as my father-in-law makes out.'

She watched him heap the sticks together and strike two small rocks to create a spark, then he went back to his haversack, drew out a knife and started skinning the rabbit. His fingers were quick, deft, and she thought suddenly of Tomas.

'Can I ask you a question?'

'Of course.'

'Did Tomas say anything to you – about why he was leaving?'

Magnús stopped what he was doing and looked up at her. 'No. Should he have?'

'I suppose not. It was just so sudden. And he and Freyja were friendly.'

'Then I'm sorry for Freyja.' He skewered the rabbit over the fire. 'Nothing fancy, I'm afraid.'

'We've eaten less than that in years when the hay's been bad,' she said.

'Of course. I forget you're a farmer's daughter.'

'And yet I sound just like a real person.'

He crouched down in front of the fire. 'Now you're forgetting who I was raised by.'

'Where were your parents?'

'They gave me up. My mother did, anyway. Ran away when I was one. My father died before I was born. But they'd been workers for old Baldur, so he took me in. Fridrik's story was similar, although he was a good few years older than me. He must have been eleven or so when I was born – Baldur put him in charge of me.'

'I'm sorry.'

'Probably why my father-in-law distrusts me.' He took out his watch and examined it, turning it over and over. 'I come with no real family – no name.'

'At least he let you marry her,' Gudrún said. 'Snæfellsnes people aren't always so reasonable. He could have had you killed instead.'

Magnús smiled. 'You're right, I suppose – I should be thankful for small mercies. Although I like to think my wife would have objected to my murder. We were very close back then.' He carried on turning the watch but looking straight at her now, making her feel oddly dizzy. 'I enjoy talking to you, Gudrún Einarsdóttir.'

'I'm glad,' she answered, although her mind was busy with what he'd said immediately before that.

He pocketed the watch, and turned the rabbit instead, over the flames. Gudrún smelled the crisping skin and felt her mouth water.

'Why did you get rid of Freyja?' she asked.

Magnús looked surprised. 'Get rid of her?'

'Why did you let her go?'

He shrugged. 'My wife runs the household, Gudmundur runs the farm. I have no influence over either.'

'Why did Rósa let her go, then?'

'I couldn't say.'

'Is it because Freyja fell in love with you?'

His face, which had been wary, relaxed into an expression of amusement. 'I've never heard any such accusation.'

'Surely you've noticed how she behaves around you?'

'What about her behaviour led you to think that?'

'She won't look you in the eye, she doesn't talk to you.'

He laughed. It was the first time Gudrún had heard it, she realised, and it was almost as big as him. It was an attractive laugh, delighted, sincere.

'Is that how women show they're in love?'

'Not all.'

'How would Gudrún Einarsdóttir behave?'

She tried to shrug but her shoulders were stiff from sleeping on the floor. 'I suppose I would tell him, so I could find out if it was reciprocated.'

'You wouldn't worry about being unmaidenlike?'

'I wouldn't worry about conforming to a role I didn't choose for myself.'

He looked her directly in the eye. 'I like that you're tough,' he said, and her heart began palpitating so strongly she was sure he would see it through her clothes. 'I admire it greatly. But you're not as tough as you think, Gudrún Einarsdóttir.'

Maybe that was true, she thought. She could be someone different with him. Up here, in this cave, she could be whoever she wanted to be. She could be someone that men would choose over Freyja.

She felt a pang even thinking it, and tapped her fore-finger against her heart. Freyja was safe, she told herself. She would know otherwise.

'What is it?' Magnús asked.

She thought about unburdening herself, telling him the real reason that Freyja had disappeared, at her part in it. She longed for him to reassure her, so much that although she braced herself to speak, at the last minute she couldn't say the words. What would he think of Freyja, if he knew she'd let Tomas take advantage of her? What would he think of Gudrún driving her away?

'What is it?' he said again.

'I'm hungry,' she said. 'When will we eat?'

1975

'YES?' AMMA SAID, INTO the telephone.

'Amma, it's me.'

'Go on.'

'I'm calling you from the hallway,' Sigga said. She sat on the bottom step, clasping her hands around her knees and cradling the receiver between her shoulder and ear. 'I don't know who can hear me.'

'Why should that be a problem?'

'It's just—' She stopped, closed her eyes. 'The body in Snæfellsnes – the one they found in the ice cave . . .'

'What are you telling me?' Amma asked, and her voice sounded tighter than usual.

'Nothing. Just . . . you seemed kind of upset about it the other day, and . . . it was just after that, and then what you said about wanting to move because of the mountain. I wondered if it was anything to do with your sister?'

Amma breathed in sharply, then went silent; for a moment, Sigga thought they might have been disconnected.

'Anyway, they're moving the body to Landspitali . . .'

'Thank you for letting me know.'

'So it isn't your sister?'

'I don't *know* who it is,' Amma said. 'I just . . .'

There was another silence.

'Will you come with me to the hospital?' Amma asked eventually. 'Before the rally. Say twelve o'clock.'

'Of course,' Sigga said, and Amma hung up.

Sigga replaced the receiver and crossed over to the front door, slipped on her shoes and went out. She could walk around town until twelve; for whatever reason, she didn't feel like going back into breakfast.

She saw Pabbi straight away, standing at the garden gate with his hands in his pockets. He was rocking back and forth on his heels as if he was waiting around for something, or someone.

'Pabbi,' she said, and he turned around with a start. 'How did you even get out here? I was just in the hallway.'

He looked back over her shoulder. 'I came through the back garden and around the side,' he said eventually.

'Didn't you want anyone to know you were going out?'

'It's not that.'

'I was going to go for a walk,' she said. 'Do you want to join me?'

He looked at his watch.

'Just a quick one,' she said.

'All right,' he said. 'A quick walk and then I have some errands to do.'

She took his proffered arm, and they set off.

'How's the speech going?' Pabbi asked.

She shrugged. 'Okay. I don't know. I feel kind of differently about the story at the moment.'

'Hmm,' Pabbi said.

They'd reached the crossroads with Frakkastígur, and the smell of the harbour – fish and salt, oil and seaweed – floated up to them. Sigga glanced down at the grey water of the North Atlantic, and then up the hill. A group of young men with sideburns and denim jackets were standing beneath the peeling sign for Fiskbúð, arms crossed, watching them.

One of the young men was leaning against a parking meter, and she saw him spit onto the sidewalk without taking his eyes off them. It suddenly struck her that if someone wanted to hurt women the rally would make it much easier for them by gathering all the women in one small area.

You're being paranoid again.

But she tugged at Pabbi's arm. 'Let's walk faster, I'm getting cold.'

They kept on walking until they were down by the harbour, and then onto the jetty and along it towards the far end. They passed low blue shacks and small fishing vessels docked close together. A low stone wall with lamp posts set into it ran along the right-hand side; beyond the wall, the Soviet satellite tracking ship, *Kosmonaut Vladimir Komarov*, was floating in the middle of Kollafjördur Bay, its hull brown with rust.

They perched on the harbour wall. Sigga pulled her coat around her and squinted at the ship; it always felt like a bad omen to her when the ship was in the harbour. She didn't know why. Had there been a ship in the day of the incident? She couldn't remember now, although she could remember the feel of the harbour wall under her thighs, scratchy and cool, even in the sunshine. Pétur and Pétur's friend had lain along it on their bellies, spitting into the water below, competing to see who could gob the farthest. They'd let her tag along that day for some reason, and she'd been flattered, because they were ten, and practically grown up, and she wasn't even seven. It was Pétur's friend who suggested it, in fact. He even held her hand on the way to the beach. But when they were there he changed. He called her a baby, and pinched her hand. He laughed at her clothes – hand-me-downs from Pétur – and when he and Pétur lit up the cigarette he'd brought along, he blew smoke in her face. She'd been about to go home when he dared her to jump in the water. She wouldn't even have thought about doing it, except then Pétur had joined in too, chanting 'sissy missy' at her, over and over again until she couldn't hear anything else in her head.

But even then she hadn't, so Pétur had pushed her.

But Mamma had been angry with *her*. The morning after she'd got out of hospital she'd found Pétur sitting in the rowan tree in the garden. She'd climbed up next to him and straddled the branch, feeling the bark scratch the inside of her thighs as she gripped on.

'What did you tell Mamma?' she asked.

He addressed the branch. 'I said I pushed you, just a little, but you weren't expecting it, and you lost your balance.'

Birds called to each other nearby. The sun came out and flooded the garden with sunshine. The smell of grass and wildflowers rose up to where they were sitting as a cloud in the heat, fogging Sigga's mind. But there was something about the way Mamma had looked at her when they were all sitting around the dining table the previous night that was at odds with this warmth, this haziness, and she suddenly understood what it was – Mamma wasn't on her side. Even this time. *There must be something very wrong with me*, she thought, *to make Mamma so cross all the time.*

Pétur was looking just above her head. 'It doesn't matter anyway, right? You're okay – that's what matters. That's what Pabbi says.'

Sigga said nothing.

210

'Okay,' Pétur said. He looked at her quickly, then away again. 'Okay, good.' He jumped down from the branch and went indoors.

A wind blew in from the water, carrying a spray with it that caused them to draw back hurriedly from the edge.

'Shall we continue walking?' Pabbi asked, in a way that made her sure he was hoping to get away.

'Okay then,' she said, to spite him.

They turned and headed inland. Sigga could see the water of Tjörnin a few hundred feet ahead of them, grey and glittering in the light of the street lamps that were already turning on. Along the far shore were the Big Houses, as her family called them: embassies mostly, but some residential properties too. That was where she would choose to live, Sigga thought, with a balcony overlooking the pond. They could drink their coffee on the balcony during the summer, hot wine in the winter. They'd have to wait years on a single salary before they could afford one; another reason for her to put off having a baby and work instead.

When she thought about her future, it was always imprecise. She'd tried to think about what would make her happy, what she wanted, but it was only little moments that she could imagine fully: the balcony, the water, the coffee. Everything else was a fog of longing and ambition, anticipation. And she didn't know how to work towards something she couldn't picture, that was the problem.

They were skirting the pond and Sigga looked down at a flock of geese who were paddling near the road. The water had a dark, oily sheen to it that hid the birds' feet from

211

view. It was barely twelve thirty, but it seemed later. They stopped for a moment and she leaned her head on Pabbi's shoulder and it felt nice, normal between them again.

'I haven't seen Olafur at ours the last few nights,' Pabbi said, after a while. 'Is everything all right between the two of you?'

'You notice things like that?'

She lifted her head and saw he was smiling.

'Of course I notice,' he said. 'That's a parent's job, isn't it, to spend their time watching and worrying about their children?'

'Do you worry about the boys?'

'Not as much.'

'Because they can look after themselves?'

'Because I've never sat by their bedside in a hospital,' Pabbi said. 'I hadn't realised exactly how small I was. Loving you and the boys filled me up, made me feel big, but when I saw you in that bed, your hair all over the pillow . . .' He put his arm around her shoulders and pulled her in for a hug. 'That's one of the drawbacks of knowing what the different tests mean. The doctors were worried.'

'But I was fine,' she said.

He was quiet for a bit. 'You know, I'm still not used to seeing you so grown up, not having to bend down to hug you,' he said after a while.

'I've been tall forever, Pabbi.'

'When I think of you – there was this dress you used to wear. A pink one, and Eva put you in pigtails. And I'd come home from work and there'd be this blur of pink and hair and you'd throw yourself at my legs.' He sighed. 'I wish I'd been around more often. It was just . . . work was demanding.'

'I remember that dress,' Sigga said after a moment, because he seemed sad, and it wasn't his fault, she told herself. Of course work had been demanding.

'And I'd scoop you up in it. You always smelled like milk. Milk and soap.'

'You always smelled like that cologne Mamma used to buy you.'

'And Gabríel smelled like the outdoors, and Pétur smelled like liquorice.'

'Probably because he was always stuffing it in his mouth,' Sigga said.

Pabbi raised his eyebrows. 'What is it? Is Pétur being annoying?'

'Always.'

He laughed. 'Look, I know he's insufferable, but Gabríel said he was really good at calming him down after he and Ragga found out she was pregnant. Maybe you should give him a chance.'

'Maybe he doesn't get any chances after he tried to drown me.'

'He didn't *try* to drown you.'

'Fine, it was an accident. But he wasn't even sorry.'

Pabbi took a step back, holding her at arm's length. 'Sigga, he cried the whole time you were in the hospital.'

'He did?'

'Of course.'

'It's not how I remember it,' Sigga said.

'Well, you were six, and you weren't there,' Pabbi said, gently, and she laughed, despite herself. 'He was sleeping in our bed because he was waking up screaming, thinking you were dead and it was all his fault.'

Her stomach was pitching again, like the last time she'd thrown up. 'How do I not know this?'

'I don't know. You never seemed to want to talk about it, after that first night you got back from the hospital, so—'

She twitched away from him. Maybe this was the problem, all of them tiptoed around each other, never asking questions. But she could ask him about Ísafold, anyway. 'Pabbi . . .'

'Yes?'

No, she couldn't do it. 'What do you think of Olafur?' she asked instead. 'Do you hate him as much as Amma does?'

Pabbi took off his glasses and polished them on his sleeve. 'Should I?'

'Of course not. I don't know what she's got against him.'

'She just wants you to be happy.'

'Because she knows all about true love, right?'

He gave her a sideways look. 'She had a child under difficult circumstances,' he said after a moment. 'And she knows that connects you to someone for life.'

'Having a child with them, you mean?'

'There was someone I loved before I met your mother,' Pabbi said. 'She was called Elísabet. She was Ava's great-great-niece, and she came to stay with Ava for a little while when we were both children.'

'She's the one who played Helga when you were Bárdur?'

'That's her. Her father died, and her mother had a new baby who was sickly and Elisabet was sent away until the baby and mother were feeling stronger, which didn't seem right. Anyway, I thought she was very beautiful and very sad and very alive all at once. And when we grew up, I wanted to marry her, but her mother didn't approve of my situation.'

'What situation?'

'She thought people should know where they'd come from and I didn't know anything about my father.'

'Didn't you ask Amma to tell you about him, then?'

'Of course I did,' Pabbi said. 'But she wasn't ready back then.'

'And you weren't angry with her?'

'I was. I wrote to the parish priest in Snæfellsnes, to see if his name was recorded at my birth. I thought, whatever reason Mamma had for keeping him from me, she wouldn't hold on to it forever, not when she saw me happy and able to marry the girl I loved.'

A wind started up, tracing circles across the pond, and Sigga crossed her arms around her chest for warmth, one hand on each shoulder. 'Then what happened?'

'His name wasn't recorded. And Elisabet wouldn't have married me anyway. She was too pragmatic. Her mother found her an older man who'd made a lot of money in Canada, and she married him, then moved to Denmark and had two sons.' He gave her a small, tired smile. 'From what I heard, her husband had a pretty nasty temper, but she's stuck it out because of the boys.'

'Oh.' She knew it wasn't the point of his story, but there it was again – Amma's past being kept secret. But Amma had asked *her* to go to see the body.

She checked her watch.

'I've got to go,' she said.

She got to the car park at Landspitali at five minutes to twelve. Amma was already there, stamping her feet against the cold.

'You didn't tell anyone about this, did you?' she said.

'I don't even know why we're here. Is it the body?'

Amma gave Sigga a look that was hard to read. A little defiant, a little scared, maybe, then nodded.

'Come on, then,' Sigga said, although her mouth was dry again.

They passed through the main doors and stopped in the empty reception area. Sigga didn't have to look around to see the scuffed linoleum, the pine dado rail, the potted Yuccas, the strip lighting; she'd been here often enough with Pabbi, and hospitals probably looked the same the world over. The only other one she'd been in was in Akureyri, but she didn't remember much about that.

Amma went to talk to the man on reception, and Sigga watched her point at the sign for the morgue, saw the man frown and pick up the receiver of the telephone in front of her, jab his fingers against a few of the buttons. Amma took off her scarf and gloves and bunched them up in her hands. Sigga scuffed her shoe against the floor and nodded at a passing porter.

Five minutes or so later a tall, thin man in a white coat appeared and shook Amma's hand. He had a dark ginger beard and a very pronounced widow's peak. Sigga joined them in time to hear him say: '. . .very irregular. Normally, we would expect the police to arrange a visit.'

'Why would I go to the police?' Amma asked. 'The body's here.'

'How did you know that?'

'That was me,' Sigga cut in, and the man looked at her briefly, frowning. 'I know someone who knows the chief of police in Snæfellsnes.'

'And does *he* know you're here?'

'No.'

The man's frown deepened. The receptionist blew his nose loudly into a tissue and dropped it into a wastebasket next to his chair. Over the tannoy, a doctor was being paged. Sigga looked at Amma, who was wearing the patient expression she used to deal with Mamma when Mamma was being unreasonable.

'I would have thought you would be glad if someone could identify the . . . deceased,' Amma said.

'Yes, but—'

'My grandmother came from the region,' Sigga said. 'She moved here after a family tragedy about sixty years ago.' She tried to imbue her words with a sense of meaning while staying vague. She didn't look at Amma, but felt her stiffen, and the man's frown disappeared.

'I see.' He put a hand on Amma's shoulder. 'I suppose I can tell the police afterwards.'

'We'd appreciate that,' Sigga said. She dared to look at Amma and saw the skin around her nose and mouth was pinched and bloodless. 'Do you definitely want to do this?' she asked, trying to take Amma's hand.

Amma pulled hers away. 'Let's get it over with,' she said.

They followed the doctor to the lift, and down to the basement, then along a bright, quiet corridor. The doctor, striding ahead, was giving them a little potted history of the hospital, but Sigga was concentrating on Amma, who had started to slow down.

'I'm glad you're here, actually,' the doctor said as they neared a set of double doors. 'There are a few personal effects to show you, too. Clothes, mostly, and a necklace of some sort that was found with the body. Perhaps you could have a look at those first—'

217

'Amma?' Sigga said, just as Amma put out her hand as if to catch the wall, and stumbled.

Sigga caught her, and saw her eyes were unfocused, her skin even paler than before.

'I need some help,' she called, and the doctor turned, mid-flow, and made a noise that sounded half concerned, half annoyed. He hurried back and took Amma's wrist in one hand.

'Her pulse is good,' he said after a moment, as Amma's eyelashes started to flutter. Sigga and the doctor lowered her to sit on the floor, and the doctor left, muttering something.

'You fainted again,' Sigga said, trying to catch Amma's eye. 'Amma, you have to tell me what's going on.'

'It's the smell down here,' Amma said.

'It's not the smell.'

The doctor returned with a paper cup of water, and watched as Amma drank.

'I don't think it's a good idea to go ahead with the identification,' he said.

Amma shook her head. 'I'll be fine. But I want to go in alone.'

'Why?' Sigga asked.

'Sigga, please. No questions just now.'

'You can wait back up in reception,' the doctor said. He checked his watch. 'Shall we . . . ?'

Amma nodded and they helped her up. The doctor kept hold of her arm and the two continued along the corridor while Sigga watched them, then they pushed through a set of double doors on the right and she turned and headed back upstairs.

She sat in one of the padded, orange chairs in the lobby, avoiding the receptionist's gaze, and tried to remember what the doctor had mentioned just before Amma had fainted again. An item of jewellery. A necklace, maybe. That would mean it was a woman's body. Amma's sister – the one who loved kjötsúpa and would have given years of her life for their cat?

She gazed at the walls, reading the headlines on the sun-bleached posters: *Don't poison the air that they breathe. Blood is life: donate today. For health's sake, wash your hands.* More instructions and rules about what she was supposed to do, even from pieces of paper.

Amma and the doctor reappeared a few minutes later, Amma looking grey still, but walking by herself.

'Shall we go?' Amma said, coming over to Sigga as the doctor stopped to say something to a passing nurse. 'Sorry to keep you waiting.'

'Did you know who it was?' Sigga asked.

'No.'

They were almost at the doors by the time the doctor looked up. 'I'll inform the police,' he called, and Amma kept on walking.

'Why does he need to tell the police?' Sigga asked.

'They need to know who it isn't, I suppose,' Amma said, and Sigga was sure she was lying. She took Sigga's arm. 'Let's get out of here.'

1911

THE RABBIT WAS TENDER and delicious, a subtle meatiness to the flavour that tasted better than ptarmigan and mutton and any meat Gudrún could remember eating before in her life.

They ate in silence. After they'd finished Magnús went to the mouth of the cave and came back with handfuls of snow.

'For your thirst,' he said.

She took some and put it in her mouth, letting it melt completely before swallowing.

Magnús sat on the floor opposite her, crunching pieces of ice and polishing his pocket watch.

'Why do you do that?' she asked him.

'Do what?'

She looked at the watch. He closed the lid with a snap and returned it to his pocket.

'What's wrong?' he asked.

'I was just asking about your watch that you keep playing with—'

'But you're not really thinking about a watch, are you?'

'What do you mean?'

He leaned back against a large rock and lifted his chin so he was looking along his nose at her. Gudrún had the sudden thought that it was exactly the way Jules Verne looked at a mouse, as if he couldn't decide whether to eat it or not, and a shiver of anticipation – not unpleasant – ran through her.

'Women never reveal what they're really thinking,' he said.

'We don't?'

'You're naturally deceptive. Just as men are naturally strong.'

'You have a low opinion of your species if you think those are our two defining qualities.'

'Look at the animal kingdom. The males hunt and the females entice them to mate. It's the way of the world.'

The air in the cave was turning cold, and she pressed her palms between her thighs for warmth. 'But we're not animals,' she said.

'Yes we are.'

'We're humans. And women are just as human as men. We do the things we do because of experience, because of where we were born, and who raises us, and whether anyone teaches us to pour coffee into the saucer before we take the first sip, and if we meet a stranger with a lisp on a Wednesday when the moon is full.' She was talking quickly, and stopped for breath.

He took his hand out of his pocket and ran it through his hair. 'It may be that I'm terribly dense, but I'm afraid I don't follow.'

'I'm trying to say.' She paused. How to phrase something that she felt to be so intrinsically true she'd never bothered to think of it in words? 'It's chance. You know not all men are the same, and not all women are the same. We're not just biology.'

'Of course there are differences in station.' He met her eye. 'And a woman will act differently in society depending on her looks, but strip all that away and the desires are the same.'

'And what are they?'

'To have children, to have a man love her, and to wield power over men.'

'Please—'

'You know the New Testament, don't you?'

'What's that got to do with it?'

'Women have the power and influence to soften men's sternness, and if you could just stick to that, society feels the effect in thousands of ways.'

'How do we soften you hard men, then?'

He smiled. 'By depending on us.'

She turned away. 'If you don't stop talking, I'm going to be sick.'

'You don't think you might be a little dependent on me now?' he asked, affably.

'Now is different.' She flung her arm out to indicate their surroundings. 'And when we're not injured up a mountain, we still can't build palaces, or write laws, or cure diseases, but we can simper and ask for your help? Is that our great magic?'

There was silence for a moment, then he spoke again. 'Your eyes change colour when you're angry, did you know that?'

'Not being able to see my eyes, I can't say I've noticed.'

He laughed. 'Our heroine from the *Laxdæla* certainly takes no prisoners.'

Gudrún's skin turned cold, then hot. Her ears started ringing, then fell completely silent, as if they were stuffed with wool.

'Don't mock me,' she said.

His face turned suddenly serious. 'I'd never do that. I think too highly of you.' He took the nail of his left thumb in between his teeth. 'I'm sorry if you thought that was my intention.'

'No—' She stopped, confused. 'It was a misunderstanding.' How could Freyja have stood being in the same house as him? she wondered. To have strong feelings for him, to have him nearby, and not be able to reach across and take his hand in her own. It would have been unbearable. She could almost believe that she felt the same way, except with her it was just the tiredness, the fact that she was worried about Freyja, the unreality of it all.

But she should have looked after Freyja better when she came back from the Big Farm. Maybe none of this would have happened if—

He stood. 'Please excuse me.'

'Where are you going?'

'I've drunk nearly a whole flask of coffee.' He pulled the sleeves of his jumper down around his wrists.

'Oh.' She was suddenly aware of her own urge to pee.

'With any luck, I won't be set upon by an eagle. Then we can continue this debate.' His voice was brisk and cheerful, the voice of someone who regretted something they had said recently.

'Can you . . .'

'Yes?'

'I've been drinking too.'

'Oh. Of course. What do you need me to do?'

'Take me outside with you.'

'Of course.'

He held out his hands. She gave him hers and he slowly pulled her up to standing.

'Ready?'

She nodded.

'I'd forgotten you were so helpless,' he said, and smiled. 'It must be the way you argue.'

They limped their way over the rocky path back to the opening, then up the corridor, through the porch and to the ledge outside the cave. It was longer and harder than Gudrún had remembered, but Magnús was patient.

He turned away while she untied her belt and lowered her trousers, then turned back to help her squat down, purposely keeping his eyes above her head.

'I'll be on the other side of the ledge,' he said. 'Call me when you need me again.'

She waited until she could no longer see him out of the corner of her eye, then released her muscles and let out a stream of urine. It hissed as it hit the snow, and she felt a wave of relief pass through her. When it had stopped, she took a moment to let the air dry her, looking out at the world from where she crouched. The snow had settled, and everything below her was a cold, dazzling white. Above her, the sky was as deep and dark as the ocean, except for a sprinkle of stars, like the blue-green phosphorescence she sometimes saw in the water at night. Sea sparkles, Papi and all the fishermen called them.

'I'm ready,' she called softly, and sensed hidden life all around her pricking up their ears at her voice.

Magnús appeared as if from nowhere, padding across the snow as quietly as she'd spoken. He put his arms around her and lifted her, then held her up while she fumbled with the trousers and belt.

'Finished,' she said into his shoulder.

He looked down at her and they smiled at the same time.

There was a muffled boom from above and then a roar.

'It's the glacier,' Magnús said.

'I know.'

'Of course you do,' he said, but it wasn't unfriendly.

They stood for a moment in the opening, watching the sky. A faint light blossomed above them, a pale curve that seemed almost cloudlike. Gudrún could see stars winking around and behind it at first, but as they watched it grew brighter and firmer, until it was a deep emerald colour, blocking out any other light around it. It started to swell, washing over the black until it was four times the size it had been at first, then all of a sudden rays of colour shot out above and below it, pinks and blues and yellows shimmering, fainter than the immense green body in the centre, and rippling in the breeze so that the effect of the whole was of continual, glittering movement. It was stretching now to either end of the horizon, lighting up the vastness, and Gudrún thought of it dancing above Papi and Freyja, wherever they were, and a lump came in to her throat. Without thinking, she leaned onto Magnús's shoulder, and felt his arm come out to steady her; he left it there, around her waist, his fingertips brushing the top of her hip, and the excitement she'd felt at his first touch came flooding back.

'It's beautiful, isn't it?' Magnús said.

'Yes.'

'Funny how you stop noticing it down there.' He breathed in. 'There's something about being up the mountain that feels closer to God. I don't mean purely physically.'

Gudrún breathed in too. The air tasted sweet in her throat, nourishing. 'I don't wonder that Bárdur chose to exile himself here.'

'You think that's what it was?'

'Of course. He couldn't live among the others after what he'd done.'

'Perhaps he would have ended up here anyway, even without the killing. He was different, after all. Elemental, as well as human.'

Gudrún shrugged. 'How can we know? He did kill, and he did leave.'

'But he atoned for his actions,' Magnús said. 'He helped others. He could have gone back.'

'I don't know. Can someone atone for what he did?'

There was another silence between them, then Magnús shifted, holding more tightly onto her.

'How does it make you feel?' he asked. 'Being up here?'

'Smaller. But more . . .' she searched for the right word, 'connected to others. It feels good to be reminded of something more permanent than ourselves.'

He turned on the spot and looked up at the peak. 'I wonder what it looks like for the birds.'

'I'm sure nothing looks as remarkable when you're soaring above it,' Gudrún said. As soon as she said it, she had the strange sensation that her words had fallen in between them, that he was no longer listening. She glanced at Magnús and then away. He was looking in the direction of the Big Farm, at the twinkling lights in the distance that meant people were sitting down to dinner, to thaw themselves next to the fire, to talk about their days. She wondered if he was thinking of Rósa, wishing he was in bed with her. And, at the same time, she let herself remember that he'd said he and Rósa were close 'back then'. *So not anymore*, a voice inside her said.

'There's something I need to tell you,' he said.

But what of it? You're here to find Freyja, and he's married.

'What is it?' she asked; she thought she heard a tremble in her voice and prayed Magnús hadn't picked up on it.

'That afternoon, after I found you at the church—'

'Yes?'

'I said something to Tomas.' He looked at her, then quickly away. 'I told him I was going to keep an eye on him, make sure he didn't abuse your generosity.'

Gudrún's ears buzzed. 'But I'd said he wasn't a burden.'

'I know. I'm sorry – I thought I was protecting you, but now . . . I wonder if that was why he left?'

'I don't think that's a mystery anymore.'

'I'm truly sorry,' he said.

She shook her head. 'It doesn't matter now, anyway.'

'We should go in,' he said.

'Yes.'

They turned and started the journey back. After a few steps, Magnús stopped and crouched down. His fingers fumbled for something on the ground.

'Look,' he said.

He was holding out a rock, just large enough to fill his palm. It was bluish-grey, speckled with white, and coarse-grained. At first, she thought it was nothing special to look at, but as he turned it in the moonlight, the white speckles flickered green and then back again.

'It's reflecting the sky,' she said softly.

'Yes.'

This moment, she told herself, *is important somehow.*

'What is it? I've never seen it before.'

'Neither have I.' He held it out. 'It's heavy.'

She took the rock in her hand, feeling the weight, the roughness of it. It was unexpectedly warm against her skin. She tried to give it back and Magnús waved it away.

'It's yours,' he said. 'A gift.'

'Thank you.'

'It reminds me of you.'

'A rock?'

'Yes, a rock.' He gave her one of his smiles. 'It's not too polished. Rare.'

When she and Freyja were younger they'd swum naked in Kirkjufell waterfall, slid into its green depths until all of their long, white limbs were submerged and shone through the water.

She didn't know where the memory came from, and squirmed, thinking of it.

His smile grew. *Please God*, she thought, *don't let him be able to read minds.*

'Thank you,' she said again.

'My lady,' he said.

She slipped the rock into her trouser pocket and took the arm he was offering.

Her ankle was throbbing again by the time they reached the remains of the fire.

Magnús placed her gently in front of the ashes. 'You did well.'

She watched him build another fire and light it, her body and mind heavy with sleep and cold and something else.

He came and sat next to her. 'I have some coffee left.'

'Don't you want it?'

'I want you to have it.'

'We should save it for the morning,' she said.

They were quiet for a moment; Gudrún closed her eyes and listened to the crackle of the flames, smelled the woodsmoke and the coffee. The lingering scent of roasted meat. She sensed all this but her mind was out at sea with Papi, and in a crevice with Freyja, and even back in their garden, watching her mother hang up the washing. She couldn't shake the feeling that something important was happening, something big.

Magnús broke the silence.

'Do you think Rósa puts on airs?'

'No.' She opened her eyes hurriedly. 'I was just saying things.'

'But you two aren't close?'

'I don't know her.'

He looked at her; his eyes were darker in the light of the fire, deep as lakes now. 'You don't have to hide it from me.'

'Why not?' she asked, although she already knew what he was going to say before he said it.

'My wife and I aren't close either.'

'Oh?'

'She's too much under the influence of her father.'

'How does he influence her?'

'He doesn't seem to have much faith in my intellect, shall we say.' He paused. 'They think of me as decoration.'

'I see.'

'Do you?' His voice was bitter. 'A man has to be useful, otherwise what point is there to his existence?'

'Does existence have to have a point?'

'You think we should live purely for pleasure?'

Gudrún thought of the years growing up when they'd shared one meal between three, of the nights huddled in layers of clothing because they had a hole in the roof and no time to mend it. 'Some existence has no room for meaning to it.'

He took her hand. 'I'm sorry – I forget. I've been comfortable for so long.'

She felt a tingle where his fingers were pressing against her skin, and prayed her hands weren't clammy to touch.

'I didn't always have it easy,' Magnús said. He smiled, but it was tired.

'No, you said you grew up in a room much smaller than our badstofa.'

'I was almost bent double by the time I was twelve, the roof was so low. And even after I left, I lived hand to mouth too. Baldur had nothing to spare me.'

Her mouth was dry. 'And then you met Rósa?'

'Yes.' He ran his fingers up her arm to her elbow and stroked the hollow there. 'Maybe that's why I stay now. You probably despise me for it.'

'No. Of course not.'

She wondered if Freyja had noticed, if that was why she had defended Rósa, because she felt pity for her loveless marriage. If that had been why she had let herself fall for Magnús. Gudrún looked at him; his face was drawn, eyebrows furrowed and lips pressed tightly together, but it made him seem childlike, almost lost, and she felt a pang of sympathy too.

'I'm sorry—' Her tongue stuck to the roof of her mouth and she swallowed to bring back some moisture and her teeth clashed together.

Magnús looked at her quickly.

'You're cold,' he said.

'A little.'

'Take my coat again.'

'You need it too.'

'Then let's both sit inside it.'

He held it open, and she shuffled closer until he could wrap it around her. They were pressed against each other, bodies firm and smelling of animal. Gudrún felt light-headed.

'You know,' Magnús said. 'Rósa wasn't always so ill-tempered.'

'Oh?'

'She was fun when I first met her.' He drew the coat more tightly around them. 'We were younger, of course – about your age.'

Gudrún licked her lips. 'Respectfully,' she said, 'I don't want to talk about your wife.'

Magnús laughed once; it sounded nervous. They looked at each other. They were so close, their noses were almost touching, and she could feel his breath on her cheek. He blinked and the swoop of his eyelashes against her skin sent thousands of tiny shocks around her body.

'I don't know anyone like you, Gudrún Einarsdóttir,' he said. 'You're quite infuriating, you know?'

Her heart was hammering in her chest. 'You're much worse,' she said.

She smiled, but he looked serious. Then he leaned forward an inch, and their lips were touching. Just brushing against each other at first, and Gudrún was surprised how soft his were, and how much she wanted them to press against her own. Her arms came up of their own accord and wrapped themselves around his neck, pulling him into the kiss until they both broke apart for breath. He stared at her.

'I've wanted to do that since we first met,' he said.

Gudrún felt a swelling within her, as if a part of her that had always existed in theory was suddenly made real. 'Oh?'

'Yes,' he said. 'Don't tell me you're lost for words?'

'. . . No . . .'

He grinned, showing all his teeth. 'I should have done this hours ago then.'

Gudrún smiled back weakly. *Please don't devour me*, she begged him, although really the idea didn't frighten her.

He took her face in his hands and kissed her again. She was impatient and bit his lip and he yelped and twisted his hands in her hair. Then he pulled back and removed his coat and laid it down on the floor of the cave. He guided her back onto it, and lay down on top of her, holding her gaze the whole time until she had to break it or burst out screaming. She turned her head and saw the white bones of the rabbit picked clean and discarded on the ground next to her.

1975

THEY FOUND A SPOT on the grass outside the prime minister's offices, where Ava had said she would meet them, and stood close together. The sky was grey and the air itself seemed sluggish, until the sun emerged from behind a cloud, and at the bottom of the hill the city suddenly lay in a pool of light.

'This is something, isn't it?' Amma said.

'Uh-huh,' Sigga said.

At first she felt hemmed in, and panicky, but after a while, her heart slowed down, and she was able to look about.

The only space was around a covered stage that had been erected at the far side of the square. A female-only choir was gathered around a microphone and Sigga could hear singing. The rest of Lækjartorg was filled with bodies, with the clock tower in the middle rising out of the crowd like the last dry point in a flood. *There must be thousands here already*, she thought. And still the women kept pouring in.

Amma seemed calmer to Sigga and she tried to focus on the stage, trying to forget about the baby, the body, the fainting. *Just enjoy it*, she told herself. Everything else could wait. But there was something inside her brain that she couldn't reach, as if grabbing at an object sliding around on glass; she didn't know if it was a memory, a thought, a sensation, but she knew that when she caught it, it wouldn't be good. *And Amma lied to you. Why would she lie?*

As Sigga watched, a short, round woman in a leopard-print coat and large glasses stepped from the back of the stage to the microphone and spoke into it.

'And now for more singing.' She turned and beckoned a few women who were loitering behind her. 'Come on, let people see you. I'm not going to stand here like a Christmas tree.'

There was laughter among the crowd. The women stepped forwards. A slight breeze had sprung up, and Sigga saw the music sheets in their hands quiver. The singing started.

'Isn't that the neighbour we met the other day?' Amma said, nudging Sigga.

Sigga looked and saw a woman on the edge of the crowd, a few rows back from where they were standing. She was wearing big sunglasses and a colourful silk scarf tied around her head. There was a small placard in her arms and she shifted her weight from one leg to the other every ten seconds or so, as if rocking a baby. Around her, women were joining in with the song, but she seemed to be silent.

'Oh yeah.' Sigga's mouth was dry, as if she'd swallowed sand. 'Ísafold.'

Amma called out Ísafold's name, and she swivelled her head from side to side as if trying to see where the voice had come from. The placard was pressed tightly to her chest now. Eventually, she spotted them and started to make her way over.

'Hello again,' Amma said, when she reached them.

'Hello,' Ísafold said, in a slightly breathy voice. 'I was looking for your father earlier, Sigga. Do you know where he went today?'

Was that what his errand was? Sigga shrugged. 'I haven't seen him for a while.'

'I didn't realise how many people there would be here.'

'I don't think anyone knew exactly,' Amma said. 'Just goes to show the feelings run deep.'

Ísafold had been looking at the ground, fiddling with her sunglasses; now she lifted her head and started when she noticed the two of them paying her attention. 'I'm sorry. I'm feeling a little jumpy today. I don't spend much time in crowds.'

'We're all friends,' Amma said, gently.

Ísafold blushed.

The choir had finished and they trooped off the stage. A woman in a dark polo neck and grey double-breasted coat stood up and started addressing the crowd loudly and nasally as 'sisters in the struggle'.

'Who's this?' Sigga asked.

'She's one of the trade union women,' Amma said.

'Something unique happened at the Loftleidir conference in June,' the woman went on. 'Women of all classes and political parties stood together and proposed that all women in Iceland take a holiday today.' She paused. 'And the result is this huge crowd here.'

There was clapping.

The woman's voice climbed higher. 'After today, we won't go back.'

'We won't go back,' someone shouted from the middle of the crowd.

'For all of us, for our whole lives, whatever our class, whether married or unmarried, whether we like men or women, we have lived under the power of the fathers. We are only allowed whatever power or freedom they see fit to bestow upon us, and only for as long as it pleases them.'

There was cheering now. Some women were stamping their feet, placards were being punched into the air. Sigga shifted. Her stomach gurgled and she realised she was actually ravenous. She wondered if she could slip away to the hot dog stand without anyone noticing. Then, a moment later, it passed, and she felt slightly sick at the thought of eating.

She looked around and saw Amma and Ísafold leaning in towards each other, a slight frown on Amma's face as Ísafold was speaking. Sigga hesitated, not wanting to join in, and felt a tap on her shoulder.

'Sorry.' It was Ava. 'Have you two been here long?' She peered over Sigga's shoulder. 'You three.'

'She's not with us,' Sigga said. 'She's just my next-door neighbour.'

'Oh?' One side of Ava's mouth lifted in a small smile. 'And I'm an ex-neighbour. At least I know where I stand, I suppose.'

'No, it's her.' Sigga pressed her hands against her belly, then realised what she was doing and dropped them to her sides. She leaned closer to Ava, lowered her voice so Amma wouldn't hear. 'I just think she wants to spend a bit too much time with Pabbi.'

'Oh, well.' Ava's mouth made the half-smile again. 'Who wouldn't want to? Where do you think you get your good looks from? Although Pétur's the one who *really* looks like him.' She took a step back, and considered Sigga.

'You look like your mother, too. Something about your eyes. Maybe it's their shape.'

'I don't think I'm like her at all.' Sigga's chest pinched at the thought. If she looked like Mamma, then Mamma would have felt closer to her, the way she did with Pétur. She would have tried to understand Sigga, instead of treating her like a changeling with her head in the clouds.

But Mamma had her own ideas about womanhood. That was the problem. Women were for making babies, raising children, even when it didn't seem to bring them joy. Even when one of the children nearly died and she could only get angry with them. And Sóley was right – Sigga always believed Mamma when Mamma said the problem was her.

Stop it, she told herself. *Why can't you just* stop *thinking about it? And anyway, Amma always wants to spend time with you – so there can't be anything wrong with you.*

To her left, Ísafold laughed at something Amma had just said and the hairs on the back of Sigga's neck rose in protest. She was feeling trapped again, and shifted, bumping into the woman in front of her, who turned around and looked at her, curiously.

'Sorry,' Sigga muttered, and the woman turned away again.

'Are you all right?' Ava asked.

'What's going on with Amma?'

'Is anything?' Ava's tone sounded cautious, or maybe she was just being paranoid.

'Who knows,' Sigga said. 'She never tells anyone anything.'

'She's always seemed pretty straight-talking to me,' Ava said.

'Do you know what happened to her sister?'

'She died.'

'But *how*? Isn't it weird that I don't know that? And I don't even know what Pabbi's father was called. Is *he* dead?' She looked over at Ava. 'And if he isn't, why aren't they together? Was he married?'

Ava raised her eyebrows. 'Is that what you heard?'

Sigga winced. She'd never really considered it. What would it mean about Amma, that she would come between a husband and wife like that? What would it mean about her grandfather, and Pabbi, and by extension her? She was suddenly sick at the thought that the two people without whom she wouldn't exist could be such strangers to her.

On the stage, the trade union woman was building to some sort of climax, it seemed. Placards were waving wildly towards the front.

Sigga turned her head and caught Ísafold's eye. 'Why were you looking for Pabbi earlier?' she asked, loudly, and saw the surprise on Amma's face.

'Oh, we had an appointment together,' Ísafold said. 'He's been very helpful.' Her expression was almost wistful. 'It must have been wonderful growing up with such a good father.'

'It was,' Sigga replied, irritated, although she wasn't sure exactly why, or how she wanted Ísafold to behave. Did she want a confession? 'I had a really happy childhood.'

'I haven't seen your boyfriend around for a little while,' Ísafold continued, and it took Sigga a moment to realise she meant Olafur. 'You know, I saw the two of you in the library together a couple of times, when I used to work there. I think you were studying for something, and he brought you sandwiches. I always thought he seemed very sweet to you.'

'You must be one of those people who sees the best in others,' Amma said.

'Yeah, well,' Sigga said. 'I haven't heard you and your husband recently. You're very loud, you know.'

Ísafold bit her lip so hard it turned white. Amma glared at Sigga.

'How did you meet your husband?' Ava asked as if Sigga hadn't said anything unusual.

'He was the one after my high-school sweetheart,' Ísafold said. She touched her sunglasses again, and seemed to calm down. 'We used to go to the same café for lunch – I always thought he was so handsome. And then, one day, he sat down at my table and said he was taking me out to dinner.' She laughed. 'That's Stefán – totally direct.'

'Sounds very romantic,' Ava said.

'Oh yes.' She was curling and uncurling her fingers around the placard pole.

'And you don't have children?'

'No. Stefán wants children.' She took a step back. 'Excuse me, I'm just going to find a bathroom.'

Sigga watched Ísafold picking her way through the crowd. She was weaving slightly, as if she was drunk.

Amma stepped in front of Sigga, hands on hips. 'What was that about, young lady?'

'People keep giving her the benefit of the doubt,' Sigga said. 'I don't think she's as helpless as she pretends.'

The trade union woman finished her speech to catcalls and stamping. The mood was high; Sigga could see them all around her, full of light and air, as if they could start floating at any moment. But she was too heavy. Her legs ached, her feet pressed into the ground, feeling every lump and hillock. Sweat dripped slowly down her temples and ran into the corners of her eyes, stinging.

'I want to go home,' she said.

Amma looked at her blankly.

'We'll go home then,' she said, eventually. 'Ava, I'll call on you tonight.'

'You two can stay—' Sigga started.

Amma took her arm. 'Nonsense.'

They had to fight through the crowds to get out, and around the junction with Bankastræti, she saw Sóley with a group of older women, one of whom looked identical to her. They were standing with their arms around each other's shoulders, cat-calling and waving placards, and Sigga felt another pang.

'Sóley,' she called, and Sóley looked around and grinned.

'Sigga,' she called. 'This is my mother. Mamma, this is Sigga.'

'Nice to meet you,' the woman said, smiling. 'I've heard a lot about you.'

'This is my grandmother,' Sigga said. 'Amma, this is—'

The crowd started clapping the new speaker on stage, and there was a general surge forwards; Sigga and Amma were pushed up against Sóley and her mother, who tried to make room for them.

'Were you leaving?' Sóley asked.

'Yeah.'

'A bunch of us are going to Prikid afterwards, if you fancy?'

Sigga looked at Amma, who shook her head.

'But you should go,' she said, 'be with women your own age.'

'Maybe I'll see you there,' Sigga said, and Sóley squeezed her shoulder quickly and they carried on pushing their way out.

Mamma and Pabbi and Pétur were all home when they got back and the lights were on, glowing against the fading afternoon. Mamma was in the kitchen and the house smelled of fried onions and sausages. Pabbi and Pétur came out of the living room, Pabbi holding his reading glasses, and looked at them expectantly.

'Is it over already?' Pabbi said.

'No.' Sigga hung up her coat. 'I wasn't feeling well.'

'Let me take your temperature,' he said, and walked over with the back of his hand outstretched.

Sigga ducked away from him. 'It's fine.'

'We walked from Hlemmur,' Amma said. 'And heard most of the speeches. We didn't miss too much.'

'Is there any wine left?' Sigga asked Pétur.

'I think so.'

'Good.' She went into the kitchen, and found Mamma by the stove, pushing sausages round a pan with a spatula.

'I got the last lot,' Mamma said. 'The shops all sold out apparently. Crayons too.' She frowned when she saw Sigga take the wine bottle out of the fridge.

Sigga ignored her, poured herself a large glass and took a big gulp. The others came in too and she waved the bottle at them.

'I'm on call tonight,' Pabbi said.

Amma shook her head and Pétur sat at the table, looking faintly amused.

'I can make coffee?' Mamma said.

'If you were going to anyway,' Amma said.

'I wasn't,' Mamma said, 'but it's no trouble.' She made a big show of filling the kettle and switching it on. The sound of the water starting to heat joined the spitting from the pan; otherwise, the room was quiet.

'What's wrong with everyone?' Sigga asked, and took another gulp of the wine.

'You'll have to be more specific,' Amma said.

'Gabríel called,' Mamma said as if Sigga hadn't spoken. 'Asking for you, Sigrídur. What are you two plotting?'

'Nothing,' Sigga said.

'Uh-huh. Well, there haven't been any more tremors since yesterday.' She turned back to the pan. 'I asked him when my next grandchild was coming. None of us are getting any younger.'

Pétur rolled his eyes. 'He's only twenty-five, Mamma.'

'I always thought thirty was the best age for men,' Amma said, starting to unwrap the scarf from around her neck.

'What's the best age for women?' Sigga asked.

'How old is Juliet?'

'You mean *Romeo and Juliet*?'

'Yes.'

'Twelve,' Sigga said.

'And how old's Helen of Troy?'

'Ten,' Pabbi said. 'Some say seven, but Diodorus has her as ten. That's when she's abducted by Theseus, anyway.'

'Well, there we go,' Amma said.

'That's disgusting,' Mamma said.

'Anyway,' Pétur said, 'I don't know if they want more kids. Gabríel says he still gets nightmares about childbirth. *I* still don't understand why he was in the room.'

'Oh, you're both such *babies*,' Amma said, but she smiled.

'What's it like?' Sigga asked.

'I'm sure you've heard about it before.'

'Tell me something about it that means something – that no one else talks about.'

'I can't,' Amma said. She saw Sigga's expression. 'Really. There are limits to our imaginations. We can't imagine God, and you can't imagine childbirth.'

Sigga let her hand graze against her waistband, imagining she'd felt a pop underneath it, a tiny foot striking out. She felt sick again and drained the rest of her wine.

'The hardest part is afterwards,' Amma said. 'I cried for weeks after Thórfinnur was born. At anything, really.'

Pabbi polished his glasses on his shirt and placed them back on his nose. 'That's perfectly natural, of course. No reflection on me as a child, I'd like to point out.'

Mamma poked harder at the sausages. 'Why is it natural for mothers to be sad?'

'It's hard when the thing we want comes true,' Amma said. 'We lose all the things it isn't.'

She looked at Sigga, who felt suddenly dizzy. Amma was right; she'd never thought of it that way before, but it was true. In a way, it was how she felt about her story. Something that had been in her head, something possible, imagined, had come down to the realm of reality. And it had an end; it couldn't be changed now.

'I just don't understand why it's so fashionable to degrade motherhood,' Mamma said. She was getting annoyed, Sigga could tell. 'We have uteruses, don't we? What else are they for? *That's* the natural element.'

Sigga poured herself the dregs of the wine and drank them in one go. They went down the wrong way and she started spluttering and coughing, and for a moment she couldn't draw a breath, just like in *the incident* when she'd hit the water. She'd been expecting the cold, but it was the cold and the punch all at once that had taken her by surprise and she'd cried out. And then she'd known she was in trouble, because there was water in her mouth and her nose and her eyes. She felt it in the back of her throat, like the urge to sneeze, or cough, and tried to hold it there, tried not to open her mouth again, and all the while her heart was trying to squeeze out of her eardrums, trying to escape back up to the real world, trying to save itself because she was going to die down there, the rest of her, even though she was kicking and wriggling with all her strength—

'Sigga, are you all right?' Pabbi asked.

She looked at Pabbi, looked away again. The memory was spreading now, making her shiver as if she were actually underwater.

And Mamma – she'd always told herself Mamma had been angry because she loved Sigga, because she wanted to protect Pétur. And Sigga never stood up for herself, never told Mamma how it made her feel to be blamed.

Boys will be boys, Sigga. But it was always *her* living with the consequences, that didn't seem fair. Who was protecting her?

She tilted her chin up. 'I think I'm pregnant,' she said.

It was so quiet they could have heard a bubble pop. She looked at each of them in turn. Amma's pupils were so big, Sigga had the sudden thought that she might be able to see through them and into her brain, see what she was thinking, even as she stayed silent.

'Did you hear me?' she asked the room.

'Fuck,' Pétur said eventually.

'How?' Pabbi asked, calmly.

'Well, guys, when a man puts his—' She had an overwhelming urge to laugh, and covered her mouth.

Mamma threw the spatula into the pan. 'Have you lost your mind?'

'That's pretty rude.'

'You're drinking.'

'So?'

She took a deep breath, as if Sigga was being particularly irritating. 'You've just told us you're pregnant.'

'It's my fucking body.'

'It's *not* just you in there anymore,' Mamma said.

'And what if I don't want it?'

'You're just saying that to hurt me.'

'No, Mamma. What if I never want a baby?'

She took a step back. 'Is that true?'

'I don't know.'

'We could explore—' Pabbi said, and took his glasses off again, as if he didn't want to see properly.

She could taste salt in her mouth and realised she was crying, hated herself. 'I don't even know why I told you,' she said. 'It's not like you care.'

'Of course we care,' Amma said. 'Sigga, you mustn't—'

'Then why are you keeping secrets from me? And you are too, Pabbi—' Amma put out her hand, as if to take Sigga's, but she ignored it, 'You're too busy with your new *friend*, and you're both walking around like I don't exist, and Mamma—'

'Of course this is our fault,' Mamma said.

'Give her a break, Mamma,' Pétur said, sharply, and Mamma gaped at him.

'It would be nice if it wasn't *my* fault, for once,' Sigga said. Her voice caught at the top of her throat and came out ragged. 'I didn't ask to be different to you, and I didn't ask to be born. I know how miserable I've made you and I'm sorry, okay. I'm fucking *sorry.*'

'Oh, Sigga,' Amma said.

'Forget it,' she said, pushing past Pabbi in the doorway. She grabbed her coat and went out, slamming the door behind her.

1911

GUDRÚN HAD NEVER KNOWN she could feel so full. It was a wonder, the way she ached for the fullness, even while it was happening. And at the same time there was pain. A sharp pain at first, and a heaviness on her that felt as if she couldn't draw breath. Every time he moved she remembered her ankle and tensed, knowing how it would send fire up her body if he knocked into it.

'Relax,' he said, 'I have you.'

She tried to relax. She was terrified, and hungry for him and astonished at herself. She dug her fingers into his back, she arched her own back, she let out a sob—

And then it was done, and he was holding her and she realised she was leaking.

She raised her hand and stroked his cheek. 'So *that's* why people have so many babies.'

He laughed, then rolled off her, and a rush of cold air mixed with the hot fluid down there.

'You're very special, Gudrún.' He propped himself on one elbow and slid his hand inside her jumper, cupping her breast.

'Am I?'

He bent and kissed her mouth, and she felt her nipple harden underneath his fingers.

He pulled back and looked at her. 'What do you want?'

'Want?'

'I'll make it my mission to give it to you. Whatever you desire in life.'

She smiled.

'What's funny about that?'

'It would be funny if it wasn't so obvious you've gone mad.'

'How am I mad?'

'I don't know how – maybe the cold, maybe being up the mountain. Maybe you'll get better when we go down again.'

'I meant what's mad about wanting to make you happy?'

'It's mad to make it your life's mission, anyway. What about Rósa? You told me once she doesn't like it when you take too long on your errands. What will you tell her when you never get them done at all? Don't laugh.'

He caught her hand and brought it up to his mouth to kiss. 'I can't help it. I've never met such a Martha.'

'Martha?'

'Mary's sister. Don't you know your scripture?'

She felt a searing pain in her chest. Sister.

'Oh, that.' The fire hissed nearby and Gudrún turned to see it was almost completely burned down to embers. It would serve her right if she froze during the night. Freyja was out there freezing too, and she'd forgotten her for a moment while— 'Yes, I know it.'

'So you aren't a heathen. Father Fridrik will be relieved.'

She faced him again. 'Please don't mention Father Fridrik.'

'You're forgetting that he's been a good ally to me.'

'Oh yes, of course. Saintly Father Fridrik.'

If our cave exists, then another one does too, she told herself. *Freyja's in it right now, staying warm and dry.*

Tomorrow we'll find her. There's nothing I can do tonight in the dark and with this ankle, anyway. Stop thinking about it, about how you drove her up here in the first place, or you'll go mad and then you'll be no use to anyone.

She let out a yell of frustration that bounced off the walls and died abruptly.

'Are you all right?' Magnús said.

He was looking at her.

'Yes.'

'I won't talk about him if it bothers you.'

'Do you ever go back?'

'Back where?'

'To the farm – where you both grew up.'

'No. I left there when I was twenty-one and I never returned.'

'Why not?'

He unlaced their fingers and laced them again. 'There was nothing there for me anymore.'

'Where did you go after that?'

'Reykjavik. I lived there for five years and then I came here. With Rósa. But this is getting away from my original question. What do you want?'

'I want to find Freyja,' she said, before she could stop herself.

'We will,' he said, in such a way that she believed it. 'But not tonight.'

'I know.'

'Freyja's a smart girl – she'll have found somewhere to shelter, just like us.'

'I know, I know.'

She looked at their intertwined fingers. On top of it all, she'd made herself into a hypocrite. She'd warned

Freyja against giving herself away, against putting herself in a weak position, and she'd done exactly that with Magnús.

'Then I want nothing except your whole heart and soul,' she said, as lightly as she could, wanting him to know it was in jest, and yet not wanting him to be in jest himself. 'I want to know that I'm the only woman you've ever loved and that if I died you would pine away from sorrow. But apart from that, nothing.'

'How can you even doubt it for a minute?'

She smiled, despite everything.

He lifted her jumper and leaned over her. 'I would never have guessed how beautiful you were,' he said, looking at her breasts. He put one in his mouth, and sucked gently, then kissed her breastbone. Then her navel. Then the dip in between her hips. Then down, further down.

Gudrún closed her eyes. Magnús's tongue was flicking over her. She felt her womb begin to answer, squeezing her from the inside out. She wondered if this was right, if it was meant to be happening. She cried out in alarm, in pleasure, and then, finally, the walls broke. She was drowning, dying, an image flashed across her eyelids – the ship, incomprehensibly, the one that Tomas had arrived on, that lay on the floor of the ocean.

She opened her eyes and took a great, shuddering breath. Her whole body was shuddering too. Magnús sat back; he placed a hand on her stomach and slowly she felt herself returning to her body.

She reached down and pulled up her trousers.

'Don't cover up on my behalf.'

'I'm cold.'

He looked around. 'The fire's almost out.' He dressed quickly and started moving around, piling up sticks again. 'We don't have many left.'

'Oh.' She hauled herself to an upright position and moved back to her old rock, where she'd first sat when they found the cave. So much had changed since then.

'What are you thinking?'

She ran her tongue across her lips to wet them. 'I don't know.'

He stopped and looked at her. 'I don't want you to think we betrayed Rósa.'

'Haven't we?'

'My wife and I don't share a bed anymore.' He walked over and took Gudrún's hand, kneeling in front of her. 'We haven't for a long time.'

Gudrún felt a shooting pain in her chest. 'Have you taken lovers before, then?'

His voice was low, 'I've never met anyone I've wanted to be with before.'

She turned away, not wanting him to see her eyes fill up. It all suddenly seemed so hopeless – Rósa would never let her have Magnús, even if she didn't want him herself. Even if something more came of this night – and something more could. She shook her head at herself. How ironic it would be if she was a mother now too.

'I've made you unhappy,' he said.

'I suppose I played a part myself.'

'I wouldn't make you unhappy for the world.' He raised her hand to his lips again and kissed it lightly. 'I want to protect you, Gudrún. You make me feel alive, like a real man.'

'That's not . . .' Her heart was beating madly, as if she'd been running. 'You *are* a man, whether you run the farm or Rósa. I don't want to be a way for you to prove what we both already know.'

'Of course you're more than that.'

'But not enough.'

He looked at her. 'What do you mean?'

'I mean – you'll never leave Rósa, or tell her about us.'

He smiled, but it didn't reach his eyes this time. 'I thought Gudrún Einarsdóttir didn't want to take a husband?'

'I don't want to be a secret either. I want the man who loves me to talk about me, to be able to kiss me in public.'

He let go of her hand. 'You don't know what it is to be really poor, Gudrún.'

'Don't I?'

'You have a family – you weren't owned by someone from childhood. You wouldn't ask me to jeopardise my position if you knew what I'd gone through.'

'Don't lecture me about ownership,' Gudrún said. 'Married women still can't own property because it passes automatically to their husbands. We can't vote, except in local elections, and we can't—'

'You like playing the crusader for women's rights,' he interrupted, and there was a warning note in his voice, 'and it's endearing, but this isn't playing, Gudrún Einarsdóttir. This is real life, and it's harsher than you understand. Don't do anything rash.'

She was quiet for a moment, trying to unpick her thoughts. 'Maybe I was more fortunate in that respect, to have a family. But you *are* a man, and even if Rósa has more power than you in your household . . .' She hesitated. It was suddenly important to her that he understood what she wanted to say. 'You have friends now who'll vouch for you, and opportunities because of your sex. You say you want to work – someone will employ you. You would be fine. Our customs, our language, our law all determine what role we play in society and your role is always above ours.' She saw him shake his head and plunged on. 'If you want proof, then think of motherhood. Women are bound by motherhood in a way that men aren't. No wonder Freyja was scared—'

He looked up sharply. 'Freyja?'

She bit her lip.

'What does Freyja have to feel scared about?'

'I shouldn't say.'

'What does Freyja have to feel scared about?' he asked again, bluntly.

'She's carrying.'

He raised an eyebrow.

'She . . .' she gestured helplessly. 'She ran away because she couldn't face it. And I didn't help. She was terrified and I just thought about myself.'

Magnús stood up and started pacing. Whatever intimacy they had built had suddenly vanished; his face was locked up to her now. 'A baby?' he muttered.

Gudrún felt a stab of fear. She cursed herself for letting it slip, for having deceived him in the first place. 'I'm sorry. I know I led us up here under false pretences. I just wanted to make sure she didn't do anything—'

He turned on his heel to look at her. 'She came up here to kill herself?'

'I think so.'

He let out a long hiss of breath. *'Freyja?'*

'Yes.'

He smiled then. 'Surely you're mistaken.'

'She left a note,' Gudrún said. 'And we fought, the night before.'

'A baby,' he said again, but as if to himself. 'How far along is she?'

'I don't know for sure.'

He was standing next to the fire, lost in thought. He took out his pocket watch and rubbed his thumb over the glass, and his hand was trembling.

Gudrún felt a creeping shyness that almost stopped her from asking, 'What are you thinking?'

'We need to find her quickly,' he said.

'Are you going out now?'

He looked at her carefully. 'It's too dangerous to walk around here in the dark.'

'Yes – I know.'

'In the morning.'

'Yes, of course.'

'We should probably get some rest, then.'

'Where will we ... ?' Gudrún asked, and heard the timidity in her voice.

'Here's as good as any place,' he said, and indicated to his coat, still spread out on the floor of the cave. Gudrún turned away, unable to look at the spot where they'd shared something intimate so recently. It was almost unbelievable now, in the face of his coldness.

They lay together on his coat. Magnús cradled her head in the crook of his arm, but he wouldn't look at her, just stared unblinkingly at the ceiling. She lay there rigidly. She could feel the little rocks underneath the coat sticking up into her back; there was no danger that she'd fall asleep. She couldn't be asleep around him. He might get up and leave her. Now that she'd given in, he was losing interest in her, she could sense it, and the revelation about Freyja had sped it up somehow.

The air being sucked in to her lungs was suddenly not enough, as if she was much higher up the mountain. She clenched her fists, down by her sides.

'You're so stiff,' Magnús said.

'It's not very comfortable, sleeping in a cave.'

'I've slept in worse places.'

'When we were younger, we slept on the beach in the summer. Sometimes, anyway.' She forced herself to relax, uncurl her fists. 'Once, we woke later than usual and the tide was already in. All I could think was – how stupid it would be if we died like that. So close to home, and from something so ordinary. Falling asleep and never waking up.'

He closed his eyes. 'And now? How would you like to die now?'

'Now, I think we all have to die somehow. Does it really matter how?'

He was quiet for a moment, and she thought he'd fallen asleep until he said, 'If your ankle is no better tomorrow, perhaps I should go out alone and find Freyja.'

'Oh?'

'Now that I know it's even more important. We can't delay when she's . . . in this state.'

'Yes, you're right,' she said, although inwardly she was screaming: *Don't leave me here.*

She shifted slightly.

'Why are you trying to move away?' he asked. 'Stay next to me. I have you.'

His eyes were still closed, and his voice was changed, with none of the warmth from before.

'I'm sorry, Magnús,' she said.

He was silent.

'I should have trusted you.'

'Let's not talk about it now,' he said.

I won't be made foolish, she told herself. *I won't let you make me foolish*.

After a while she heard his breathing change, felt the slackening of his arm around her, but even so, she kept up her mantra all night.

1975

PRIKID SAT ON THE corner of Bankastræti and Ingolfsstræti, with red walls, and a red-and-green archway over the door. Through the window, Sigga could see a large group of women standing towards the back, blocking the stairs. They were swaying a little, and laughing; some looked like they were singing. A bartender was wiping the curved bar in front of him in languorous strokes with a dirty towel. Behind him was a glittering tower of glasses.

She pushed her way through the door. The lights above the bar had been switched on, creating a homey, orange glow, and the place smelled of cigarettes and sweat and perfume; the faint sound of Edith Piaf was playing from a radio.

She hadn't been inside in a while, although she used to come by loads with Gabríel. If Mokka was hers, Prikid was Gabríel's, and she wished suddenly, furiously, he was still in Reykjavik.

Sóley was perched on one of the vinyl stools at the bar, smoking and jabbing her finger into another woman's chest. She was wearing the same dungarees that Sigga had first seen her in, and an oversized, red woollen jumper underneath. It looked more like a man's jumper, and Sigga wondered briefly if it had belonged to a former boyfriend. She hung back, shy for a moment. There were so many things about Sóley she didn't know, so much life she'd lived before they'd met, and it suddenly seemed impossible that she could ever uncover it all. Then Sóley glanced over and grinned at her, and Sigga crossed the room and stood next to them.

'As I was saying,' the other woman said, 'language is everything.' Her glasses slipped down her nose and she pushed them up again with one finger. 'If you "father" someone, all you're doing is providing sperm. "Mothering" someone implies nurturing, caring for them, maybe forever.'

'Yeah. Language didn't just appear, you know?' Sóley said, looking at her cigarette. She was holding it between two fingers, her forearm pointing away from her body, her elbow digging into her side. It looked uncomfortable, unnatural even, and for some reason it made Sigga want to smoke for the first time.

'No, of course not. It grew out of societies, and men controlled society, so they also controlled the development of language.'

'Sure.'

'I never thought of that,' Sigga said. She was amazed, suddenly, at all the things she'd never thought of.

'Oh yes.' The other woman signalled to the bartender, who ambled over. 'Three brennivín,' she said, and he ambled off again. 'In a way, I feel sorry for men.'

Sóley hooted. 'I knew you were nuts.'

'No, it must be hard, to be so jealous of your own power.' The woman pushed up her glasses again. 'They've made it to the top of the tree, and everything they do is a scramble to stay up. Everything is to control us, keep us down. Language, sex—'

'You don't think they might like sex?' Sóley asked.

'It's anxiety-inducing. Men have to ignore us as living, breathing people. We're territory to be conquered.'

'That's fucking awful,' Sigga said.

'If they think about it too much, they're going to think about death.'

'Excuse me?' Sóley said.

'Because we all come from a woman. And if you follow that line of reasoning you remember once you were nothing, and one day you'll be nothing again.'

'Then don't have sex,' Sigga said.

Sóley shook her head. 'What's the point in life without sex?'

Sigga remembered her smiling at Pétur in the kitchen. 'I forgot how obsessed you are with it.'

Sóley blew smoke at her and grinned again.

The bartender returned with the brennivín and they clinked glasses and drank. Sigga felt it burning on the way down and closed her eyes. She vaguely heard the other woman saying something to Sóley and when she opened her eyes, it was just the two of them; the other woman had wandered off to join the big group behind them.

'How are you guys, anyway?' Sóley asked, stubbing out her cigarette. 'You and the boyfriend who you clearly don't like sleeping with.'

'I don't know. It's all a fucking mess.' She sat on the vacated stool and half smiled at Sóley. 'I just told my family I think I might be pregnant.'

'Holy *shit*.'

'Yeah.'

'What are you going to do?'

'I know what *you* think I should do, right?'

'Look,' Sóley said. 'A baby's a fucking miracle, don't get me wrong. I just think . . . it's your life that gets turned upside down now. So you should have a choice. It's not destiny, just because we have vaginas.'

'I know.' Sigga bit her lip. 'I just – *I* never wanted to have to make that decision.'

'Sigga,' Sóley said, and grabbed her hand. 'You can want or not want this baby. You can want *and* not want this baby. Fuck anyone who says there's only one right way to feel about it.'

She hugged Sigga, and Sigga let herself relax for a moment, concentrating on the feeling of one of the dungaree buckles digging into her chin. *This is how they should have reacted*, she told herself, and bit her lip again to stop herself crying.

'It'll be okay,' Sóley said. 'It'll be okay, okay?'

'Okay.'

Through the window over Sóley's shoulder, Sigga suddenly noticed streams of people going by. *I've missed something*, she thought, and was angry at herself. She pressed her fingers against her eyes until red dots appeared behind her eyelids. She lowered her hands, but kept her eyes closed, listening to the excited voices around her, the hacking cough coming from the direction of the bartender, and beneath it all, the radio, the presenter's voice barely a mumble. Then, suddenly, a knock on the glass, and she opened her eyes and saw Pétur standing outside.

She drew back from Sóley and put up her hand, automatically.

He pointed at the door and raised his eyebrows, as if asking a question, and she shrugged.

'My brother's here,' she said.

'Okay.' Sóley kept her face neutral.

They watched him push his way inside and walk over to them.

'Hey,' he said.

'Hey.'

'Amma said you might be here.'

'Did she send you?' Sigga asked.

'No.'

'Right,' she said, and felt deflated, and annoyed with herself at the same time. Of course Amma wasn't thinking about her – she was too busy visiting morgues and lying about dead people.

'Look, I'm sorry how everyone was earlier, about the . . .' He looked at Sóley, then back at her. 'You know. It was shitty.'

'I told her,' Sigga said.

Pétur cleared his throat. 'Oh? Well, I just came to see if you were all right.'

'I'm going to pee,' Sóley said. 'If the barman comes over, I'll have the same again.'

She climbed down off her stool and walked past Pétur. Sigga saw their hands brush against each other, and it seemed almost unconscious. She looked away.

'I don't know,' she said, after a moment. 'If I'm all right, I mean.'

'How far along are you?'

'Probably not that far. Six weeks, maybe?'

'How does Olafur feel about it?'

She looked at him warily. 'I haven't told him.'

'Okay.' He moved closer to let a group of women pass from the back of the bar to the booths in the front. 'Are you going to?'

'I don't want to think about it right now.'

'Okay, sure.'

She finished the rest of her brennivín, wincing at the burn. 'Thanks, by the way,' she said.

'For what?'

'For coming to check up on me. And for standing up for me earlier.'

'Of course.' His cheeks began to flush. 'I don't hate you, Sigga. I don't know why you always thought I did. You two were the ones who left me out.'

'What are you talking about?'

'You and Gabríel. You always liked him more.'

She felt a familiar irritation beginning to rise, and stopped herself.

The bartender brought the brennivín bottle back and gestured at the empty glasses on the bar, and she nodded.

'Did you cry when I was in the hospital?' she asked, taking a sip when the bartender had finished pouring. 'Pabbi said you cried.'

'You mean after you'd nearly drowned?'

'Yes.'

'You thought I didn't?'

'Yeah.'

He let out a long breath. 'I'm sorry, then. I cried loads.'

'I'm sorry too.' She took another sip. 'Maybe it was just easier thinking you hated me than thinking Mamma did.'

Pétur took the glass from her and drank. 'Mamma doesn't hate you.'

'No?' She leaned back against the bar. 'She acts like it. But maybe you can't see it because you're her favourite.'

'Well, maybe I'm only her favourite because you always went to Pabbi whenever you were upset, and Gabríel was a grown-up by the time he was four. I was the only one who seemed to need her.' He passed her glass back. 'I know she's difficult sometimes. But she wasn't always. Gabríel says she used to laugh a lot more, and I kind of remember that too.'

'And she stopped when I came along, right?'

'No – it wasn't just you. She just got kind of sad, and then it never really went away.'

'Was it because of Pabbi?'

He gave her a sidelong glance. 'What do you mean?'

Maybe the problem was her imagination, in that she could only imagine people doing the worst thing. But anyway Pabbi hadn't been pleased to see her and Amma that day she had met him and Ísafold coming out of the basement, and anyway she'd seen them now.

'Was it?'

He shrugged. 'I don't know. I don't think it was just one thing, you know.'

'Oh,' she said, and took another sip of her drink.

'Turn it up,' someone called, and the girl nearest the radio leaned over and twisted the knob until Minnie Riperton's voice drowned out all others in the room.

There were blue and red and purple spots dancing at the corner of her vision, and when the women around her shook their heads to the music, their hair rippled like seaweed, making Sigga feel dizzy. Everyone seemed to be arranged in a circle, arms slung over shoulders, heads thrown back, singing loudly.

Why had Mamma stopped laughing? She didn't want to think it was anything to do with Pabbi, but he'd said himself he should have been around more. And she didn't want to think it was because of her, but babies were hard, and babies that cried all the time were even harder. And Mamma could have been a dancer in Norway. Her life could have been like Sigga's last summer, except she would have eaten fish and brown cheese and lingonberries, and gone out with the other dancers on the spur of the moment to swim in lakes, or camp in forests, or look for trolls.

It came to her then that Mamma regretted becoming a mother. And she was right, in a way – what was the point of getting an education, learning a skill, working hard, when as soon as women got pregnant the world was closed to them? How could there ever be equality when parenthood really meant motherhood?

She took another sip of the brennivín and slid off the stool.

'Where are you going?' Pétur asked.

'I've got something to do,' she said. 'You stay here. Flirt with Sóley, it's fine. She seems to like you for some reason. I'll see you back at home.'

Ísafold seemed surprised when she opened the door. 'Sigga,' she said. 'Did I leave something at the rally?'

'Not really,' Sigga said, and stepped forwards until Ísafold had to move back, and she was halfway over the threshold. 'I wanted to talk to you about something.'

'It's not really a good time,' Ísafold said, looking over Sigga's shoulder.

'Well, I want to talk about it now and it's cold outside.'

For a moment, Ísafold seemed to be debating with herself, then she stepped back again, and Sigga came into the house properly. Ísafold shut the door quickly behind her.

'Can I make you a coffee?' she asked.

Sigga looked around. She was feeling the effects of the wine and the brennivín, and the edges of her vision were a little blurred, but even then, she could tell the house wasn't as cosy as hers. They were in a little vestibule – about two metres by two metres – that opened onto the kitchen and then from there to another hallway, where she guessed the stairs would be, and then another room. There were no pictures on the walls, and no little ornaments on the hall table, no pile of shoes underneath the coat rack. The carpet was dark red and the walls a mushroom-brown. There was a smell of cleaning – carbolic soap and freshly ironed clothes – and the sound of a television turned right up coming from a few rooms away.

'Yeah, okay,' she said. 'I'll have a coffee.'

They passed out of the vestibule. The lights in the kitchen were much brighter, and Sigga blinked once or twice, not just against the lighting, but because the room had bright yellow walls, yellow laminate countertops and orange laminate cabinets. In the middle of the room was a small, round kitchen table and an island unit with a sink and little cabinette behind it. A yellow telephone hung from the wall, missing its cord.

'It hasn't worked for a while,' Ísafold said, following her gaze. 'Anyway, coffee.' She went to the cabinette and took out a coffee pot and started filling it. 'What did you want to talk to me about?'

'Has my dad been here?' Sigga asked.

'Maybe,' Ísafold said. 'I can't remember.'

'Are you sure?'

Ísafold turned and gave her a strange look.

'I mean,' Sigga carried on, 'the time you two spend together *is* memorable, isn't it?'

'I hope you know I'm very grateful to your father, for all his help.'

'Of course you are.'

'Sigga . . .' Ísafold's cheeks were pink. 'I think I know what you're getting at, and you've got it wrong. There's nothing happening between me and your father.'

'Funny,' Sigga said. 'Because I can't smell any damp in here.'

'Well, that wasn't exactly true—'

There was the sound of a key scraping in the lock, and the front door opened. Ísafold jumped, knocking the jar of coffee onto the floor and spilling its contents in a heap at their feet.

'Shit,' she said, quietly, her eyes filling up.

'It's just coffee,' Sigga said.

'It's fucking cold in here,' a man's voice said from the vestibule. 'I thought I told you to turn the heating on half an hour before I got home.'

Ísafold dropped to the floor and began sweeping the coffee grounds into a pile with her hands. She was talking to herself, too quick and quiet for Sigga to hear.

'Answer me, then,' the man's voice said, and then a figure appeared in the doorway. Sigga vaguely recognised Ísafold's husband.

Ísafold got up from the floor. 'Stefán,' she said, in a strange tone, 'this is Sigga, from next door.'

'Hello, Sigga,' Stefán said. He came into the kitchen, bringing a musky smell of cologne with him. 'What's this, a social call?'

'Yeah,' Sigga said, after a while, 'I guess so.'

'We should offer you a drink then.'

'I'm just making coffee,' Ísafold said.

'I meant something a little stronger.'

There was a mugginess to the air, a sense of electricity. Sigga shifted her weight from one leg to the other, and tucked her hair behind her ears. Stefán smiled at her with one corner of his mouth. He had a kind of Clint Eastwood vibe, now she thought about it. Tall, strong jaw. Big hands.

'Are you sure you don't want a coffee?' Ísafold asked.

She seemed to be crumpling in on herself, shrinking, without actually moving. Sigga, watching her, had the sudden sense that she was looking the wrong way through a telescope; everything was very clear, very far away.

'Didn't I just say I wanted something stronger?' Stefán said, louder this time. He went to a cupboard in the far corner of the kitchen, shaking his head, and took out a bottle of rum.

Ísafold silently fetched him a glass and he poured himself a slug without taking his eyes off Sigga's breasts. 'So why tonight?' he said.

'Can't I be friendly?' Sigga asked and folded her arms in front of her chest.

There was a tiny ripple of movement, like a muscle had twitched in his jaw, then he smiled at her. 'You're not trying to get your claws into my wife, are you?'

'What?'

'That fucking joke today, the rally. I'm guessing you went to it. Do you know what feminism does?'

'What does it do?'

'It encourages women to leave their husbands, kill their children, become witches and fucking dykes.' He took a drink of the rum. 'So, if you think I'm letting you put any of those ideas in my wife's head, you can think again.'

Ísafold was silent, but Sigga could feel her working, as if all her energy was going into staying still, and quiet and upright. Stefán smiled again.

'I should probably go,' Sigga said.

He took a mouthful of rum. 'Smart.'

'Okay.' Her fingers and toes prickled with a rush of blood. *Are you going to leave her here?* 'Are you ... ?' She tried to meet Ísafold's gaze.

'She's fine,' Stefán said. 'She's where she belongs.' He reached out and put his hand on the scruff of Ísafold's neck, like a cat carrying a kitten. 'I give her everything she needs, don't I, Ísa?'

Ísafold smiled weakly at Sigga. 'Nice to see you,' she said.

Sigga went into the vestibule, deliberately walking the other way around the island so she wouldn't have to pass him. Her hands were shaking when she tried to open the front door, and for a moment she couldn't get the tumbler to turn, then, when she did, the door scraped against the floor, sticking. She tugged at it, increasingly frantic as she heard footsteps approaching from the kitchen.

'You should be more careful,' Stefán said, behind her, and his arm reached past her head. Her heart was thudding so hard she could feel the vibrations in her throat. 'See?' He pulled the handle, the door opened smoothly, and she fled.

1911

THE SKY AT THE ENTRANCE to the cave changed slowly from deep purple to light grey, bottom-up, like a sink draining colour into the horizon. The cave changed too, grew forms and edges, sharp points at the ends of stalactites.

Gudrún could feel Magnús waking. She forced herself to roll closer to him and smooth her face into a smile. Maybe it was the shock of the news that had made him seem cold to her last night, she thought. Perhaps he would be his old self again this morning.

His eyelids flickered.

'Good morning,' she said.

'What time is it?' Magnús asked, but not as if he was expecting an answer. He drew out his watch and looked at it quickly. 'Eight o'clock. We'll make a start when the sun comes up.'

'Whatever you think,' Gudrún said.

He frowned slightly and she bit her tongue. It was too much, she was being too different.

She pushed herself to stand, then at the last minute remembered her ankle, and winced as the pain shot up her leg again.

'Poor Gudrún,' Magnús said. He drew circles on the watch face with his thumb. 'That settles it. I'll look for Freyja by myself.'

'No, no. It'll be fine if I don't put too much weight on it.'

'I thought we agreed on this last night?'

'I . . . don't want to be left alone.'

'Well . . .'

She could feel him wavering and looked at her feet. 'Please.'

He came over to her and put his hand on the scruff of her neck and rubbed the skin there. 'I didn't know you had it in you to be afraid?'

'Everyone's afraid of something,' Gudrún said.

'Not everyone has the sense to understand that.'

He embraced her and she let him, made herself relax into his arms. They were strong around her, sturdy, and he still had that musty, appealing smell to him. She felt a warming tingle below her stomach and hated herself for it.

They left the cave as the sun was peeping over the edge of a blushing sea. The sky was the colour of pure copper, the colour of ten–year-old Skúli's hair, and the air was clear everywhere, and fresh. Gudrún stopped for a moment to fill her lungs with it, as if they'd been in the cave for months rather than one night. This air was part of the mountain, she knew, as if the mountain went further than just earth and rocks. It carried on up into the atmosphere, proud and vital; it tasted like clarity in her throat, like confidence, and she knew suddenly she could do it, knew she could save Freyja. And maybe win Magnús properly at the same time.

'Luckily the snow isn't too thick,' he said.

'No.'

'Hold my hand as we walk.'

'Thank you.'

They made slow going, which only gave her more opportunity to scour the landscape. Once or twice she saw the yellow of the fox again, and smiled to herself, recognising a friend. No one else was visible on the mountainside. The search party would be setting off from Rósa's now, if they hadn't already, she knew, this time to find three lost sheep rather than one.

Magnús walked in front of her, clearing the path and testing the rocks before they clambered over them. They were headed west but on a level, never climbing too far up or down from where they'd started. After a while of following him, the thought flashed through Gudrún's mind that he seemed almost to know where they were going, that this search was more purposeful than the previous day. But that was her imagination, she told herself. Or maybe the fresh air had had the same effect on him as it had on her.

They were walking for almost an hour before Magnús stopped and half turned in her direction. Gudrún looked over his shoulder and saw the entrance. Just like their cave, it was small and hidden, this time by a drift of snow. She squeezed his hand and pointed.

'Look.'

He nodded.

'We should look inside.'

Magnús took out his watch and put it away again without looking at it. 'God willing, she's in there, safe.'

'Maybe I should go in first?' Gudrún said. 'You stay out here unless I call you.'

Magnús ran his free hand over his face; he seemed hesitant, almost rueful. 'What if the cold was too much for her?'

'Let's hope not.'

She dropped his hand and hobbled towards the cave. She took a moment at the entrance to check for bones, sniff the air for the scent of wild animal. Nothing.

'What are you waiting for?' he called.

She heard him take a step towards her.

'I'm just behind you,' he said.

She could sense him fidgeting behind her, sense his eyes on her back, and felt strangely afraid.

'It's fine,' she said. 'I'm going in.'

'Go on, then.'

She moved forwards again, suddenly keen to get away from him.

'Freyja?' she called, then again, louder the second time. What if she wasn't here? But she had to be. She took another step and stopped, letting her eyes adjust to the gloom. If she wasn't here then maybe Gudrún had been wrong and Rósa right. Maybe she didn't know her sister as well as she thought. Or worse, what if Freyja *was* somewhere on the mountain but Gudrún had lost her ability to navigate? If Freyja was the one thing she couldn't find.

'Please, Freyja,' she said, and she heard the crack in her voice.

Something stirred inside the cave. Gudrún braced herself.

'Freyja, it's me.'

'Gudrún?'

It took a moment to find her. She was sitting on the floor with her knees drawn up to her chest. Her eyes were wide and her hair tangled. Her skin was pale, with a blue tinge, and she looked so delicate, so much like a doll, or a child, that Gudrún could have cried.

'I thought he'd be here, Gunna.'

'Who?'

'Tomas.'

'But why?'

'*He* knew,' Freyja said. 'He knew this mountain was special to me. I thought he would leave Tomas here, as a warning. I'm meant to be *his* – he told me that.'

The thought that, perhaps, she had come too late after all flickered through Gudrún's brain.

'Oh God.' She came forwards and threw her arms around Freyja's neck. 'Oh God. Oh God, oh God.'

Freyja whispered something into her hair, and Gudrún drew back.

'What did you say?'

'I didn't want to leave him here,' Freyja said.

Gudrún took a deep breath, and then another. 'Magnús,' she croaked, and Freyja's eyes widened. 'Magnús,' Gudrún yelled. '*Magnús.*'

'Is everything all right in there?'

'Something's happened.'

Freyja was shaking her head, babbling softly to herself. Gudrún leaned forwards and held her, squeezing her sister's body to her until there was nothing between them. 'It's okay, shush. It's okay.'

'Gunna,' Freyja said, then Gudrún felt her go rigid in her arms.

She craned her neck to see Magnús standing at the entrance to the cave, looking over her shoulder at Freyja.

'Magnús,' she said. 'It's Freyja. I think she's in shock.'

He breathed out slowly.

'She thought Tomas was up here.'

Freyja pulled away from her. Gudrún looked back to see her staring at Magnús, her arms wrapped protectively across her midriff as if trying to shield it from view.

'Did you hear me?' Gudrún asked, trying to break the moment between the two of them.

He took a step forward. Something passed over his face that Gudrún didn't understand at first. It looked almost like pity, but not quite.

'Do you still think that?' he asked.

'No,' Freyja said.

'I told you I saw him buy a ticket for the boat,' he said. 'Why would he be hiding up here?'

'I thought you said you saw him board the boat?' Gudrún said.

'Did I say that?'

'Yes. I was sure . . .' Her head was pounding, and her ears were clogging up with blood. *Something's wrong, something's wrong.*

His eyes flicked over to her, then back to Freyja. 'Then it's even less likely we'll find him here.'

'I can ask the captain,' Freyja said. 'Next time he's in port.'

He licked his lower lip once.

'Didn't you see him board then?' Gudrún asked. Perhaps if she pressed him more it would all be cleared up.

'Maybe I saw someone who looked like him.' He put his hand in his pocket. 'I saw him buy the ticket, and later, I *thought* I saw someone who looked like him boarding.'

'But . . .' Gudrún looked at him and it was as if they were underwater; she saw him shimmer and change shape in front of her, and felt a coldness seeping in. She knew.

Bile rose in her throat and she swallowed quickly. How did she know? Or had she always?

He was Freyja's first. Magnús.

He was behind the silences, and the sleeplessness and Freyja pleading with her. And the blushing, the flinching – it wasn't because Freyja loved him, but because she was afraid of him. She'd felt ashamed, she'd told Gudrún. What had happened between them? What had he done? And not only Freyja – that hand at Rósa's party. The one that had felt so comfortable pushing aside her skirt and touching her where no one had before. Uninvited and under cover of darkness. She'd assumed it was Tomas because she'd heard him nearby, but it must have been Magnús who'd caught her after all. He'd been close enough for that.

She turned away just in time before throwing up.

He was at her side, solicitous. Stroking her back and murmuring in her ear.

'Poor Gudrún. It's been so difficult, with your ankle, and now finding Freyja like . . . this.'

Don't touch me, she wanted to shout, but she stayed silent. She couldn't let on.

Freyja sobbed once. 'Where is he then?'

'I don't know,' Magnús said.

Gudrún met his gaze; that green again. But now she knew it was the green of a snake's skin, the green of sea lettuce that grew along the shore, smothering other plants and suffocating the fish. She dug her fingernails into her palms.

'What do you think, Gudrún?' he asked.

He was looking at her; she tried to keep her eyes open, unsuspecting. He was doing the same – she could almost see his thoughts ticking behind the curtain – and she felt a bubble of laughter rise up her throat.

Don't, she told herself. *Don't become hysterical now. There's so much more mountain to face first.* And running alongside those thoughts was the question: *How was I so blind?*

Another voice came to her. *They hide themselves in the deep.*

'Papi,' she whispered, under her breath, and felt her eyes fill up with tears. Papi, who was out at sea, alone, at this very moment, setting, hauling, cleaning, storing, his arms aching from the work and his skin tingling from the cold. All for them, so he could keep them safe and fed. What would happen to him if he came back to find both daughters had perished in a blizzard up the mountain? He would die.

Survive then, she told herself. *Think only of how to survive, you and Freyja. That's all that matters now. If he doesn't know you know, he might let you live.*

'Tomas could have changed his mind about the boat,' she said. 'Maybe he had an accident on the way back from Arnarstapi. Or it might not have been an – accident. Maybe he was still upset after the shipwreck.'

'And he wanted to hurt himself?'

She felt Freyja stir at her elbow. *Don't let him know, don't say anything.*

'He *wasn't* upset,' Freyja said.

'He was, darling. He was always walking around with that hangdog look. Oh God,' Gudrún said, and threw herself into Magnús's arms. 'I can't bear it.'

She felt his hand patting her back, heavily. 'It's a shock, I know.'

'I'm so glad you're here,' she said, although every part of her body shrank back from him. Her self, her innermost self. She'd let him inside. She'd welcomed him, even.

'Of course I'm here,' he said, and she heard the triumphant note in his voice.

She straightened up and turned around.

'Magnús helped me when no one else would,' she said. She tried to catch Freyja's eye, but Freyja was staring at the floor. 'We started out yesterday and got snowed in nearby.' She glanced at him. 'She's cold, and tired.'

'I need to take her down,' Magnús said.

'I know.'

Freyja covered her face with her hands.

Where had it happened? The barn? She could suddenly see it – see Freyja at work: sweeping, collecting eggs, and then his arms around her. Would she have struggled? He was strong enough that it wouldn't have made a difference. Then turning her around and pressing her up against the wall; a quick lift of her skirts.

Or perhaps it hadn't been like that at all. Perhaps he'd admired Freyja, perhaps they'd flirted beforehand. But still, it came back to the barn. It came back to a man who felt enfeebled by his wife; who felt the world owed him compensation; who felt free to take it from another woman. Now that she'd found it in him, the urge for violence, she couldn't not see it. Images reeled through her head: fingers prodding, gripping, twisting lips together to cut off any shout for help. A knee in the middle of the back, pinning the body down—

Rage burned inside her. She welcomed the rage, stoked it. If not for the rage, she would collapse inwards, disintegrating into a jumble of shame and disgust. She would hate herself, and not him, for what they had done. For her vulnerability.

'Gudrún?' he said, and she realised he had been talking for a while.

'I'm sorry . . .'

'Will you wait here? I'll send the others to collect you as soon as I'm down – we're down.'

'Of course.' *Don't let him know, don't say anything.*

Gudrún took Freyja's wrists in both hands and gently prised her fingers away from her face. 'Freyja, Magnús is going to take you home. I'm injured, so I have to stay behind or I'll slow you down.'

'*No.*'

Magnús took another step closer, seemingly involuntarily, because he appeared to check himself, and put on a sympathetic expression.

'It has to be this way,' Gudrún said.

'You can't stay behind,' Freyja said quietly.

'I'll be fine. It's more important to get you to safety.' She stroked Freyja's cheek. *Pay no attention to what I say now*, she thought, *just trust me*. She thought it over and over again, as loudly as she could, and on the third time, Freyja met her eye. She looked tired. *Nod, darling*, Gudrún thought, but Freyja simply blinked at her.

'Come on, Freyja,' Magnús said soothingly. 'You can lean on me.'

Gudrún saw her recoil and pressed down on her shoulder, to give her weight, support. 'Go. I'll be with you soon, I promise.'

Freyja hesitated.

'I promise,' Gudrún said again.

Freyja took Magnús's hand and stood slowly. He smiled encouragingly at her, then slipped his arm around her waist. 'We're about halfway up, here. It should only take a few hours to get to the bottom.'

'All right,' Freyja said dully.

'Just stick close to me, though. Some of the going is quite steep.'

Watching him touch her Gudrún felt light-headed, fizzy, as if her body was slowly dissolving and she was going to float up into the air as bubbles of rage.

Don't let him know, don't say anything.

'Good luck,' she said, making an effort to keep her voice normal.

He held his hand out and she took it, amazed at herself. He squeezed once, smiling that smile that she knew so well by now, then turned and guided Freyja outside.

She waited until she could no longer hear Magnús's voice speaking softly to Freyja, or see their shadows on the snow around the cave, and then another few minutes just for luck, then left the shelter herself.

There they were, a hundred feet or so to her left, tracking their way down the slope. Magnús was behind Freyja, and he had one hand on her shoulder. Freyja's head was bowed. Just one more minute, then she could start to follow them, keep an eye on them. Her ankle would slow her down but not too much – it was better than yesterday, anyway.

She wondered, fleetingly, what he was thinking, if he was planning how to stop Freyja from revealing what he had done to her, how he had killed Tomas. And he must have killed him, Freyja was right, otherwise why the deception?

Plan away, she thought, *but it's no use. I know now. Even if you threaten her, bully her, I can keep her safe.*

It didn't cross her mind that he would really hurt Freyja. He loved Freyja, she knew that now, in the only way he could love anyone – twisted, possessively. He'd said she was his. He wanted her too much to do anything to her. No, everything – the morning sun, the mountain air, the fox that had been shadowing them – was on her side, Gudrún's side; everything would help her because she was on the side of the righteous, and they were in Bárdur's territory now. She felt powerful, almost elated. She could have pitied him, for how cold and miserable his soul must be, but then she thought of young Freyja, holding her arms out to be picked up – and she couldn't pity him.

The wind started up, whipping her hair against her face. Gudrún pulled her coat tighter and slipped her hands into her pockets, curling her fingers to make fists for warmth. For a moment, she didn't realise, then it hit her – the rock was gone.

She had that same feeling of being underwater again, but this time it was because all the oxygen had been sucked out of the air. He had the rock – that's what he'd been doing with her trousers. And she'd waited too long, she'd let them get too far ahead.

She started running, ignoring the fire in her ankle. Scrambling down towards them as quietly as she could, slipping down the slope and scraping herself as she did. Once she fell forwards and landed face-first in a fresh pile of snow, but she barely noticed. She was impervious to the cold, to the wind that pushed at her shoulders. She looked down and was surprised to see her shadow had disappeared, or at least, was hiding from her. She made no sound – she was part of the mountain, she was the fox, she was gaining on them. And now she was close enough to hear snatches of what Magnús was saying, see how he'd stopped Freyja and was gripping her upper arm with his left hand. His right arm dangled by his side. They were near a ledge, not close enough to slip, but close enough that Gudrún felt her stomach heave in fear. She was still twenty feet or so from them.

'. . . I'm sorry,' Magnús was saying. He was facing away from Gudrún, but the wind seemed to blow his words straight at her. 'You know how I feel about you.'

Gudrún stopped, crouched down, started to crawl.

'But you have to see – I can't let you do this to me.'

Now Freyja's voice, smaller: 'What did you do with Tomas?'

'Oh him.' Gudrún could almost hear the shrug in his voice. 'I slit his throat.'

'Is that what you're going to do to me?'

'No – this has to look like an accident. People are searching for you.'

'Where is he?'

'He's somewhere in the lava field. Did you really think I'd drag his body up a mountain?'

'I thought . . .' Freyja said. 'I showed you that cave. I thought it was a message, for me.'

'I suppose it was too easy after all,' Magnús said as if he hadn't heard her. 'He was so eager to talk, once I said I had something to tell him about you, that I might be able to help the two of you. He followed me like a puppy.'

Freyja sobbed.

'You can't actually have cared for him.'

There was silence for a moment, and Gudrún stopped crawling, then Freyja spoke again.

'So what are you going to do to me?'

He lifted his free arm, and showed Freyja something. Gudrún knew, without seeing it, it was the rock. She crawled on, one knee in front of the other.

'What will you tell everyone?' Freyja asked. Her voice wavered, but it was getting louder, and Gudrún's chest tightened with pride.

'I'll say you fell as we were climbing down. Or perhaps you threw yourself off. Women are liable to lose their heads once they've been caught.'

'Caught?'

She was close now, five feet away. *Move slowly, slower than that, get onto your feet, don't let the snow crunch.*

Stop, he's moving too.

Magnús had let his left hand fall away from Freyja.

'I wish I didn't have to,' he said. He slipped his left hand into his watch-pocket, and at the same time lifted the right hand, rock and all, above his head.

Gudrún sprang. He must have caught sight of her out of the corner of his eye because he was turning as he swung the rock through the air. Gudrún felt her shoulder connect with some part of him – his stomach? At the same time, her ears singing with blood, she heard a faint crunch.

Magnús was down. She crumpled to her knees. Flecks of red appeared on the snow around them.

'Oh,' she said. She looked around with eyes that didn't focus; a dark shape was lying nearby, but it seemed to be moving, undulating. A dozen Magnúses trying to sit up.

'Gunna,' Freyja shouted from a hundred miles away. 'Gunna, get up.'

Gudrún shook her head. Dark spots had appeared in the corner of her vision and it took a moment to connect that with the rock that was by her side. She put a hand up to her left temple and felt warmth and a wetness under her fingertips. Magnús had hit her with the rock and now she was bleeding. Or maybe he'd split her head in two – whatever had happened it was the worst pain she'd ever felt.

'Get away from him, Freyja,' she said. Her voice was thick and sluggish.

Freyja was by her side, tugging at her arm.

Magnús sat up, clutching his stomach; he seemed to be breathing heavily.

'Stay away from her,' Gudrún called, and felt a shooting pain in her skull.

He took a long breath. 'I thought you were different, Gudrún Einarsdóttir.'

Gudrún looked at Freyja. Her eyes were liquid, horrified. She clapped a hand to her mouth. 'Freyja—'

He was on hands and knees now. 'But you're all the same.' He took another deep breath and pushed himself to stand. Staggered back.

'Stay away from her,' Gudrún called again.

Freyja was tugging harder on her arm, pulling her up.

Magnús took one step forwards. 'I thought you cared about me.'

'Stop,' Gudrún said, but now she couldn't tell if she'd said it out loud or not. Her head; she felt as if she might be dying.

Another step. He was almost within reach of her now and she tried to push Freyja away, behind her.

'*Stop*,' she said, this time for real.

'It'll be your fault,' he said, and lunged at her.

He had her. Her arms were pinned down at her sides and he was dragging her towards the ledge behind him. She was struggling: kicking, digging her heels in. Freyja was on the ground, trying to stand up.

Gudrún ducked and twisted, knocked into him, a frantic energy pulsing through her. She couldn't die. If she died—

'Stop *fighting*,' Magnús said. He pushed his face into hers, his skin red with anger.

'Freyja,' she called. 'Help me—'

'*Hold your tongue.*'

She bit his chest, hard, feeling her upper and lower teeth knock into each other through the skin. He screamed and she wrenched her arms free and twisted away.

'Freyja—'

She was flagging, her ankle was on fire, and she knew the next time he took hold of her she wouldn't be able to fight him off.

Then suddenly Freyja was running towards them. Out of the corner of her eye, Gudrún could see Magnús was distracted, still clutching his chest. Her determination came surging back, filling every part of her, and she spun around just as Freyja reached him. Then their hands were on his body, together. His head whipped up, eyes meeting her gaze, and Gudrún pushed him with all her strength and felt Freyja do the same. It was as if the whole mountain were behind her, behind them. She saw the panic in his eyes, felt his hand reach out and grab at her throat, catch on her necklace, then the chain snapped. He went over the ledge and for a moment there was silence, then: a scream and a thud.

Gudrún sank slowly to her knees. Her head was throbbing, burning up, and she wanted nothing more than to lie in the snow for a while. Cool, dazzling snow. She put her hands down and let her head hang for a moment.

'Help me.' Magnús's voice from somewhere, somehow.

'He's still alive,' Freyja said. She was standing near the edge.

'Goddammit,' Gudrún said. She heard the bubble in her voice and spat blood onto the white.

She crawled forwards. Magnús was lying on another ledge twenty feet below them, his leg bent at an unnatural angle. He looked up at them, his face screwed up in an expression of fury, ugly suddenly.

'It's broken,' he said. 'You have to help me up.'

Gudrún wiped the blood from her chin. 'Freyja,' she said. 'We need to get you home.'

Freyja was looking down at Magnús.

'*Freyja.*'

'Yes?'

Gudrún held out her arms. 'If you can help me stand, I can walk down.'

'*Whores*,' Magnús shouted.

Freyja slipped her arm around Gudrún's waist and helped pull her up. They started walking; Magnús was still shouting, but Gudrún closed her ears to it. She was bleeding, and after a moment, Freyja took off her grey scarf and wrapped it around Gudrún's head.

'You brought this with you?' Gudrún asked.

'Yes.'

'You never meant to kill yourself, did you?'

'I don't know.'

Gudrún looked at her.

'I thought I did, after he disappeared,' Freyja said. 'I thought it was my fault that he died—'

'No.'

'But I knew it was Magnús – I *knew* he was lying. And then, when he spoke to me in the garden, he almost admitted it. I could tell he wanted to boast about it.'

'Of course he did,' Gudrún said. 'He wanted to frighten you into doing whatever he wanted.'

'He wouldn't have touched Tomas if it weren't for me.'

'You're not responsible for the actions of a maniac, Freyja.'

'And I knew he would never leave me alone.' She rubbed her eyes with the heels of her palms. 'But then, I was glad when I woke up this morning.'

'I'm glad too,' Gudrún said.

They clasped hands. Gudrún took a deep breath. 'I should have listened to you. He would never have left like that.'

'No,' Freyja said quietly.

'I'm sorry. I was wrong about him, and what I said about you – I should never have judged you.'

'We don't have to talk about it.'

'Poor Tomas.' She heard her voice shaking. 'I'm sorry – I don't know why I'm—'

Freyja leaned her head against Gudrún's shoulder. 'You never got to say goodbye to him either.'

'No. But I didn't – you were . . . How are you not falling apart, Freyja?'

Freyja looked at her. 'I've got a baby to think about.'

Gudrún stopped, put her hand on her chest. 'You're right. A beautiful baby.' She let out a long breath. 'Can we sit – for a moment? My ankle is hurting again.'

'Of course.'

They sat on a boulder, looking out at the world. The sun was golden, pulsing in a pure blue sky. Birds wheeled through the air, floating, swooping, plunging down the rock-face and spurting upwards again like a geyser. Their movements were so free, so joyous, that Gudrún laughed, feeling her whole chest expand.

Far off in the distance, she could make out a snaking line of yellow coats, the search party come for them, and she blessed each and every one of them.

They stood and began climbing down again. Once, Gudrún stopped and looked behind, at where they'd been. Magnús may have still been shouting after them, but if he was, the breeze snatched at his words and bore them away.

The rescue party found them near the bottom a few hours later. Skúli had brought a stick, to help walk on the ice, that he lent to Gudrún with her sore ankle, and Freyja smiled at her when he passed it over.

'Thank you, Skúli,' Gudrún said, very solemnly, and he nodded.

'Where's Magnús?' someone said.

Gudrún took Freyja's hand. 'Didn't he make it back last night?'

'No.' They exchanged looks.

'He left me here,' Gudrún said. 'We almost made it down in the storm, but I hurt my ankle and he said he'd find help.' She pointed at the lava field between them and the Farm. 'I saw him set off.'

The men muttered to themselves. 'He's a fool to cross it in the dark', 'Probably sank', 'Lost a horse that way last June . . .'

'We need to get you home now,' Gudmundur said. 'We can come back for Magnús when you're safe.' He looked doubtfully at the lava field and back again. 'He's probably at the Farm already – we could have missed him. We'll go there first.'

There was a round of throat clearing, even while they nodded. Gudrún squeezed Freyja's hand.

'Of course,' she said. 'I'm sure that's where he is.'

1975

THE KITCHEN LIGHT WAS on behind a closed door. Sigga knocked once, then opened the door. Mamma was sitting at the table in her dressing gown, a cup of coffee in front of her.

'Sigrídur,' she said, looking up. 'Where did you go?'

'I went round to our neighbours' house,' Sigga said, coming further into the room and closing the door behind her. Her legs still felt shaky, but if she leaned against the door, they might not give her away.

'Oh?' Mamma said. 'Why?'

'I wanted to tell her something. And then . . . and then her husband came home, and he was kind of threatening and I just wanted to get out of there.'

Mamma's fingers looked bloodless against the coffee cup, as if she were gripping it extra hard. 'What did he do?'

'He was mean.' Sigga took another step into the kitchen. If she looked to her left, she would see the window above the sink, and out of that onto the side of the house next door, *his* house, so she didn't look to her left.

'Anything else?' Mamma asked.

She felt cold suddenly, and gripped the back of the chair in front of her until the feeling passed. 'I think maybe he hits her.' She pulled the chair out and sat down, rested her elbow on the table and cupped her chin in her hand.

If she kept on making little movements like this, maybe the trembling would stop. 'She seemed afraid of him. And I just left her there.'

'You had to,' Mamma said. 'He's a grown man, Sigrídur. He could have hurt you.'

'But what if he was angry that I'd gone round? What if he hurts her?'

Mamma went to the sink and started filling the kettle. 'Your father is trying to help her,' she said, without looking at Sigga.

'You guys knew?'

Mamma put the kettle back carefully, switched it on. 'She came to see him a month or so ago. He *is* a doctor – people come to him for all kinds of help.'

'I saw them around town,' Sigga said. 'I thought they were acting kind of strange.'

'He's trying to find her somewhere to stay,' Mamma said.

'Why didn't you tell me?'

'It's confidential,' Mamma said. 'I'm not even supposed to know. And it's not your responsibility. It's not your father's either, for that matter. I keep telling him to go to the police.' She looked up at the ceiling, towards her and Pabbi's bedroom. 'But – you know your father. He's a good man.'

Sigga clasped her hands together. She felt a bubble of relief, and guilt, too, that she'd assumed something else had been going on. 'He *is* good,' she said, and suddenly she started crying.

Afterwards, after the tears had stopped, after Mamma had made her a sweet tea, for the shock, Sigga felt better.

'Do we have anything to eat?' she asked.

'Will sandwiches do?'

'I suppose so.'

Sigga watched her bustle around the kitchen, gathering the rolls and butter and cold meat. Outside the kitchen it was dark and quiet; she wondered if the party at Prikid was still happening, whether Pétur and Sóley were still together, and suddenly hoped they were.

'Pickle?' Mamma said.

'Yes please.'

'Do you remember how you used to eat pickles straight out of the jar?' Mamma said. 'And peanut butter – you used to smear that on them.'

'I remember.'

'Salty nut snacks, that's what you called them.' Mamma smiled at her and Sigga smiled back, and as she did, she remembered something else. The night after she'd got out of the hospital, as she was brushing her teeth, Mamma had come into the bathroom and caught her up in a hug. It hadn't been a gentle hug, like Pabbi gave, or a tickling hug, like Gabríel's. It had been all elbows and clasping, so tight Sigga had felt her ribs grinding together. Then Mamma had let go. She'd looked at Sigga for a moment, eyes shining, then turned and walked out of the bathroom.

Thinking of it now made her feel like crying again. 'Why do you never say anything nice about me, Mamma?' she said, and Mamma stopped buttering the roll, looking surprised, then a slow flush spread across her cheeks.

'I say nice things,' she said.

'No. You always make me feel like I've done something wrong, or I'm about to do something wrong.'

'Is that what you meant, earlier?'

'Partly.'

'I'm sorry,' Mamma said. She took a deep breath. 'It's not my intention. My mother was strict with me and my sisters, and I didn't want to be like her.'

'I know,' Sigga said.

After a moment, Mamma went back to the sandwich, and Sigga sipped at her tea. It wasn't Mamma's fault she was the way she was. History repeats itself and a family's nature stays the same. Except—

'Here you go.' Mamma put the sandwich down on the table and sat facing Sigga, cradling her own cup of tea.

Sigga picked up the sandwich. 'Are we going to talk about it?'

Mamma's eyes glazed over slightly. 'Do you want to?'

'Yes.'

'How far along are you?' Mamma asked, quietly.

'I don't know. I didn't notice that my period was late until the last week or so.'

'Why didn't you tell me?'

'You know why.'

'I suppose I do.' Mamma blinked slowly.

'I don't want a baby right now,' Sigga said. She took a bite of her sandwich. 'Maybe in the future, but not now.'

'There was a woman in my neighbourhood,' Mamma said. 'She never married, never had children and we all assumed it was because she didn't like them. Kids used to throw stones through her window, people wouldn't talk to her in the line for bread, things like that.'

'Mamma – I can't do something just because I'm expected to. That's not the right reason to have a child.'

'I just want you to know that it's harder to swim against the tide,' Mamma said. 'And I don't want you to think motherhood is easy ...' She took the other half of the sandwich from Sigga's plate and held it carefully. 'Maybe there are times when I've felt sorry for myself, and questioned – but I'm not sorry for you three. Does that make sense?'

'I think so,' Sigga said.

'Good.'

'But that's partly what we were marching about yesterday.' Mamma opened her mouth and Sigga carried on, hurriedly. 'I don't know if it's going to work, but, you know, maybe motherhood doesn't *have* to be so hard. That's it.'

Mamma paused. 'Okay,' she said, after a while. 'I don't know that the world is going to change, but if you believe it can ...'

Sigga took another bite and chewed slowly. 'Did you ever talk to your mother about why she was the way she was?'

'She had six children to raise.' Mamma shook her head. 'But maybe I should have tried. It was a shock to me, how open your father and grandmother were with each other when I was first getting to know them. Maybe I didn't handle that very well, either.'

Sigga tried to stifle a yawn. She could feel the food in her belly as if it were weighing her down, tugging at her eyelids. She pushed back her chair to stand.

'Where are you going now?' Mamma asked.

'To bed.'

'All right,' Mamma said, and she looked at Sigga, then quickly away again. 'We'll talk more about this tomorrow. If you want.'

'All right,' Sigga said. 'Goodnight, Mamma.'

*

Sigga woke suddenly with a bad taste in her mouth. The curtains were open, and outside, the sky was a dirty grey. She turned her head to look at the alarm clock: 6 a.m. again. She slid out of bed and pulled on her jumper and skirt from the previous day. Strange to be going through the same motions as yesterday when yesterday seemed a million years ago.

She crept along the corridor to the bathroom to pee, then made her way slowly downstairs. No one was stirring yet, apart from Loki, who followed her and rubbed himself against her ankles. She tickled behind his ears and opened a tin of tuna for him, then took a bag of kleinur from the bread bin and stole out of the house. She tried not to look directly at Ísafold's house, but for a moment, and just out of the corner of her eye, she was convinced one of the curtains moved.

She took the same route as always, crossing Frakkastigur and turning left towards the sea, then right again on Grettisgata. On the left side of the road, the street lamps were still bathing the sidewalk in a dim, orange glow. The right side of the road was still crammed with parked cars, still mostly Fords. The green Mini had been moved.

Olafur wants a Ford, she thought to herself, then immediately – *oh yes, Olafur*. She had to talk to him, and sooner rather than later.

Amma was in the kitchen, peering into the fridge, when Sigga opened the front door. She straightened up, quickly.

'It's only me,' Sigga said.

Amma gave her a half-smile. 'Better than the Deacon of Myrká.'

'Can I come in? I brought kleinur.'

'Always.'

'You're up early,' Sigga said.

'I couldn't sleep,' Amma said. 'I kept thinking about you.' She cleared her throat, and said, 'I need to—' at the same time that Sigga said, 'I wanted to—'

They stopped, smiled at each other.

Sigga held up her hands. 'You go first.'

'No, you,' Amma said.

'I'm sorry about the tantrum yesterday,' Sigga said.

Amma blinked. 'Oh, Sigga. You needed me, and I . . .' She pressed the backs of her hands against her cheeks. 'You have nothing to apologise for. I was caught up in remembering something. And sometimes I forget how young you are – you're so clever, and brave. I should be looking after you more.' She gestured at the table. 'Sit. I was going to make eggs and coffee.'

'I'm going swimming in a minute,' Sigga said. 'I'll eat after that.'

'Just a kleinur then?'

They sat and took a kleinur each from the bag. Sigga nibbled at hers.

'And your father,' Amma said, suddenly, as if remembering something. 'The reason he was with Ísafold—'

'I know,' Sigga said. 'Did he tell you?'

Amma nodded. 'After you left.'

'I just don't understand the way she was talking about her husband yesterday,' Sigga said. 'When Ava was asking her all those questions. She made him sound so romantic.'

'You mustn't think that monsters are always strangers,' Amma said, slowly, 'or that people can't deceive you, or that you can't love a brute for the brief moments when he treats you well ...' She dusted the kleinur off her hands. 'It's a hard lesson to learn, darling, because it doesn't make sense, but there it is.'

'Okay,' Sigga said, and it wasn't enough, but also it was, because she wasn't even nineteen yet, and there would be plenty of time to learn about people and why they did the things they did, and she had Amma back again and that felt good for now.

Amma got up and switched on the radio, then sat back down again. Outside the window it was still dark, and all the street lamps were lit and all the lights were on in the houses, but soon the sun would come up.

'Amma,' Sigga said, after a moment. 'I want to ask you a question.'

'Go on.'

'Were you lying yesterday? When you said you couldn't identify the body.'

Amma drew her thumb down Sigga's cheek and pressed it gently against the middle of her chin. 'I was, and I'm sorry about that.'

Sigga's heart thumped. 'Was it Pabbi's father?'

'No,' Amma said quickly. 'It wasn't him. Tomas was very different to Magnús.'

'What was he like? Will you tell me now?'

'He was very handsome,' she said, after a while. 'And he loved life, even though it wasn't always easy. It seemed like fate when he came into my life. Something bad had happened, then Tomas was suddenly there. When I was with him it felt like I could obliterate the bad memory, and fill it with love.'

'Was the bad thing your sister dying?'

Amma cocked her head at Sigga.

Sigga could feel her cheeks heating up. 'Sorry – I just . . . you've never said when it happened, or how. And then that story about the body in the mountain, I kind of thought it might have been her. It's crazy, I know—'

'She died of influenza,' Amma said quietly. 'My father too. Before the big wave in 1918, there was a smaller one in 1912 – that was the one that got Papi and Gunna.'

'Fuck.'

'So many people were gone suddenly. And I felt like my family got lost among them. Like they weren't different to anyone else.' She smiled sadly. 'I had to sell our farm. As soon as the priest had buried them, I came here with your father, to start again.'

'And you never went back?'

'No. I couldn't bear to. Gunna was the brave one.'

'Braver than you?'

'Oh, yes. And tough. But kind, too. She saved my life once, you know. I was on the mountain in a storm, and she came to get me.'

'Are you kidding me?'

Amma cleared her throat. 'Look, I know I've been distracted recently – and I fainted, I know that was scary for you. But I didn't want to drag you into it.'

'Drag me into what?'

'Why don't you come by after your swim? I'll tell you more about it then.'

'Do you promise?'

'I promise.'

*

The water was cool, slipping over her like silk as Sigga powered up and down the lanes. She touched the tile at the deep end and stopped, tucking her elbows into the channel that ran along the wall to the drains on either end. She rested for a moment. Somewhere to her right, a lifeguard coughed; other than the two of them, the hall was empty and the sun not yet up.

It felt good to be in the pool. As she'd climbed the stairs from the changing room, there'd been a moment when she'd felt shaky, almost scared to see the water. But then she'd turned the corner, seen the glitter of the lights reflected on the surface of the pool, smelled that familiar smell, and the shakiness had disappeared.

She kicked her legs unhurriedly, letting the water slow them down, watching the sky lightening little by little, until all of a sudden the day broke open like an egg. Her lower back was aching and she breathed out, trying to push away the pain. It was a throbbing pain, dull, and it took a moment before she recognised it, but when she did, she could have laughed. Her period. Finally.

She held onto the lip of the channel and let herself sink until she was submerged up to the halfway point on her goggles. This was her favourite view – half under, half above water, with the boundary changing in little waves and ripples. Everything above the line was so sharp, so bright, and everything below so soft and blurry. Like her body, she thought, suddenly. Beneath her skin, she was soft. But strong too. She could make another human in there, when she wanted to. *If* she wanted to.

She would see Olafur tonight. And then London, she could see where that led. Life was opening up, starting to *happen*.

She ducked underwater. Look how much strength she had propelling herself through the water, kicking her legs, scything with her arms.

She pushed off from the side.

1911

DOCTOR JÓHANN TUTTED WHEN he saw his patients, and scolded Rósa for not sending for him urgently.

'I heard you were attending the women at the new farm,' she said meekly.

He waved his hand impatiently. 'Nothing that the midwife couldn't have handled.'

Rósa looked away, then stood and paced the room while the doctor cleaned Gudrún's wound.

'How did you say you got this?' he asked.

'A rock,' Gudrún said truthfully.

'It's a nasty one,' he said. 'But you'll live.'

'And Freyja,' he said, turning to her. 'I understand you've been unwell.'

'Not unwell,' Freyja said.

The doctor frowned, and Rósa stopped pacing.

'I was told . . .' he said, then readjusted his glasses. 'Ah.' He turned to Rósa. 'Would we be able to find a bed for this examination?'

'Use mine,' Rósa said.

The doctor and Freyja went out, and Rósa sat in the same chair as she had the last time Gudrún was here.

'Coffee?' she asked.

'Thank you.'

Rósa watched Gudrún drink, her hands twisting in her lap. Eventually she looked away. 'My husband . . .' she said. 'The men said he left you before dark.'

Gudrún let the coffee sit in her mouth for a moment. She could taste the bitter note from the chicory root, taste the creaminess from the milk. Even Rósa's coffee was perfect.

She swallowed. 'Did you know?' she asked.

'Know what?'

'About Magnús and Freyja.'

She watched the skin on Rósa's neck turn red and the colour travel up to sit on her cheeks. 'I beg your pardon?'

The headache was back, and Gudrún pressed her fingers against her eyes, trying to push it inwards. 'So you didn't?'

A servant came into the room, followed by Father Fridrik, carrying his hat, and Rósa turned her head.

'The priest is here, Madam,' the servant said.

'So terribly worrying,' Father Fridrik said, moving towards Rósa, and holding out his hands, then, at the last minute, seeming to realise the hat was in the way and trying to shove it under his armpit. 'I've been praying for his safe return since I heard the news.'

Rósa let him drop a kiss on the back of her hand. 'Thank you, Lauga,' she said.

The servant shuffled out again. Rósa kept her head turned in the direction of the doorway.

'You didn't?' Gudrún pressed her.

'I don't even know what you mean by Magnús and Freyja—'

'You know exactly what I mean,' Gudrún said. She removed her fingers. 'He hurt her.'

Father Fridrik tutted.

'I don't believe you,' Rósa said.

'Has he done this before?' Gudrún persisted.

'I can promise you my husband never laid a finger on me.'

'But to others?'

Rósa looked back at her.

'He has, hasn't he?'

'All lies,' Father Fridrik broke in, and Rósa shot him an irritated look.

'So there *are* stories,' Gudrún said.

Rósa stopped, smoothed out the folds of her skirt. 'The eve of the wedding his landlady paid me a call. She said they had been . . . intimate. Magnús had never been her lodger. She told me he had left the farm in the north in a hurry. One of the milkmaids had claimed he had . . .' She shrugged. 'But she was jealous, afraid of being lonely again. I thought she was making it all up.'

'A hysterical girl and a bitter spinster,' Fridrik said. He was standing in between the two of them, legs spread in a wide, unnatural-looking stance, his hands clasped behind his back. 'Neither one carries much weight, don't you think? And you would be surprised by how often women do fabricate, when they don't get their way.' He wagged his finger at Rósa. 'I could see the looks your husband attracted even as a child. And when I came back from my religious training, he was already besieged by this . . . milkmaid. But I set him straight. I taught him not to trust a libidinous female – always a sign that Satan has a hold over her.' He sniffed. 'She didn't like that, of course. As soon as she realised she couldn't get him to marry her, that's when the stories started.'

'What happened to her?' Gudrún asked.

'I found a different position for her at another farm.'

'Rósa,' Gudrún said, without taking her eyes off Father Fridrik, 'how did Birta meet her husband?'

'Who?' Rósa asked.

'Birta. The girl who died in childbirth recently. She used to work here, Freyja told me.'

'Oh, her.' Rósa sounded peeved. 'She got lazy after a while. She was always moping about the place, or complaining about being tired. It was you, Father, wasn't it, who suggested she would make a good wife for that man.'

Father Fridrik began to look uneasy. 'Was it, now?'

'That's interesting,' Gudrún said.

'I'll admit I can be an incorrigible romantic.' He cleared his throat. 'Perhaps I should come by later. I've quite a few other parishioners to see today.'

'If you have other demands on your time . . .' Rósa said, coldly. 'I wouldn't want to keep you.'

He dithered for a moment, looking between the two of them. Gudrún raised an eyebrow at him and he seemed to make up his mind.

'I'll certainly come back as soon as I can,' he said.

They watched him back out of the room, half-bowing.

'Well,' Rósa said. 'If there's nothing else . . .'

'I have a question,' Gudrún said. She drummed her fingers on the arm of her chair. 'Why did you let Freyja go?'

'I noticed Freyja was falling behind in her duties. She seemed upset about something and I thought perhaps she was missing home.' Rósa leaned back in her chair. 'I did worry about her, whatever you think of me.'

'So you sent *her* away?'

Rósa closed her eyes. Gudrún noticed, for the first time, a web of faint lines that spread out from their corners.

Outside, a few of the men from the search party were speaking in low voices while ponies stamped their hooves in the garden and birds twittered on the rooftop. Gudrún

306

lifted her coffee cup to her mouth and drained it. A sunbeam found its way into the room and played on the wood panelling. The sky was blue, and cloudless; it could almost be July.

Doctor Jóhann came bustling back in.

'Well, she'll live too,' he said. 'And more besides her.'

Rósa opened her eyes wide and looked at Gudrún.

'Thank you, Doctor,' Gudrún said.

He came and patted her cheek. 'Your father won't know what to do with himself,' he said. 'I remember how he laughed when the two of you were born.' And he smiled.

Once he had gone, there was a long silence. A few times Rósa opened her mouth, then shut it again. When she did speak, it was in a timid voice, 'Will he come back? Magnús?'

'Who can tell?' Gudrún said. 'Possibly not.'

'I see.'

Rósa's voice was thick, with grief or regret, Gudrún wasn't able to tell. She wondered at all the emotions in herself, too. Anger; pity; guilt; a strange tenderness towards the other woman. *If we have nothing else in common*, she told herself, *we have his deception*. But she, Gudrún, had Freyja to take care of. And there was a baby on the way.

'Well.' Gudrún pushed herself to stand. 'If you don't mind, I'm going in to see my sister.'

Freyja was sitting up in bed when Gudrún drew back the curtain separating the badstofa and the bedroom. The blankets were drawn up to her knees and no further, and her hands were resting in her lap. Sitting down, and in her borrowed nightshift, the slight swell of her belly was visible, and Gudrún felt the breath catch in her throat.

'Hello,' she said.

'Hello.'

Gudrún came in and sat on the edge of the bed. She put a hand on Freyja's leg, revelling in its reality, its solidity. Only two days ago, she'd been afraid she'd never see it again.

'Doctor Jóhann seemed pleased with you,' she said.

'I thought so too.' Freyja traced a pattern on her belly with her finger. 'I suppose the news is out now, then.'

'How does it feel?'

'Good.'

'Yes?'

Freyja looked at her, and her eyes seemed bluer than ever. 'I don't know how to describe it – there's a *person* inside me.' She smiled. 'How is it so ordinary and so extraordinary at the same time?'

'One of life's great mysteries.'

'And I loved Tomas. At least I'll always have part of him with me now.'

Gudrún took a deep breath. 'I could help you look after it,' she said, and was surprised that she really meant it.

Freyja shook her head. 'You always look after me. I can't ask you to anymore.'

Gudrún leaned forwards so their foreheads were touching. 'I'm your sister.'

'I know.'

'Well then.'

'I'm in trouble if this baby is as determined as you.'

'I hope it's as strong as you,' Gudrún said, and felt hot tears crowding her throat.

They were quiet for a moment.

'Shall I leave you to rest?' Gudrún said eventually.

Freyja yawned, then laughed. 'Maybe.'

Gudrún stood up, wiped her cheeks, and pulled the blankets up higher. 'Keep warm,' she said, and kissed Freyja's forehead. 'I'll be back later. I'll send Rósa in with a hot drink.'

'Thank you.'

Rósa was nowhere to be seen when she came out from behind the curtain. Gudrún left word with one of the maids to brew a moss tea and then, to make sure Freyja wasn't disturbed, she slipped out the front door and started walking. She hadn't planned where to go in particular, but her feet took her naturally in the direction of home, and past it, to the cliffs where she and Freyja and Tomas had spied the seals.

A breeze had started up, and it blew the hair back from her face, carried the smell of salt up from the water and into her lungs. She breathed deeply. Somewhere, just beyond the horizon, was Papi. She knew, somehow, that today would be a good day for him, that the fish would swim straight into his nets.

She sat on the edge of the cliff and let her feet dangle. She could sense the mountain behind her, but she wouldn't look at it. She looked out to sea instead, at the dark blue water stretching to meet the light blue sky, at the flurry of gulls, wheeling and diving, casting shadows below them. She looked at the sunlight playing on the surface, the little ripples and flashes of silver, shoals of herring on their way to the fjords, and, not far behind them, greenish-white bubbles rising lazily to burst on the surface.

It took a few moments for her to recognise the bubbles as the *vaða*, as the fishermen called them, and when she did, her heart thumped painfully against her chest. And suddenly it happened: the sea changed from blue to luminous green and the water seemed to swell, boiling with fish. She felt her breath catch in her throat, then, with a whoosh that she could hear from almost half a mile away, the whales broke through the surface, mouths wide open to catch the herring as they fell.

She pressed her hand against her chest to calm the frantic knocking underneath, but it wouldn't stop. And still they kept coming, whale after whale, and clouds of white vapour rose in the air as they blew noisily from their blowholes. Some were feeding, some were merely surfacing, blowing out, and diving again. And once, not far from the pod, one threw itself into the air in a movement that looked like nothing more than pure delight. It hung for a moment, white belly facing out, tail flukes just skimming the surface, then fell back again to hit the water with a smack, flinging out a glittering curtain of spray.

Of course she'd seen whales before. But this time she was surprised by their size, their strangeness and familiarity at the same time.

Then, just as suddenly, they flexed their backs and dived in a long, smooth, certain motion, lifting their tails so the dip between the flukes was the last thing she saw of them.

Afterword

My first introduction to the world of the sagas wasn't via a saga at all, but through *Beowulf*, the Old English epic poem set in Scandinavia during the sixth century, and an example of Germanic heroic legends. In my last year of primary school, my class and I read what I can only assume was a highly abridged version, before writing and illustrating our own interpretations. Reading it years later, my attempt reveals two stark truths. One, that I was clearly enthusiastic about the feasting element of the age (an entire page is devoted to a list of all the foodstuffs the Danes lay out for Beowulf and the visiting Geats). And two, that it was the female character, Grendel's mother, who really fascinated me. Grendel, the first monster, is dispatched with barely a second thought. The third monster, the dragon – who kills Beowulf – merited a description about the same length as the items of the feast. But Grendel's mother, the second monster, is the adversary truly worthy of the name. Not only is she fierce and dangerous, but my eleven-year-old self seemed highly sympathetic to the rage motivating her attacks; her son has been killed by Beowulf, of course she's out for revenge.

Revenge plays a large part in the Icelandic Sagas that came some centuries afterwards. This is because the society they portray, the Old Norse society, was an honour culture. And given the sagas' positioning as the amalgamation of the fictional and historical, they are especially valuable sources for modern readers trying to understand the world they depict. Or at least this is true of the most common form of the Saga – the *Íslendingasögur*, as the family sagas are known. These are prose narratives that describe real events that occured (primarily in Iceland) between the ninth and eleventh centuries – starting when the first Norse settlers migrated across the North Atlantic – although all were set down on paper over 200 years later. (The family sagas stand in opposition to the chivalric and legendary sagas – the descendents of *Beowulf* – whose events take place before the settlement of Iceland, and are purely literary products with little historical accuracy.) From these *Íslendingasögur*, we can make various assumptions about the character of the people who founded the Icelandic commonwealth: concerned with honour, glory and loyalty; reactionary enough to have withdrawn to this remote island, and outside the course and influence of the states of Europe, but with a clear sense of self. From the beginning, a social contract was established to invent a set of laws and observe them, and – unlike the other historical texts of the Medieval period, which were mostly written in Latin – their literature was written in the vernacular. I think it speaks to a certain pride in their identity as 'Icelanders', borne out by the desire to preserve and record local and personal interests, and details.

The oral traditions of Iceland suited a compilation of tales bound by a common local setting or association with a particular family. Naturally, since the written tradition grew out of this oral one, the *Íslendingasögur* often feature the migration to different parts of Iceland and conflicts between families once there. And the saga composers' preocupation with preserving a record of actual life in the past means the proportion of time spent on everyday, 'unheroic' details set them apart from other heroic literature. Not all characters can be Njal, or Bárdur. Some are dull or slow, or just perfectly ordinary. Just as in my own novel, where there is space for both the uneventful cooking of the *vinnarterta*, and the desperate charge up a volcano in a blizzard to save Freyja.

The sagas provide details and clues on the social values of the age, too. For women, living in an honour culture meant that their sexuality was supposed to be at all times under male control. Indeed, in the newly formed Icelandic Commonwealth, 'unlawful' sexual relations such as sleeping with an unmarried woman (with a permanent residence) faced a criminal penalty, regardless of the woman's consent to, or even desire for, the sexual act. It was her male guardians who were perceived as being wronged here, highlighting how women were denied ownership of their physical selves. Somewhat depressingly, this theme was one I was compelled to write about centuries later because of the relevance it still holds today.

When I first started to think up my novel, besides wanting to set it in Iceland, a country I'd lived in and loved, I wanted to explore the lack of autonomy women face, be it over their own bodies, how they are allowed to make their way in the world, or sometimes even who they are allowed to love. Iceland, with its compressed modern history and its progressive achievements (the world's first democratically elected female president, regularly topping the World Economic Forum's survey for gender equality), felt like a good backdrop against which to examine these issues. After discovering the Bárdur Saga (a late example of the *Íslendingasögur,* written in the four-teenth century), I recognised several parallels between it and the story I had already begun to imagine. Bárdur compels Helga to follow him home, away from her lover, even though she 'had no joy after she left Skeggi. She grieved and faded away ever after.' Similarly, the separation between Freyja and Tomas is not of her own doing, but the result of another man's jealousy and sense of entitle-ment.

Then there is the parallel between Helga, forced to raise her half-brother for twelve years, seemingly (as it appears to modern readers) as a punishment for slighting her father's honour by transgressing sexual norms, and Sigga, worrying that she might be pregnant, and how that will put paid to her dreams of further education, travel, living freely with only her own wants to attend to. In these two cases, we see that the state of motherhood, if not actively chosen (and sometimes even when it is) can be a bind and an oppression.

To modern readers, the sagas contain many incidents and details that seem fanciful. But to their original audience, these were far less likely to strain credulity. In this, I include not only the 'heroic' acts that attest to the contemporaneous moral laws underpinning the narratives, but also the mix of realism and the supernatural to be found in them. Even before moving to Iceland, I'd heard of how the Department of Transport will only build new roads if they can be assured there will be no upheaval to the 'hidden people', and during my time there I discovered that many Icelanders even build miniature houses in their gardens for the elves. Once you have spent any time on the island, none of this is surprising. It's not an environment that recommends itself to human habitation. The mountains explode fairly regularly; caves open and disappear; you can go to bed one night with clear skies and empty pavements and wake the next morning to snow drifts up to your waist; in the coldest months of the year, the sun disappears after only a few hours. The landscape feels otherworldly, certainly beyond our control. Why shouldn't it be home to creatures that we can't see or control?

I wanted a glimpse of the supernatural in my own book, so as the novel progresses Gudrun (already possessing the gift of seeing things for where and what they really are) increasingly takes on Bárdur's role, and her story becomes more intertwined with his. I also wanted the climax of the 1910/11 storyline to have the narrative satisfaction of the sagas and to echo their moral laws, although it is Gudrun, not a male relative, who takes action to avenge the wrongs enacted on Freyja. Conversely, I wanted the 1975 storyline to be more bound by reality and its limitations. Heroism/mythology and reality coexist to the world of the sagas, and the Bárdur references in my novel tie *my* family (Gudrun, Freyja and Sigga) to the mythical history of Iceland. It elevates them, makes them larger than life, but also makes the point that these stories are not new. The problems women faced before are those they are still facing, generations later. Who among us isn't tired of history repeating itself? I want my female characters to be sympathetic – like Grendel's mother – even in rage, even if they kill.

* For anyone wishing to know more about the history of the Icelandic Commonwealth, I can recommend *Epic and Romance*, by W.P. Ker. And for an illuminating (and troubling) read on the history of sexual assault depictions, the article "Rape in the Icelandic Sagas: An Insight in the Perceptions about Sexual Assaults on Women in the Old Norse World" by F.C. Ljungqvist.

Acknowledgements

There are a number of writers I am indebted to. For beautifully written depictions of the countryside, of unforgiving weather and camping without comforts, I turned to Lavinia Greenlaw's *Questions of Travel: William Morris in Iceland*. For extensive research and excellent ethnographic details, Margaret Willson's *Seawomen of Iceland: Survival on the Edge* was invaluable, and for inspiration as to how to write about the Icelandic people through their landscape and their stories, Sarah Moss's *Names for the Sea: Strangers in Iceland* was a book I returned to over and over again. And no one can write about mountains without first reading *The Living Mountain* by the wonderful Nan Shepherd. When thinking about the sagas, I found *Epic and Romance: Essays on Medieval Literature* by W. P. Kerr, not only fascinating, but accessibly written. *Notable Shipwrecks: Being Tales of Disaster and Heroism at Sea*, published by Cassell and Company, helped me imagine my own shipwreck. In Reykjavik, the National Museum of Iceland and Árbær Open Air Museum were excellent resources with exceedingly helpful and knowledgeable staff.

The idea of 'motherhood' is so large and so unwieldy, and my own experience of it was so fresh when I started writing this book, that I don't think I could have clarified any thoughts on it without Adrienne Rich's seminal *Of Woman Born: Motherhood as Experience and Institution*.

Anne Enright's *Making Babies* was not only thought-pro-
voking, but frequently made me smile.

One of the great joys of writing a book set in Iceland
was that I felt I should expand my knowledge of Icelandic
literature. I can now list (in no particular order) Sjón,
Halldór Laxness, Einar Már Guðmundsson and Auður
Ava Ólafsdóttir among my favourite writers, as well as the
various authors of the Sagas.

I'd like to thank everyone at Manilla for their enthusiasm,
their kindness and most importantly, all the free books. I'm
so pleased to be joining such a talented list of authors and
such a dynamic publishing house. A special mention must
go to Arzu Tahsin, for her encouragement and her nuanced
editing; the book is a thousand times better for it. And
another mention to Sophie Orme, for her understanding
of this book and her humour. I'm endlessly grateful to both.

I'd also like to thank: my agent, Caroline Wood at
Felicity Bryan, who really champions her writers and who
always believed in this book.

My writing group, whose feedback I am immensely
grateful for, and even more for their friendship.

My family and friends for being brilliant, always. My
mother died while I was in the middle of this book, and
their love and support meant everything to me.

Our neighbours and friends in Iceland. Special thanks
go to Elisabet Hafsteinsdóttir, who read the manuscript
and patiently explained how terrible I was at spelling
Icelandic names, among other invaluable notes. I owe
her countless drinks and am very lucky to have her.

And last but not least, my partner, Tom Feltham and
our son, Noah. Motherhood has been a joy for me because
of you two. Sorry for eating all the biscuits.